James Pycroft

Dragons Teeth

In two volumes. Vol. 1

SALZWASSER VERLAG

James Pycroft

Dragons Teeth

In two volumes. Vol. 1

Reprint of the original, first published in 1863.

1st Edition 2022 | ISBN: 978-3-37500-645-7

Verlag (Publisher): Salzwasser Verlag GmbH, Zeilweg 44, 60439 Frankfurt, Deutschland
Vertretungsberechtigt (Authorized to represent): E. Roepke, Zeilweg 44, 60439 Frankfurt, Deutschland
Druck (Print): Books on Demand GmbH, In de Tarpen 42, 22848 Norderstedt, Deutschland

DRAGONS' TEETH.

DRAGONS' TEETH.

BY THE

REV. JAMES PYCROFT, B.A.

IN TWO VOLUMES.

VOL. I.

LONDON

1863.

PREFACE.

THE continued popularity of my other works convinces me that truth pleases longer than pure fiction. I offer another tale, of the nature of a "literary Mosaic tesselated with FACTS."

If anything in the story of "Hannah Hengen" seems improbable, three cases can be cited in which Woman's wit has achieved as much, or more.

J. P.

27 Gloucester Gardens, W.

May, 1863.

CONTENTS.

DRAGONS' TEETH.

CHAPTER I.

OUR STORY BEGINS WITH A FAMILY DISAPPOINTMENT.

WHETHER I was an otter, in a former state of existence, or whether the soul of Izaac Walton migrated into my body, I cannot say, but certainly—without committing myself to such ingenious speculations—I never could see the trout leaping at the May-fly without a natural yearning and impatience to be hunting the waterfalls and filling my basket with those beautiful gold and speckled creatures. So heartily do I agree with Archdeacon Paley, that the man who has never felt the spring of a fine trout or a salmon for the first three minutes after he is hooked—plying the rod from point to butt, and flinging himself desperately some feet above the water—has yet to learn the highest thrill and tumult of the breast.

One day, at the end of May, 18—, I was thus pleasantly and exultingly employed on the estate of the late Thomas Walford, when I perceived some very loud and animated discussion between old Richard of the lodge and one of the keepers.

"You cannot have had much sport to-day, Sir, I fear," said Richard, as I came up to him and stuck my rod carelessly into the ground; "and till some time this evening, about sunset, you won't have much. Do you know, Sir, I have often thought what a very strange thing it is that the fish should all be of one mind at the same time. If some of our trout in this water won't rise, there is not one of them that will rise—not, at least, as should be; or if they do, it is only to play with the fly, and not to take it. It's the same in shooting; if some of our birds are shy, then all of our birds begin to be shy, and it's a long shot at all of them."

Here old Richard paused philosophically for a solution of this phenomenon. But presently—seeing that I was rather looking to him to solve the mystery, and finding also that, for this striking unanimity in the animal kingdom, I had no conjecture worth offering—old Richard continued:

"And these, Sir, are nothing but poor dumb creatures, these are—that I say are always of one mind—so very much of one mind, that you can always know where to find them and how to have them; and, in short, you can count upon their ways and doings quite regular: but, contrariwise, it's quite different with Christians, for human creatures are never of one mind; and as I was just now saying to Robert, while your honour was fishing round the mill-pond, that there is not a kennel of dogs where there's half, if you look all England over, the snarling, the snapping, and the quarrelling that there has been about our manor-house ever since master died."

Richard Wyatt was known as "a character" about that part of the country. Though such characters—shrewd and observing, though unlettered men—are not as surprising as we are accustomed to think; only, after all we pay for school and college, we are too apt to conclude that we may claim a monopoly of mother-wit; though there is no possible reason why the talk around the blacksmith's forge, the tap-room, the ready reckoning of the chandler's shop, and the strife of tongues on market-days, should not sharpen up the rustic intellect, and fill up a little of the gap that would seem to separate between the master and the man.

And now, as my morning's sport proved quite a case in point, and the trout seemed positively unanimous in not rising, I thought I could not do better than to sit down on the bank and indulge in a quiet chat with Richard. He had evidently something on his mind, and all bearing on a subject in which I was really interested, having heard a little before. I was, therefore, glad to be a patient listener while he supplied the missing links, and enabled me to make out the following connected story.

It soon appeared, that all the quarrelling to which he alluded was about two little babes—two poor, helpless, little infants—most helpless, most powerless to look at, but yet so mighty in the eye of the law that they even were powerful enough effectually to divert a stream of wealth from the family of their uncle, General Colton,—bidding timber to grow and rents accumulate for twenty-one years, till the elder or the survivor of the babes aforesaid should have attained to the years at which discretion is supposed by courtesy at all times to make its appearance.

Indeed "'twas strange, 'twas passing strange," for the unprofessional mind to think of, but there lay two little innocents in their cradle—still, whether sleeping or waking, they were guarded, not only by the yearning of a devoted mother, but by the inviolable majesty of the law of England, as administered by the great Lord

Chancellor, who—rather than one tittle of their remotest right should fail—would have their cause pleaded before him by one learned counsellor duly instructed for each of them, and would himself sit, day after day, with a knotty question, just as patient and as scrupulous as if he were adjudicating for the highest and the noblest suitor in the land.

The appearance of these two babes, expected little and wanted less, proved a very sore disappointment to General Colton.—So very near had the General been to the summit of his ambition in realising the comfortable independence, as well the county influence of Richcourt Manor, yet, after all, had missed it!

Who has not, at one moment of his life, grasped in his sanguine imagination some envied boon—measured it, and calculated it—even laid his plans and made up his mind what he should do with it, till at last his ideas have already enlarged and swelled to the full measure of the desired possession, but, dashed from the pinnacle of all his hopes, has been compelled to fall back upon his own far humbler state of things—a state actually shrivelled, shrunken, and insipid from the contrast?

Yes, there was one commanding spot and summer-house, with round thatched roof, called

Belvidere, and there Richard had often espied the General, as he called it, "a regularly taking of stock." For, Richard always fancied he could read the inmost thoughts of the General as, in his sanguine imagination, he cut down timber, formed ornamental water, planted out eye-sores, and disclosed new views, with the same lively interest as if he were already the proprietor of Richcourt Manor.

But Richard Wyatt wanted no such master as General Colton; and Richard's likes and dislikes, Richard's sympathies and antipathies, were not hard to read; especially when he returned to the General very short answers to many a question which seemed, in Richard's homely phrase, "a making free with what wasn't his'n," and too much like "reckoning the chickens before they were hatched."

But we left the two master Walfords lying in the cradle. But how they came there, and how the fortune of one, at least, of these little innocents was made before he was born, with all the advantages of having the rutty road of life made smooth and easy, and the hard work ready done, with everything as soft and comfortable as can be at the outset, so as to promise a pleasant life-long journey—all this shall be the subject of the following pages.

CHAPTER II.

SHOWING WHERE ALL THE MONEY COMES FROM.

IT is wonderful what a wealthy old gentleman John Bull is. If we calculate even the money that he is robbed of, and the leakage of his pockets, it is equal to the revenue of a petty state. Fifty millions a-year he loses by bad debts in bankruptcy, and as much more, in some years, in foreign loans and bubble companies. In Liverpool alone he loses more than half a million a-year by pickpockets and other thieves; besides many other proofs, it were easy to point out—as the shipwrecked mariner said when he espied a gallows—of a well-to-do and of a well-ordered and flourishing establishment.

But the question is, Where does all the money come from? How is it that the enterprising family of John Bull contrive to get together so much more money than they know what to do with?

It all proceeds from such patient and persevering members as Thomas Walford; men who begin life very painstaking, and end life very avaricious. First of all, they make money that they may live; and, last of all, they live only that they may make money; and go on, simply from the force or impetus of habit, striving, saving, paring and scraping, for the mere pleasure of adding cipher to cipher, and parchment to parchment; oftentimes with as little real use or enjoyment of their hard-earned riches, as if they were dotting down and mapping so many acres of the sky!

However exaggerated a picture this may be of some rich men, it was true to the life of Thomas Walford; it is equally true of many another soulless and office-dried specimen of humanity at the present day.

Thomas Walford began the world with nothing; and since he never saved a penny, of which he did not at the same time learn the value, from the hard labour and self-denial required to earn it—he commenced by laying, stone by stone, a very sure foundation for his future fortune.

Thomas Walford began the world as a clerk in the office of Messrs. Catcham and Keepham, who were called "general merchants;"—a kind of jobbers and money-lenders, who would buy anything under price, and advance money upon anything—whether rolls of carpets for the drawing-rooms of Belgravia, or tons of oakum to rub raw the fingers of paupers in the poor-house, or of felons in Horsemonger Gaol.

The consequence was, that in the course of thirty years half the needy men in London—the men of shaky credit—men who, because they could not meet a bill to-day, felt all the more certain of doing so three months later—men tottering on the verge of insolvency, had run breathless into Catcham's office, too thankful to conciliate the managing clerk, Mr. Walford; and to borrow, on ample security (though the property of their creditors all the time), and at cent-per-cent interest, just as much money as would put off the evil hour, and give the speculation of the morrow a chance of retrieving the losses of the day.

After a while, when Thomas Walford was not at liberty to grant a loan from the money of his employers, he would yet see his way safely to lend his own; and it was not long ere his first one hundred pounds were turned into two.

The pleasant task of increasing riches—we intend no reflection on the honesty of the transaction—was the making of this managing clerk. From that hour his whole soul was in the general merchant's business. Thomas was ever at his desk—Thomas never wanted a holiday—what though all London were on the road to Epsom, what cared Thomas? he had all the excitement of gambling, and in a far safer way, much nearer home. By parity of reasoning, hunting, shooting, fishing, and the like, even if accessible, had no charms for Thomas: no, he was bagging the finest of game as he sat at his desk; fishes of all kinds were coming to his net; till at last, so excited was this money-making man, that he could hardly allow himself time to eat, to say nothing of digesting his customary shillingsworth of meat at the famous *à-la-mode* beef-shop in the Old Bailey—so eager was he to make, in the course of the afternoon, a pound or two premium, and one per cent interest for the loan of a twenty-pound note, as a timely accommodation for a week.

"There never was such a clerk as Thomas," said Mr. Catcham.

"We never had such a comfort," responded Mr. Keepham: "for, whether I stay and enjoy myself one day, two days, or even three days at a time, at my villa at Tooting, business goes on, as regular as clockwork. We are not missed in the least. Yes, Thomas is a perfect piece of clock-work—a safe peg—a sure cog in our machinery."

In course of time, both these gentlemen began to feel that life would not be worth living for—and of this commodity they had but a small remainder—were it not for the thorough ease and security they enjoyed, and all owing to the untiring perseverance and steady-going qualities of Thomas Walford. And thus, many a time since the days of Whittington, it has come to pass, that when gentlemen, like Messrs. Catcham and Keepham, have found themselves growing old, some faithful servant at command, like Thomas Walford, has proved an actual necessity to their existence, and has, eventually, become junior partner, and ended with all the profits of the firm, and a handsome legacy in the way of capital, wherewith to work it.

No doubt, there is a certain pleasure in possession, how useless soever, while the toy is new; and, no doubt, there is a secret pleasure even in rounding one of the long-wished corners of life, though it lands us nowhere, but leaves us the same weary creatures as before. On this principle, Thomas Walford may be allowed to have enjoyed some months of satisfaction, as he contemplated his own name in staircase

No. 2, in St. Helen's Court, and was complimented, among the city men, on the high position he had achieved.

Still, as time passes on the gloss of novelty passes off, and the first flutter of excitement no longer beguiles the dull routine of daily life.

An old man once complained, that the customary trifles ceased to tickle or to interest; and, at length, the same mechanical drudgery in a sunless office, and the daily quest of money, money, money, without any taste to gratify, and without the soul to enjoy more than animal pleasures, and with little zest even for them—this formed the life of the rich Thomas Walford.

Such cases, though not uncommon, when plainly stated seem like an over-drawn satire upon humanity.—To think, that the laborious owners of untold wealth should find "their schemes may prosper, though themselves unblest;" and that though God "gives them their hearts' desire, withal He sends leanness into their souls;" that is, when they live choking and clogging every inlet, and numbing each more generous feeling by the very means they take to gratify it!

Thomas Walford, now, after thirty years' hard work, was about fifty years of age, when one day, to the surprise of his clerks, his hat no more appeared, as if to mark the hour of business, upon the customary peg; and the strange news soon circulated that he had had a seizure, and was confined to his small house in Hart Street, Bloomsbury Square.

The truth was, that the long-fretted nerves had lost their tone; the heart had begun to palpitate, and a certain numbness in the fingers and dizziness in the head proclaimed that Nature meant to cry, Enough!

No ache or pain of a mere local kind would ever have proved enough to banish Thomas Walford from the daily haunts of so many years, and the one remaining idol of his heart; but when the very citadel of life itself is sapped, and the springs begin to fail, then the wrench is too strong to withstand, and the saying proves true, "Skin for skin, yea, all that a man hath will he give for his life."

Before he was one year older, Thomas Walford had been forced to realize—to retire into a very healthy part of the county of Berks, where he soon invested the greater part of his gains in the Manor of Richcourt, to which his attention had been called by his sister's husband, General Colton.

CHAPTER III.

THE SINGULARITIES OF SINGLE LADIES AND SINGLE GENTLEMEN.

Nothing causes a more agreeable state of excitement in a country neighbourhood than when one of the principal mansions, for some time consigned to housekeepers, rats, weeds, damp and dilapidations, is announced as let to some substantial city man. Richcourt Hall had long been declared "no good to anybody;" that is to say, the village doctor saw no place where the patients were not; the village lawyer missed a client; the parson got no parochial subscriptions, while the blacksmith lost his shoeing, the gardeners sighed for wages, and men of all trades and callings talked of the dullness of the times. In short, a large country house pays a number of steady annuities, large or small, to all the neighbourhood; and to shut up such a house is like shutting up a bank, as regards the incomes of those around.

And now, Richcourt Manor was announced as let, and every one who told of it spoke as usual, as if his or her organ of acquisitiveness was in a state of rather healthy activity. Squire Walford's riches, we may be sure, lost nothing by the telling. Every five thousand a-year quickly grows to ten; for the very name of a London merchant, from the days of Whittington and his cat to the present hour, suggests to the vulgar the idea of ship-loads of wealth, and heaps of golden guineas.

However, the people of Richcourt very soon found that "the London gentleman" made a country gentleman of a very exact and wary kind. The establishment, by degrees, with the aid and suggestions of General Colton, was duly organised; and dire necessity forced on Mr. Walford the unwilling acknowledgment, that whoever undertakes a large manor-house encumbers himself with a veritable "load of life."

This truth Mr. Walford realised in a swarm of "creepy-crawly creatures;" for so he called them, accustomed as he had been to the more lively movements of city life. He had yet to learn, that what he called loitering they called labour, and must be paid for as such; and when the steward, the bailiff, the housekeeper, the groom, and the gardener, and under-dittos, and all the rest of the local force, encountered him with their first accounts, there was no little surprise that, as one of them said, "he didn't know better than to expect for every penny a plain and perceptible penny's worth."

When once this manorial staff was organised, never was there more truly a fish out of water than was exemplified in the altered condition, ways, and habits, of Thomas Walford. For, now, for the first time in his life, money was always going out; whereas, money used to be always coming in. And for what was it all paid? Only to encourage waste and idleness. Paid to John for doing nothing,—paid to Will for helping John! Why, the cost of his kitchen-garden would keep a whole greengrocer's shop!

But, to say nothing of the cost, the life had no charms for Mr. Walford. After Hart Street, Bloomsbury, the very silence was distressing to him. As to the views and the scenery, all he cared for was the busy city throng; and even a cab-stand before his window, he said, would have been a sensible relief.

It was in one sense fortunate for Mr. Walford that he had various complaints, which with doctors' visits, regimen and medicine, claimed an appreciable aliquot part of his time and attention, insomuch that we never more clearly saw the truth of this remark,—that the gout sometimes answers every purpose of a quiet profession to many an idle man.

However, men conscious of an inferior pedigree are almost always ambitious of high society: and since Mr. Walford's age and intelligence, with his natural gentleness and suavity of manner, prevented the neighbours from complaining of any want of refinement, it was not long before he had the satisfaction of far more homage and attention than he ever hoped to receive.—This was owing no little to his brother-in-law, General Colton, who soon found his advantage in identifying himself and small establishment with the wealth and consequence of Richcourt Hall.

But it is "not good for man to be alone." Of this he was reminded, in one of those pleasant jests which are meant in earnest, by the Doctor; who added something about indispensable comforts, increasing infirmities, and the solace of female society. And, in this advice, the Doctor seemed only to represent the general opinion of all the neighbourhood, who, as usual, set about matching and marrying the rich old bachelor; all after their own fancy, and quite in their own way.

Nothing is more strictly a man's own affair than whether he shall live single or married; yet there is nothing which his neighbours are so ready to settle for him. The one question all the country round was, Who should be the lady of Richcourt Hall? for, the idea of there being no lady at all was not to be endured.

It so happened, that among all the families of the neighbourhood, one of the oldest, and confessedly the most respectable, was that of Sir Buller Tawstock. Every one knew that the Tawstocks were quite the leading people; and almost every one was also aware that they had very little to lead with. Even style and respectability cannot live upon air: and the Tawstock constitution evidently wanted recruiting and invigorating. It had just arrived at that point of depletion at which, we have many times observed, that even the most exclusive and particular people look about them, to exchange a little of their shadowy consequence for somebody else's solid substance. It had long been suspected that the Tawstocks had been practising one of the "genteel ways" to make both ends meet. There had been a succession of visitors, one after another, who attracted a little observation, from the fact of their appearing much more independent than most visitors, and also from their visits being as long as if they had taken a lease of the premises.

At the time of which we are speaking, the place of all these questionable visitors had been for about three years supplied by a cousin of Lady Tawstock. Her name was Miss Onslow.

Whoever spent an evening at the Tawstocks' experienced something singularly refreshing in the presence of Miss Onslow. Where a whole family seem hard, harsh, and pretentious, living in a very atmosphere of mistake and affectation, one touch of truth and sincerity lets in a ray of daylight fatal to the whole illusion. Nevertheless, the world, it seems, will never want some "who make lies their refuge;" and, like the frog in the fable, puff and painfully distend themselves, when they might be quite comfortable within their own natural sphere and dimensions.

Well, the Tawstocks were a family of this kind.—Like most other people in this world, they could name some respects in which they had been very hardly dealt with. Certain estates had not fallen in, that, by all decent regards to family, ought to have fallen into their branch: so, they had taken vengeance on the world by indulging, at all times, in very depreciating remarks on things in general: as also, in one vain and life-long attempt to rise above their proper element, forgetting that certain hissing, stupid, heavy birds, were never meant to fly.

Miss Onslow, therefore, did not appear like a true member of the Tawstock family. There was a quiet winning influence about her. She was now nearly forty years of age. Everybody was sure she must have had offers: so everybody wondered why she had never married. Some disappointment, which she could not overcome, being, as usual, made to serve as the solution of the mystery.

"If we could only plan an alliance between Mr. Walford and your cousin, Louisa Onslow!" said Sir Buller to his wife. "He can't live long; if she is not happy, she is sure to be soon out of her misery, with a good settlement to console her. What a fine thing it might be for our children in years to come!"

Suiting the action to the word, Sir Buller began—as it was invidiously reported—to make a dead set at old Walford morning, noon, and night: for, he sought every opportunity of inviting Mr. Walford to see his farming improvements after breakfast—with sometimes a luncheon at midday—and often a friendly dinner and a quiet evening.

Careful observers thought this rather strange; for old Mrs. Mitchell had shrewdly observed, "A young woman might as well enter a nunnery—she might as well make a vow of single-blessedness at once—as join housekeeping with poor and proud relations. See, child, that taken-in-and-done-for Miss Onslow; not a man will Sir Buller invite to the house, for fear he should lose her little annuity."

Miss Onslow, therefore, had long been unused to any "attentions;" she had also long, long regretted the mistake she had made in supposing that the advantages of society would, of course, be secured by the proposed domestic contract with such a family as the Tawstocks.

Miss Onslow, at length, had become almost resigned to her fate. She wore an air of resignation within doors; and had by degrees formed a very silent habit. With the sentiments which prevailed, she was rarely in unison; and being too kind and courteous to qualify or contradict every word that was said, she was, at the same time, too ingenuous to respond to a kind of falsetto that was jarring and discordant to her whole moral constitution.

But woman's life is to love and to be loved.

There is a power of goodness in them ever yearning for an object—buds teeming with loving-kindness, if they could but open—a fountain gushing with sympathies, if they could but find a channel. So, Miss Onslow every morning went forth into the highways and hedges with her maid Matilda, carrying a little basket, which spoke to the longing eyes of every cottager of tea and sugar, grits and groceries; and so did she indulge her charities with daily exercise, wherever there was a sick family or a lying-in woman. Sir Buller used to gibe and jest, and say that John Wills' legs became bad, and Molly Hobson "was took with a chill," purely out of compliment to Miss Onslow's visit.—But never mind. Charity always "blesses those who give:" and it is not given to mortal man that all the good seed he sows should bear double fruit.

Thomas Walford used frequently to meet and stop and say, "Good morning," to Miss Louisa Onslow. This was quite a new life to him. Charity forming a regular part of the everyday life of an elegant lady like Miss Onslow, invested that lady with more than mortal charms. Of course, he had often heard of Mrs. Fry in Newgate. Other instances of lady philanthropists were known to him as a matter of newspaper history; but this was fresh before his eyes; and what with the clear morning air, and the genial sunshine, and this messenger of mercy in lady-form, doing her unpretending errands among the cottages of his labourers, Mr. Walford was awed into a reverential kind of feeling he had never known before.

It was not long before Mr. Walford begged to be allowed to assist Miss Onslow with a small contribution—for so he modestly termed it: though two ten-pound notes, in an economical neighbourhood, where shillings, sixpences, and fourpenny-bits, seemed the current coin in the realm of charity, impressed Miss Onslow with an idea of something like grandeur, elevation, and largeness of views, in the gentleman's character. She did not know that her new neighbour had, all his life through, seen little charity but on great occasions: as, for instance, when Peter Manley, his clerk, was ill, and he paid for his doctor and a sea-side lodging: or, when the firm of Walford was called upon to take up its proper place in a Lord Mayor's list for a famine or a fire.

The same indescribable sensation was no little increased in the breast of Mr. Walford, when, from every cottage, there came some labourer to tell how often, as he "homeward plods his weary way," his ears were gladdened by some little comfort—all from Miss Onslow's hands. To be run after for his money was a very prominent idea in the mind of this cautious and suspicious man; but here was a lady more ready to give than to receive, and seemed too much bent on her charitable purpose to think of him.

While these were the feelings of the one party, a sense of pity and respect was prevailing with the other—that pity, so near akin to love. Miss Onslow inquired, sympathetically, about his health; recommended divers and sundry little comforts; entered freely with him into the wants and improvement of the lower orders; and, at length, awoke to a consciousness that she had a deeper interest in the felicity and the fortunes of this lonely bachelor than she would have been disposed to sum up in plain, prosaic words.

And so it came to pass, that after the customary formalities in Church and State, Miss Louisa Onslow, amidst the blessings of all the parish, was garlanded and triumphal-arched into church, and rung out it—oh, what peals of triple-bob-major they did pull!—enough to shake the old grey tower down—the daws, circling round and round, as if they never would find their nests again: and, after the customary honours, with good breakfast and bad speeches, they started off in a carriage, they did not know why, and they did not know where. In due and proper time they returned, and settled down as the much-envied proprietors of Richcourt Hall.

CHAPTER IV.

WHAT A CERTAIN RELATIVE EXPECTED, BUT DID NOT COME TO PASS.

General Colton was not a little dismayed when he found that his old bachelor relative had taken to himself a wife. What Walford could have been thinking of, he could not tell; and what Miss Onslow could have been thinking of, was no less inexplicable. A quiet, demure, self-possessed, and religious woman like her! apparently thinking only of her poor people and her prayers, and quite contented as she was! What could she possibly mean by this strange late-in-life alliance?

Contentment and resignation last just as long—especially as regards the lot of single ladies—as they cannot help it. Once open to a lady a way of escape from a forlorn, an aimless, a dreary, and a monotonous condition, and immediately her heart is all in a flutter, and a whole cagefull of crest-fallen and drooping emotions startle up, take wing in a moment, and flap every bar of their prison-house for a release.

Some thought that the old city merchant was ambitious of founding a family—an idea which caused many a laugh and many a guess at Miss Onslow's exact age. Some said, her intended had been adding field to field, and perhaps he would, but for this marriage, have devised the whole estate to the General—to change the name of Colton, and call the lands after the name of Walford. Few of these wise people considered that the explanation might be one which would also serve for many of the puzzling ventures of this life—namely, that life is motion, life is progress, and that, after furnishing his house, matrimony to Mr. Walford was simply move the next in the game of his existence:—if he did not marry, the game came to a stop; he had no other move to take, and nothing else to do.

Mr. Walford was kind and easy-going; and since the fashionable boast of making a husband's money fly, was one that would not consist with Mrs. Walford's ideas of right or noble feeling—prudence and honour being the order of the day, he soon resigned himself and his affairs unreservedly to her discretion, and let her pursue her customary village visits with a more ample purse, as also to invite her friends and relations as much as she pleased.

Mrs. Walford, it was soon apparent, had made no change for the worse. She breathed a freer atmosphere; for, living in a family in which you have little interest, is like a kind of schooling;—your days are all rules and regulations: there is a constant compromise of independence, till it eventually crushes and weighs down the spirits. Indeed, Miss Onslow had found it so difficult to modulate her expressions to a circle of unsympathetic and contradictory people like the Tawstocks, that at last she became resigned to the silent system—was with them, but not of them, and rarely spoke at all.

We are more than ever convinced that society deals very hardly with woman-kind. The estates fall almost always to the boys: they also have a monopoly of the professions. How, then, are single ladies to do justice to their friendly and hospitable feelings. These nursery and in-door plants are only seen in their beautiful perfections, and in all the expansion of their generous natures, when, so to speak, they are early planted out, otherwise, the tendrils of their finer sympathies are cramped and confined. The beautiful flower only half opens, and its charms are lost in the garden of life.

We saw our old friend Miss Onslow about six months after she was married. Her whole heart was enlarged; her once contracted looks had opened like a rose, and all her feelings and sympathies seemed to have sprung with a bound into a more genial clime and nobler sphere of action.

Mr. Walford did not live long to enjoy his happy lot. His old malady was evidently returning, and within a year of his marriage General Colton was distracted, receiving from the Doctor intelligence of a very complex kind,—namely, that there were strong premonitory symptoms of Mr. Walford's going out of the world, and about the same time of some one else coming in!

The General had good reason to know Mr. Walford's intention as to his landed property: and, failing an heir, he felt sure of succeeding to the great part of the property by right of his wife, Mr. Walford's sister.

Judging from circumstances, the sanguine man guessed—and, as the event proved, he guessed rightly—that, though a provision for the widow might be partly charged on the estate, still the high position of Lord of the Manor of Richcourt would immediately be his.

Now, the General was not a bad man: he had a respect for Mr. Walford, and quite a friendship for Mrs. Walford: for Mr. Walford was no common-place character. He had all the superiority of a man long trained to the management of large affairs, who habitually followed a strict, unswerving course, in all minor matters; actuated not more by honesty than by strong common sense. But, with all the General's regard for his kinsman, his breast now became distracted with a strange variety of contending feelings. Without wishing his good neighbour dead, his mind would obstinately run upon his remains. As Mr. Walford, like other failing men, fluctuated from day to day, though ever losing ground upon the balance, the General could not help being conscious of a little disappointment when the soft, full eye, of the devoted wife, seemed to brighten up, as hope flickered in the socket, after something favourable in the report of Mr. Wardle.

Mr. Wardle was the Richcourt doctor — so well known and trusted, that his verdict was looked for as a promise of life, or a sentence of death, all the country round.

No one could read the General's state of mind better than old Richard of the lodge, observing, as Richard did, the "negative and interrogative" way in which he made inquiries: neither did that shrewd old man fail to remark how invariably the conversation, however much it commenced in the health of the landlord, insensibly made a digression, till it ran on and ended in a deeply-interesting speculation as to what might be made of the estate.

"Why, General," said the Doctor, "a patient may live on a long time between one stroke and another with seizures of this kind. Nothing is harder to prognosticate than death. There was old Mrs. Wanley, who lived on years after she had any business to live, according to all the rules of our profession: but then women, you know, are so unaccountable in their ways, and so contradictory; many of them won't even die like other people."

In course of his many visits, the Doctor could not but observe that his friend began, curiously enough, to push forward his inquiries into other branches of medical practice. Even the health of Mrs. Walford seemed now a matter of anxiety to the General: while the effect of any sudden bereavement, anxiety, or anguish of mind, as regarded what might result to a lady in her interesting situation,—all this became the subject of inquiries, not very common with a general officer, however natural for Mrs. Broadbeam, the monthly nurse.

However, as if in mercy to the ever-constant and attentive wife, who might otherwise have wasted strength she ill could spare, Mr. Walford had, unexpectedly, rather a speedy deliverance from all the helpless imbecility of paralysis. In common language, "he died and was buried;" we may also add, that "he died sensible to the last;" inasmuch as he left exceedingly sensible instructions that in no damp charnel-house, dignified as a vault, should his poor body be bricked and mortared up; that no ashler or masonry should wall up his remains: but that in a plain, unadorned coffin, he should be carried by his own people to a grave, clean cut by the spade. And so the turf closed over him.

"It does one's heart good, dear Louisa"—so he expressed himself—"to see the hand of affection scatter flowers over those they love; but 'flowers fresh according to the season, at so much a quarter,' according to the tariff of Kensal Green, like the empty carriages of the neighbours, and all other complimentary mourning,—I call it all an idle mockery of death."

Some of his old friends, to each of whom Mr.

Walford had bequeathed a remembrance, came from London to his funeral, and discussed the virtues of the fallen city man very much in a city way. As it was from the days of Pericles downwards, funeral orations, panegyrics on the dead, and funeral gossip, have strikingly exemplified the worldly sentiments of the speaker and the feelings of the times. Pericles said of the ladies, what might as wisely be said of clergymen, that, for the most part, those are the best of whom we hear the least. But as to funeral conversations in these days, we have often thought that we see a great deal of life brought before us by the solemnities of death. We once heard a grazier's widow deriving consolation from the reflection that her departed spouse was an excellent tradesman; and though others might have equalled him in mutton, he was allowed to have killed the very best of beef.

These city men were not less remarkable in their way. They seemed to think prudence, as Coriolanus deemed valour, to be "the chiefest virtue;" and the organ of acquisitiveness to be the first to be felt for among all human bumps. They seemed to look upon the Will, and the amount it would be sworn under, as the sum and substance of the dead man's character, and as the best possible account of his stewardship, and the chronicle of his doings from the cradle to the grave.

No moralist can deny that industry is a virtue; and if so, it must follow that, when the measure of a man's wealth is the measure of his success in a kind of barter, that distributes God's blessings to the needy — every good man may regard such commercial operations with the purest satisfaction. But all depends upon the motive: and, by the mere greed of money, money, money, the merchant may be starving his own heart, while he is cheapening the food of thousands by his enterprise.

With these sentiments, the following conversation, after the Will was read, must naturally appear like a bitter satire upon the shadow-chasing folly of man:—

"Perhaps you don't know what killed him?" said Mr. Fox, a wholesale drug merchant from Mincing Lane.

"Certainly I do, Sir," said the Doctor, nettled for his own professional diagnosis. "Renewed attacks of paraplegia. He was struck down with paraplegia."

"Paraplegia, did you say, Sir? I thought you didn't know his history. No, Sir; it was tallow. As to his dealing in paraplegia, I don't know even the name of that commodity at all."

"Quite right," interposed Mr. Gill, the tea-taster. "It was the tallow that upset him. You are decidedly correct, Mr. Fox.—I mean, that was the cause of the first attack, that broke up the finest chance of business man ever could desire."

Here the Doctor began to make a question about the fumes of tallow having brought on paralysis. "White lead," he said, "was likely enough——" when the second city authority emphatically continued,—

"It was not the tallow alone, I grant you; but the tallow followed so soon after the guano, that between the two it broke his heart."

"Yes, it did indeed, Sir," said his friend. "It was that which caused the seizure: not that I mean to say the loss of the money crippled him at all; no, it was the vexation—it was the pride of the thing, that laid poor Walford low."

"Speaking as a city man, I could not forgive him for that," interposed Mr. Fox; "certainly that was a weakness—quite a blot in his commercial escutcheon. And I really have many a time remarked, that if Walford had continued in business, instead of realising when he did, he could never have half enjoyed himself after such a regular defeat and such a blunder as that tallow affair."

"But he left all pretty well, as it was," suggested the Doctor.

"Nothing at all, Sir! I call this a mere nothing to what he should have done.—Yes, it was a great pity, indeed. No doubt it is a very respectable little sum to die worth, is a hundred and odd thousand pounds, as I have no doubt we shall swear it; but then, he might have died worth half as much again if it had not been for that great,—yes, I always will say, that most unpardonable—want of judgment with that Limehouse tallow firm."

In due time the solicitor explained to the afflicted Mrs. Walford her position as regarded the property. Under all circumstances, she would have a comfortable—an ample fortune; but the command of the estate of Richcourt Manor depended on the birth of a son and heir. In that event, Mr. Walford devised the estate to the widow, until her son attained the age of twenty-one. Failing an heir, or if the heir should die before the age of twenty-one, the same command of the estate would pass to General Colton on behalf of his son, a boy of five years of age.

Few ladies ever found themselves in a more anxious position than Mrs. Walford. We say nothing of that bewildering, stunning blow by which the King of Terrors makes his power felt, in nerves unstrung, and in that general revulsion of feelings which can only be realised by those who have felt these mysterious shocks. We only glance at the two short months that yet remained to be fulfilled before the trials of maternity; but we would simply suggest that even slight events, which wound our pride or lower our consequence, will often affect us more acutely, or at least with more constant irritation, than the most momentous crisis. So, the idea that Mrs. Walford should go out of Richcourt Hall, and yield both place and precedence to Mrs. General Colton coming in, was quite enough, amidst all her anxieties, to stir up another class of feelings, and cause a very salutary diversion to the current of this troubled lady's thoughts.

Old Richard was not slow to divine "my lady's" state of feeling. Old age and the family sorrow made him a privileged man; accordingly, as his mistress walked sadly about the gardens and pleasure-grounds, he soon found an opportunity of administering a little good-hearted and natural consolation, quoting "wise saws and modern instances," and always ending with a sly suggestion that the General and his lady, "before ever master was no more, had been asking such a sight of questions about the

Manor; the wonder was, how he could possibly want to be so wise."

Of course, the General and his wife must have been very unlike other gentlemen and their wives, where there is a young family to provide for—a duty too often pleaded as ample justification for all that is selfish and ungenerous—if they did not sometimes talk over and calculate all the chances for and against that "consummation so devoutly to be wished," the pleasure of shifting their quarters into Richcourt Hall. "After such a blow, at such a time, any woman with common feeling must suffer from the shock"—the consequences could only be those most naturally to be feared—in short, "no child in common decency could be born alive;" and if the little intruder were so unreasonable as to show signs of life, "perhaps after all it might be a girl, or a poor puny boy, that could not long survive."

This is the way that, in a sanguine and excited humour, men will calculate, and become quite angry when we differ from them; till, at last, they almost persuade themselves that the event cannot be so unreasonable as to turn out otherwise: though, after all is said or done, it will turn most provokingly on wholly different issues, as if to baffle all mortal sagacity and foresight. At all events, so it was in the case of General Colton and his expectant interest in Richcourt Manor.

Such were the thoughts and calculations that, with every variety of permutation and combination, kept running in the heads of these excited family people. And, so frail is human nature, that we must confess that, almost without any encouragement with which we can criminally charge ourselves, such shadowy visitors will persist with their intrusions, and make a thoroughfare of our minds, though some persons may have more scruples in harbouring such mental vagrants, and in entertaining such roguish, vagabond imaginations, than others have.

But while man is calculating and diving into the future, time is flying; and the said future is most steadily—most unsympathetically making its appearance, as if it did not care a straw whether, when it came, we liked the look of it, or whether we did not.

In other words, it happened one morning that there was a ringing of bells and a helter-skelter in Richcourt Hall: there was a general hurrying and skurrying "up-stairs and down-stairs, and in my lady's chamber;" and a galloping off of horses, and a galloping in of the Doctor—the monthly nurse already installed in all the plenitude of her consequence: and, before sunset that day, the church bells were set ringing, and old Richard was mad with exultation, as, standing on the horse-trough outside the Richcourt Arms public-house, he harangued the assembled rustics, announcing, amidst many a "Bravo!" and triumphant cheer, that our lady had twins, and both were boys! two sons and heirs! instead of one—or, as he explained it, "one under another, in case of accidents"—though both, he was credibly informed, were the lustiest little chaps that ever had been seen—certain sure to continue the Manor in the keeping of the lady, and (he might have added) equally certain to secure his noble self in the privileges and the perquisites of Richcourt Lodge.

On the principle that ill-news flies apace, Richard promised young Sam Hodson a penny if he would put his best leg foremost up to General Colton's, to inform him of all that had happened; and particularly to say, that both the young gentlemen, as well as the lady, were doing as well as could be expected—and a pretty deal better, too.

It will readily be surmised, that these were the two babes lying in the cradle, and reposing in their innocence, mentioned in our first chapter: but, how far the elder of the two—the heir of Richcourt—was really the better for having his fortune made before he was born, and how far, to speak generally, a golden inheritance is apt to be tempered with alloy—and how far, in the scrambling race of this life, the high-bred steed proves weighted and jockeyed out of no small part of his supposed advantages—may all be gleaned from the life and adventures of the two young gentlemen of Richcourt Hall.

There is one class of medical practitioners who study the aberrations of the human mind; who, for want of a shorter appellation, are known by the uncomplimentary name of "mad doctors." These gentlemen seriously state that prosperity is so much more distracting to the mind than adversity, that more minds are overthrown by sudden riches than by sudden ruin or hard reverse of fortune.

If the effect of coming into a handsome fortune is really so apt to hurl man's reason from its throne, it is, perhaps, an instance of the goodness of Providence that a sudden fortune is almost always accompanied by a degree of anxiety and worry, amply sufficient to counteract this tendency, and to break the blow.

Such was certainly the case as regards

Mrs. Walford and the inheritance of Richcourt Manor. No sooner was she able to appear abroad, and to christen her dear babes—which she did, with the names of Edward and Nathanael—than her mind was disturbed with an announcement from her lawyer of divers threats from the General to dispute the Will, and to make forcible entry on the lands of Richcourt.

The minds of ladies are easily alarmed by vague and empty threats of setting in motion the crushing machinery of the law: but it soon became evident, that if the Will were put in the fire, her elder-born must take the lands by inheritance, as certainly as by the Will; so General Colton's disappointment and ill-humour were left to evaporate into thin air.

The General's next resource was to persuade himself and his wife that the birth of the babes made little difference. They were both sickly brats. How could it be otherwise? They inherited the worst of constitutions—a compound of London fogs and city smoke: so teething, or convulsions, or some other infantine complaints, would surely put an end to their troubles; and, obviating the waste and the folly of a long minority, would hand over the estates at once to those who were of an age to fulfil the serious duties that were involved in the very tenure of all landed property.

Mrs. Walford conceived a strong antipathy to General Colton. Not but he kept his sanguine calculations, as far as his eager and expressive looks would possibly allow him, all decently to himself. Still, woman's eye can decipher all the hieroglyphics of features ill at ease, and read the language of the looks, however varnished o'er with courtesy and smiles: nor is woman's ear less able to detect, amidst the kindest of inquiries, a certain hollow tone, when the accents of the lips find no echo from the heart.

The mother soon perceived—and there were those about her who were ready enough to repeat incautious words from the General, which plainly implied that he regarded her dear babes with an evil eye; for, with an evil eye, however unconsciously, the disappointed uncle, we fear, did regard them. And before we pronounce his offence utterly unpardonable, let us analyse our own feelings on some similar occasion. Many a man has hated the prophet, when all he really quarrelled with was his own sad doom.—Still, it was too much to suppose that the devoted mother should make allowance for that fallacy of feeling, which too often transfers to those, as innocent as her babes, the impatience which is due to other causes.

Unhappily, it was not long before the malignant aspect of this uncle's star seemed to exercise a blighting influence on the elder — for though by only two hours, he had all the rights and privileges of the elder and the first-born — Master Edward. He became a very weak and sickly child, and there were great doubts about rearing him. Whereupon the General proceeded, in his sanguine calculations, to reckon as if he were already dead, and to leave him wholly out of the equation, by which, with the aid of bills of mortality, and all the tables he could find, he was ever indulging in the doctrines of probabilities, and reducing to their very lowest terms the days on earth of the surviving Master Nat. These calculations were, of course, rather complicated — measles, scarlet-fever, chicken-pox, mumps, and all the catalogue of nursery maladies, rose up before the General's imagination as so many dark allies, ever ready, like the minions of King John, to anticipate his wish, and do his bidding.

When a man's mind is always running on one subject, however careful he may be to keep his own counsel, his neighbours rarely fail to detect and probe his little weakness. So, sometimes,

Sir Buller Tawstock, and at other times some one else—perhaps at the Board of Guardians, or the Magistrates' meeting—would jog the friend who sat next him in a sly way, and looking across the table make quiet inquiries, rather like this,—"Well, General, how are the boys? fine little fellows, they tell me—eh?"

However, after about a year, the General began to see cause very considerably to modify his calculations, because, in an evil hour, Master Ned's nursery had been shifted: it used to look over the stable-yard, to the north; but, quite accidentally, it was changed for a room to the south, with large windows that let in light and the morning sun as it rose beyond the fine open meadow-land, and did not let in, like many a Belgravian nursery, the poisonous exhalations of the stable-yard. Immediately the child freshened up wonderfully, and as the twins rode out with their donkey, one on each side, old Richard was always declaring that one pannier was as heavy as the other; "and no two rosebuds on a summer's morning could look more beautiful or blooming than Master Nat and Master Ned—one as good as t'other."

Just at this time, when the children were between two and three years of age, an event happened which showed that the General had left a very material contingency out of his ingenious calculations—namely, that he himself might die as well as the twins. If we followed the fashion set by most writers of fiction, we should pretend to record that one morning, in his study, he had just finished a new calculation which defined the exact time by which his two nephews ought in all mathematics to be dead to a fraction, when the pen dropped from the hands of this presumptuous arbitrator of the issues of life and death, and he died, as if he were intended to leave a great moral lesson of the short-sightedness of man, and the instability of all human affairs, to future ages.—In plain prose, General Colton died after a short illness.

CHAPTER V.

THE SON AND HEIR GROWS STRONG AND HEARTY.

When the General was dead and buried, old Richard began to breathe a little freely, and even Mrs. Walford admitted it was quite a relief no longer to feel that there was any human being who could not sympathise heart and soul in her truly natural and devoted affection for her two dear boys.

Time passed on. Both Ned and Nat grew strong and hearty, and one was as stout and ruddy a little urchin as the other; but already the little world in which they moved, as regarded the rural homage they received, began to show a difference. The servant-maids within-doors, and the serving-men without, in the garden, the stable, and the farm-stead—from the portly coachman to the staring cow-boy—all contrived to make Master Ned understand that he, and not Master Nat, was the Squire—that his was all "the fortune;" and that when he grew to be a man, all the horses and bow-wows, with fine carriages to drive, and heaps of golden guineas to spend at the toy-shop, and all other things he could set his little heart on, would all be his own; and then, what a great man, and how happy would he be!

The two children could not be seen picking wild flowers in the lane, or toddling through the village, but some of the simple folk would turn aside just to make sure which was the happy child. Yes, "happy" was the only word; for riches enter so naturally into our ideas of happiness, that, even with the wisest of us, it requires all our life through a constant exertion and care to correct the variation of that mental compass, which so invariably points to Money. All the wise saws and modern instances of money not being everything, of course came out sometimes, to vindicate the sense of the Richcourt people. For, no doubt experienced persons do know better; but when our desires glide so smoothly and so persistently in one way, it is very hard to make our reason lead another.

For instance, the Parson of the parish needs must have known better: still, though perhaps he finished a sermon about it on Saturday, and preached it on Sunday, yet long before Monday night he would find the heaviest of metals getting uppermost in his mind.

Mr. Wardle, the Doctor, would know better, very likely: still, as in all weathers he threaded the lanes midst driving rain or parching heat, from one sick chamber to another—albeit he carried in his bosom the untold riches of a heart that the same hard life had taught to beat for others' woe—the sight of Master Ned, "born to a fortune," tried his philosophy very hard; and he could not help thinking, how very plainly he would talk to the testy Mr. Jones, or the impertinent Mrs. Robinson, if he could but afford—what no poor man must ever think of—the luxury of speaking his mind.

Farmer White knew better: however, as he jogged along, with his feet almost to the ground, on his little shaggy pony, boding ill of his crops and grumbling at his work-people, he would stop and rub his hand across his healthful, ruddy brow, and think for a moment what great things he would do, and what a figure he would cut at market and at fair, were he only born to such a breadth of land as Master Walford.

Neither could one see old Will Webber the pauper, who had a ticket to break stones on behalf of the parish, put down his hammer, as the young Squire toddled by; or perhaps Joe Ruff, the knife-grinder, as *rotæ constitit orbis*, he stopped his whirring wheel to meditate on the inequality of worldly things; without feeling that it would take a very long lecture in moral and political philosophy to convince them, that the man who earns money enjoys himself more than the man who is born to it. Still less would they understand that money carries with it a certain blighting influence, too often fatal to the health to enjoy, to the heart to respond to the highest pleasures, or the soul to aspire above the things that perish in the using and to be all shuffled off in the quiet grave.

In short, wherever the well-known donkey and panniers, or sometimes the basket-carriage, with the footman by its side, appeared in the village, there was a kind of sensation which Molly Woodman described, saying, "It did their very hearts good to see it," simply because it set every one castle-building; it put the heavy parish imagination into a lively flutter,—with just a minute's taste of all those pleasurable sensations which make the child with its fairy tale as happy as if picking up gold and silver, as long as the airy hallucination lasts.

All this went on till the children were about

nine or ten years of age; by which time Mrs. Walford began to feel that masters and governesses at home had served their purpose, and that, for the greater quiet of her house and conscience, she must endure the cruel parting, and send her dear boys to school.

The fond mother might hardly have had sufficient strength of mind to risk all the horrors she had heard of schools. She might also have found her own heart plead too strongly against the loneliness of Richcourt Manor, when every room and every meal, and even the silence of the hall, every minute in the day, felt like a yearning void in nature—for Nat and Ned were two noisy, boisterous little fellows—had she not found a wise adviser in the Rev. Henry Raymond, the Vicar of the parish.

The Vicar soon pointed out that, as to speaking of putting the boys to school, and beginning their more public education in earnest,—all this had been going on much faster than she was aware of, a long time since.

The lady was surprised.—To what school could the good Vicar refer? What particular public education had her boys received?

The Vicar made the anxious mother look rather sad and sorrowful, as he explained that the little world of Richcourt was to her boys a school, and a very bad school, too—rich in the vulgar tongue, rife with the satyr vices supposed banished to our towns, and blighting in all the bad examples of the stable-yard or the farmer's kitchen; while the tool-house and the saddle-room, the boys' resort at all times, were insensibly becoming the standard of mind and morals to the future Heir of Richcourt!

"True," said the Vicar, "there is wickedness in all schools, but there is more wickedness out of them: and already, I think, you must perceive, that the broadness of their dialect, as well as the rural cast of their manners, prove what very apt scholars your sons can be."

Mrs. Walford felt some relief in finding that her good friend stopped here. For, more than once, had she been shocked by horrid words, and even oaths profane, and had shuddered to think of the insidious way in which other forms of evil might have been stealing upon their thoughtless and pliant minds.

The next question was, to what school they should be sent.

The mother thought it desirable that the brothers should be sent to different schools. For, already, they had had fights and bloody noses. Ned had learnt to boast of his future grandeur; and Nat, with very little reverence for the law of primogeniture, had declared that "an hour-and-a-half's start could make no such mighty difference" in the term of Ned's natural existence, that he should brag like an elder brother over him: and as to the property, of which everybody talked so much—if, when the time came to possess it, Ned did not share it with him, like a decent and respectable fellow, "he would just come and take it, and give him a precious good licking for being such a horrid, disagreeable, and shabby sort of character."

The Vicar fully coincided in the views of Mrs. Walford; the more so, as he perceived that the fond mother could not endure to send both her boys at once beyond the limits of an easy morning drive. But as the Vicar had just notions about such parental visits and interference, having long made up his mind what usually came of this kind of schooling, he thought that she had better spoil one son than two; and therefore he wisely suggested, that as Nat would, eventually, have his own way to make in the world, the sharper discipline and the wider sphere of a public school would be far more consistent with the prospects of a younger son.

While all these deliberations were in process at Richcourt Hall, there was another consultation, in which the Walford family were no little concerned, held at a house about ten miles from Richcourt, between a gentleman and his wife — a very industrious and striving couple, far too interesting not to be formally introduced to our friends.

At the small town of Sellack, one of the market-towns nearest to Richcourt Hall, lived a gentleman and his wife, the Reverend Joseph and Mrs. Watson, who received into their house "a select number" — as many as they could squeeze in — to be treated with all paternal care; the manners and morals, as well as "the natural bias of the minds of the young gentlemen," and "their destination in life," being strictly regarded.

The Reverend Joseph Watson, M.A., of Chester College, Oxford, had been known in a distant county, years before, as plain Mr. Watson,—an usher to Dr. Battersby of the Kenfield Grammar School,—a family man of small learning, and a mind just large enough to hold it; which mind, however, was always set upon the main chance.

Mr. Watson, after some years' service, finding promotion by constitutional means rather slow, decided on a *coup d'état*, and eloped with the Doctor's daughter; and since run-away girls, like run-away boys, become very penitent when their money is gone,—after the fever of parental displeasure had gone through the usual stages of "violently angry," "determined never to speak again," and then quieting down—completely reconciled, and even abusing every one who had taken up the quarrel and dared to say a word against them—the Doctor, to make the best of the difficulty, gave the delinquent Joseph a more prominent part in the school.

There is nothing to be done in school-keeping without a plausible Prospectus. The old question of " What's in a name?" is a question the Doctor would have ridiculed, as betraying a profound ignorance of the ignorance of human nature. In the commerce of thought, sounds often pass current for as much as sense. Yes, names are spells to conjure by. Charles Lamb says, that it is absurd to pretend that a man could not raise a spirit much more easily at the name of Rome than at the name of Romford! All the Graces of Oratory have been found powerless to captivate a West-end congregation till the name of Dubbins was melted into Dulile; and the Doctor always boasted, that the fifty pounds which he paid in fees for each letter of his own *D.D.*, was the best investment he ever made in his life. What cared he that D.D. was quite compatible with Double-distilled Dunce, for any learning for which it was a voucher? Long experience had taught him, that in this world you may count the wise men on your fingers, but the fools as the hairs of your head. "What do I care about the absurdity of parents' notions?" he used to say. "If they won't have sense, I'll deal in nonsense; so I never complain of lack of customers."

Such being the Doctor's sentiments, he soon pointed out that two things were indispensable for his son-in-law's wide success. "Joseph," he said, "you are like a quantity without any coefficient. You must make haste to stick 'Reverend' before your name, and 'M.A.' after it."

Both these points were eventually secured; the one by an abuse of the University, the other by an imposition on the Church.

Fact is stranger than fiction; or, no one would believe that, by mere eating of bread and butter as a proof of residence, only a few weeks in each year, without the possibility of any academical influence or refinement of mind, a University should ever have granted the same Degree which is intended to vouch for an improving course of academical study!

The title of "Reverend" was comparatively easy. Unhappily, there are rarely wanting Rectors who will importune their bishop to ordain them a curate, provide he will serve them for little or nothing—without ever considering the useless burden, and not seldom the scandal, they thus bring upon the Church.

"The Rev. Joseph Watson, M.A., of Mount Pleasant House, Sellack," was a very imposing designation, when once he was far removed from all that could throw light on the mendacious points of his early history.

On this part of the story we are the more minute, because such men as the Rev. Joseph Watson are neither few nor far between; insomuch, that the University examinations to test the proficiency of private schoolmasters and so protect parents from the most irreparable of all the cruel frauds that can be exercised—have not been instituted before they were imperatively required by the exigencies of the rising generation.

Let us not be misunderstood. There are engaged in education some of the most highly cultivated minds and the noblest natures the land can boast—men as alive to their responsibilities, as the disinterested Vicar of Richcourt. But if so, the more is the pity that such valuable members of society should be reduced to compete with mere dunces and impostors for a sphere of useful labour.

As to the Reverend Joseph Watson, we would not be understood to say that he did not intend to give a fair penny's worth for each penny in his bill; but you cannot expect a very enlarged mind with very straitened circumstances. Mr. Watson's honesty was not of the noble and chivalrous sort, but a ruder commodity for trading purposes; and whenever he did what he ought not to do in the way of extras, or left undone what he ought to do in the way of winking at vice in a boy, for fear of tempting his mother to try what another school would do for his morals, he had a semi-penitential way of blaming the carnal man instead of himself; and, "but for his duty to his family" and (even) "his duty to himself," he would act like a wholly different man altogether.

At the particular time of which we are speaking, Mr. Watson's "limited number" was limited indeed. His estate in boys was fast dwindling away, and the question was, What to do? Poor Mrs. Watson had done her very best. The very whitest of counterpanes were ready to be put on at the shortest notice, when any fond mamma was expected to have a look at the young gentleman's bed—and as quickly taken off afterwards: the packing of the school-boxes was unexceptionable; and the rigour of the small-tooth combing was worthy of a better cause. Still, boys were very scarce, and money even scarcer than boys. Two of the boys they had did not pay cash; they were only answers to their anonymous advertisements — "Pupils will be received on terms of mutual accommodation."

This kind of truck system had been pushed to its furthest limits; the Watson stores, and sundry goods and chattels, were out of all proportion to the Watson cash; and what made the measure as hazardous, as it proved unprofitable, was, that the saucy young urchins had found it out, and had adopted nicknames which might publish this economical arrangement. So, Johnny Bridgeman, whose schooling was to be taken out in kind, at the wholesale grocery and sauce warehouse in the Poultry, they had the impudence to call "Master Pickles;" while Fred. Hallett, who represented a similar arrangement with the great furnishing people in Baker Street, they as regularly denominated "Young Stool."

When, therefore, Mr. and Mrs. Watson understood that the heir of Richcourt was about, in the language of the county paper, "to commence a systematic course of study, to qualify him to discharge the onerous responsibilities which, from his large estates, would one day devolve upon him," they exclaimed both together, that this was their last chance. For, added to heavy half-yearly accounts in ready money, the rich Master Walford would be as good as decoy duck,—they had taken one young baronet cheap on purpose,—and all the silly birds from the patrician domains around would soon flock together, and Mount Pleasant would be famed all the country round.

But how to make sure of Master Walford, how to jog the memory of his devoted mother, or to influence her choice, was the difficulty; till Mrs. Watson, with her accustomed tack and female penetration, suggested that whereas the mother of Master Richardson, a lady on most intimate terms with Mrs. Walford, must daily be expecting to be pressed for her boy's schooling, now "two half-years to the bad," it might be most delicately—not suggested, of course, but simply—made to run in Mrs. Richardson's head, that by recommending the school to Mrs. Walford she would have a claim on the Watsons' gratitude, in the shape of patience and long-suffering, for ever after. Accordingly, they contrived to prefer a request to that lady, accompanied with a significant assurance, that "indeed there was no accommodation they would consider too great for so truly kind a friend."

This was the way that Master Walford was made to prop up the falling fortunes of the house of Watson; while at the same time, so all-powerful were his riches, that a lady in fashionable society positively received, however indirectly, a handsome douceur, even for recommending the school. But the Tawstock party saw through this piece of diplomacy in a minute; for, just as charity hopeth all things that are generous, so worldly feeling takes for granted everything that is mean. And during the Walford minority, so prevailing was the feeling that there was a common mine to be worked, or a golden goose to be plucked, that every hanger-on of the family suspected every one else, as if "therefrom sucketh he no small advantage."

When Mrs. Walford called at Mount Pleasant House—a name which seemed rather too complimentary to the situation—she began, as usual, to give a little history of her son's constitution, mental, moral, and physical; and to suggest the exact regimen that he would require for each—kindness and encouragement being indispensable to foster his virtues, lessons made as easy as possible for his intellect, dry shoes at all times, and a glass of port wine daily after dinner, for the preservation of that health on which so much depended.

While Mrs. Walford was thus suggesting quite a study of her son's character, Mr. and Mrs. Watson were all the time making quite a study of hers; and no sooner was she gone, and the door shut after her, than the lady and gentleman congratulated themselves, and made their observations as follows:—

Mrs. Watson. "The terms are handsome—separate room, extra—wine, extra—in short, it is very evident she will stand all the extras without a word of complaint."

Mr. Watson. "Of course, my dear: Mrs. Walford is allowed so much for education; and we never have such terms as when people are paying out of somebody else's purse instead of from their own. Had we said 100*l.* a-year instead of 200*l.*, we should have lost the boy."

Mrs. Watson. "But we must be careful what we are about. The mother has no notion of any severity. I do hope the poor boy has no *very* bad habits: I should feel so for my Harry if his bad ways were not corrected."

Mr. Watson. "Trust me for all that part of the matter. You won't catch me flogging any boy but my own; and since he knows he will have it whenever he deserves it, a little goes a long way with him. And so it would with others; but if parents are such fools they must not blame me."

Mrs. Watson. "The mother is all for 'moral measures,' that is quite clear."

Mr. Watson. "Moral measures! be hanged with them! I have no patience with such nonsense. Make them smart for it, and they'll remember it: that's what I say. They will smart enough for their vices in the sharp school of after-life. Moral measures, indeed! Who punishes us with moral measures, I should like to know? Mrs. Willett pretended to punish us for neglect, so she wouldn't pay the quarter out of principle—there's *moral* measures for you! Old Ransome slandered me out of the two Hall's and three of the Field's connexion, and, but for this last most lucky chance of young Walford, we might have been broken up and starved altogether—there's *moral* measures again!"

Here Mr. Watson enunciated far more worldly philosophy than he was aware of. This, truly, is a world of more kicks than halfpence. The severest, almost the inquisitorial forms of corporal punishment, enter largely—may I not say, exclusively?—into the economy of the Most High. The Allwise Ruler knows His stubborn and rebellious creatures far too well. With Him it is one word to ten thousand blows. With Omniscience, moral measures there may be, but they are burnt and branded into us. Witness the insufferable *ennui* of the man of pleasure; the tortures of the profligate; the tossings on the restless couch, and the gnawing of conscience at the very heart's core, of doers of iniquity of other kinds!

Mr. Watson. "I can't help remembering when I was a boy. Moral measures, indeed! A long yarn from a master, perhaps, when caught out in a lie! It only made us put on a hypocritical face for five minutes; though there was one master—a poor, pallid, ill-used usher at your father's school—he could say words that searched my very heart, and made me feel: but then, that was not as if he was paid for it—he was one in a thousand, *he* was: there is no reasoning from such a man as that. Poor fellow! he went into a consumption and died—almost at his desk to the very last; and some of his letters—they were from his mother and his sister—came into our hands—enough to make your heart bleed—he had helped to support them. Ah! that was something like moral measures to listen to him—but we shall never see his like again."

And so it came to pass, that the heir of Richcourt Hall entered "the young gentlemen's establishment, kept by the Rev. Joseph Watson, M.A., of Mount Pleasant House, Sellack;" for that gentleman took care that his full title and designation, together with "the confidence so deservedly reposed in our respected neighbour," should be prominently advertised in a paragraph in the next week's *Sellack Journal,* which journal did not fail afterwards to contain periodical notices of "the learned Mr. Watson," and "the domestic arrangements of the lady, so renowned for her motherly care of all her pupils," whenever Master Walford had recovered from measles or scarlatina, or perhaps had recited the oration of Mark Antony over the dead body of Cæsar at the great speech-day of the Mount Pleasant Academy.

Mr. and Mrs. Watson were not deceived in their calculations as to the effect the Walford connexion would have upon their school.

"Let us only find two pupils more, and we shall not have a bed to spare," exclaimed the delighted Mrs. Watson; "and, after that, I am determined that we will have cash for young Bridgeman—for there are goods and groceries enough in my closet for two years to come."

But the point to which, in the chronicles

of the Walford family, we would chiefly call attention, is this: that a school connexion flies off as capriciously as it comes on, and the slightest offence to the Walfords would, at any moment, threaten to shake the Sellack Academy to its very foundations. In other words, the master and mistress set about Edward Walford's reformation in manners, mind, and morals, under very serious advantages: they were virtually bound over, under the most fearful penalties, to keep the peace; or, to "make things pleasant" to the mother, and, consequently, to make things by no means unpleasant to the boy.

But here comes the difficulty: the correction of old habits, and the formation of new, never can be anything but a disagreeable operation. A raw recruit among our Volunteers once complained that "standing at ease" made both his legs ache. By parity of reasoning, it is easy to understand that, however pretty good children may look in the frontispiece of Mavor's *Spelling-Book*, virtue and propriety of conduct—being very much of an acquired taste—are things which, without some little unpleasantness, can only be enforced in the smallest quantities; otherwise, what Jeremy Taylor aptly calls, "that iron sinew, the unruly will," fights for the mastery

—the spoilt child writes alarming letters home, and the fond parent is soon shocked to hear what "a horrible old cross-patch" is entrusted with the son.

No great sagacity will be required to see the disadvantages under which Edward Walford's so-called education was conducted, from his tenth to his sixteenth year—the period of his residence at Mr. Watson's academy. Such terms as, "that Ned Walford was a jolly chap;" "No fellow had ever such lots of tin to spend;" or, "Such baskets of cakes and fruit, and eatables of all kinds, to give away;" were common in the town and neighbourhood of Sellack.

They might have heard, that no fellow ever had such a motive to sham sick, or was so often kept away from school, with a pony sent for his riding exercise, and every indulgence of a parlour-boarder, till he was quite a walking companion for Mr. Watson. If pressed hard with his studies, his head always began to ache; and if detected in any vicious practices, it was wiser for his master to be blind altogether: for, to punish adequately, was utterly impracticable. How could he be supposed to jeopardise so valuable a connexion as the Heir of Richcourt?

In short, of education Ned Walford had little or none, for his powers were never drawn forth. Instead of learning to go his master's pace, he went droning on at his own: and though naturally well-disposed, he was reared in selfishness and self-indulgence. Every one seemed to have nothing else to do than to think of him; so, naturally his thoughts soon learned to run on no one but himself—a victim of that cruel kindness that forgets that, so truly are we born in sin, that a young child is selfishness incarnate—a creature wrapped, like the worm, in a chrysalis of self, from which it is the highest purpose of all education to set it free, and to deliver it, like the butterfly, to a higher state of being.

And here we shall introduce no unnecessary digression if we say that, at this school, there was a master of the name of Thompson; whom the boys, always delighting in nick-names, called "Gritty Thompson." It so happened, that one impudent little urchin had come back to school, after the Easter holidays, breathless with the discovery that old Thompson was a miller, and that this identical "splitter of quills and scraper of pencils" used, at one time, to carry in the grits. Henceforth, the name of "Gritty Thompson," scribbled upon every wall, added one more burthen to the daily load of this patient man-of-all-work: for, from the days of Juvenal to the present time, the sorest part of poverty is being laughed at, or finding ourselves in a position to "sing small;" which colloquialism has always appeared to us nearest to the spirit of the original in the well-known lines:—

> "Nil habet infelix paupertas durius in se,
> Quàm quòd ridiculos homines facit."

However, the mind of poor Thompson had the happy art—superior to all the magic shifts of fairy tales—of soaring far away, and taking refuge in the future: it would fly away and be at rest. Amidst all the drudgery of the school-room, bold in the strength of his own elastic powers, Thompson conjured up pictures of a happier state of things, when he could earn books to his heart's content, and time to read them; and when, perhaps, some loved one by his side would share his honours, and smooth the deep furrows that toil and trouble were fretting on his manly brow.

Thompson was at this time little more than a boy, though prematurely thrown upon the world to act an older part. One half-year had seen him a school-boy; the next a master, nominally with opportunities for private study, in part payment for his labour. As to this part of the stipulation, his persevering spirit contrived to make opportunities he could be hardly said to find. In every country walk Thompson might be seen with his book; late at night, and long before the boys were called in the morning, the poor usher was up and deep in study: the wonder was, that the tortured brain could so long endure.

Happily, there was a good, kind, Christian fellow who lived hard by: a man of talent and a scholar—Mr. Willett Davis. Davis was one of those generous souls, a very mine of sympathy, whose hearts seem to throw out feelers—acutely sensitive to every note of woe that thrills in the bosom of a fellow-creature. Little chance was there that anything should hide the pale-faced student from his eye. He crossed him in his walk,—made his observations,—learnt his plans and simple history,—entered into his hopes and prospects,—and forthwith proceeded to do all that in him lay to give those airy hopes substantial form. In a word, Mr. Davis used often to invite Thompson to come and read with him when the boys were gone to bed—sending him home gladdened by kindness and a good supper; and fired with all the more energy for the stubborn and repulsive work before him.

But farewell, Thompson, my fine fellow, for the present: we hope one day to see you again.

CHAPTER VI.

THE PRIVATE SCHOOL-BOY AND THE ETONIAN COMPARE NOTES.

To return to Master Edward Walford. Since the tendency of his education will become yet more evident by contrast, we will pass on to take a glimpse at his brother Nat, who was all this time at Eton. For, when the two boys met for the holidays, they naturally compared notes as to their respective schools: and, if the reader will allow for the desultory conversation, that from time to time drew forth Nat's observations on the Eton system, and the wholesome tendencies of public schools in general, we will endeavour to present him with a picture as in "mosaic tesselated with facts."

"From what you tell me, Ned, the fellows at Eton would call your school, at old Watson's, as not like a school at all. Why, what good is it?

You can't do verses, and don't ever pretend to be put into Homer; and as to Virgil, a deal you seem to know about that. No wonder: you can sham sick, and shirk home half your time. Our fellows would call you a 'skulk' and a 'Molly;' for lies don't pay at Eton: but while I have to twist my brains into learning anything, the first thing you think of is how to get out of it.

"Then again, there is such a constant bother about you; only come to Eton, and see whether your tutor would let mother send after you there. When first I went I was uncommonly bumptious, and thought no end of myself, but they soon took all that out of me. At Eton, a fellow is just as important as he behaves himself. A lord or a marquis gets just as good a switching in school, if he deserves it, and just as good a licking out of school, as any one else, if he makes himself disagreeable. But, talking of that, Ned, that is just what you are growing,—disagreeable. Ah! but you don't understand what we call being 'disagreeable.'"

Ned. "Why, what have I done?"

Nat. "What have you done!—that shows you don't understand. As to that, a fellow may be voted disagreeable without high crimes and misdemeanors;—a fellow's disagreeable when he is disagreeable — when he is always thinking about himself — when he isn't in a mood for what every other fellow is in a mood —when he does not take things as they come — 'worse luck to-day, better luck to-morrow!' Why, what do you think of a fellow like Tom Whateley, switched last half, all through Richardson's fault; and when Richardson was going to tell him how sorry he was, 'It don't *mag*nify,' said Tom, 'it's all down to the day's work!' When a fellow is so mighty particular about himself, that's the chief thing in being disagreeable; and that — not to be too hard upon you — is what I mean you are growing: so you must rub up, and get over it. You wouldn't be palavered as you are by every one at home about Richcourt Manor, if you came to Eton. Richcourt Manor, indeed! Mighty grand that sounds here, but what is that to Carroty Bob's? — that's the Marquis of Broadlands — what is that to what Old Cropper — we call him 'Cropper,' because he'll crop a dog's ears against any cad in Windsor — the Duke of Windfall's his governor? A capital fellow, Old Cropper; he's my fag, and toasts crumpets first rate: so I'm never hard upon him. Why, Cropper can ride or shoot thirty miles straight on end on his father's estate! Richcourt Manor, indeed! Pshaw! —

trumpery! — about enough to fill his flower-pots!

"But as to switching, there is none to be had in your school; so, of course, you never learn anything. And you go nowhere without a master after you, for fear you should get into mischief or break your honourable noses. Now, at Eton, a fellow can go anywhere — in bounds or out of bounds — if you only make a little pretence to hide when a master's coming. All you have to do is to be back before 'absence:' if you don't, you are switched.

"Next half I am safe to pass in swimming: I can almost swim the distance now: but I must learn to swim easy, and a better style. When I can swim, I can go in the boats and row up to Surly Hall. I am already getting on at cricket.

"Now, at your trumpery private school, you don't learn to swim, or to boat; and as to your cricket, you don't know what it is. Ah! if you could play Dickey Powell's bowling, I would say something to you. You have no liberty worth having: you play, if it's worth calling play — for, after our river, and the Playing-fields, it is sad, babyish work — within four stone walls, with Mother Watson, I suppose, looking out of the window all the time; or, else you walk out, two and two, like a girls' school. I wonder you are not all ashamed of yourselves. So, not only do your fellows do no work fit scarcely for our lower school, but you have no fun either. All I find out that you do, is to shirk, and sham, and send tales home, with lots of lies at all times, as if nothing were to be done without. Send tales home, indeed! Just fancy that at Eton! Fancy mother calling my tutor to account because Master Softy or Master Moonshine had taught Master Walford some naughty words, or pulled his ears because he would not learn them! Why, I should be packed off home by the first coach —and the fellows would cut my acquaintance evermore!"

Ned. "But it seems you are 'switched,' as you call it, for everything. Isn't it horrid to be flogged?"

Nat. "Switched for everything? No, that is all a mistake. We might be switched for anything, no doubt; but, after once or so, any fellow that isn't a born fool learns to quicken his paces, mind his absences, and to have his eye-teeth sharp-set at all times, so as just to shave the post—I mean so as to steer exactly clear—neither more particular on the one hand to fetter your liberty, nor so careless on the other as to jeopardise something else."

Ned. "What do you mean by quickening your paces?"

Nat. "Why, don't you remember when Farmer Hollis sold his gig-horse to the mail, and every one said he wasn't fast enough? What said Coachee? He cried out, 'Leave me alone for that matter. I'll teach him a pace with the help of my three chestnuts and a little whipcord.' It is just the same at Eton; at first I could not learn four lines by heart, when they set me twenty, and afterwards thirty, at a lesson. So when I began to ask what was to be done, oh, how the fellows laughed! 'That's what we used to say,' they exclaimed. And if I could have written home, like you, for mother to pitch into my tutor, I never should have learned the quantity; but, as there was no helping it, I set to work late over-night, and up at five next morning. It was a near shave, and I was in bodily fear all the time; still, I just saved my bacon, and after a week or two I could learn twenty with ease."

Ned. "Then, you mean to say, they taught you to go a better pace than you ever went before?"

Nat. "A very much sharper pace. And my tutor says that's half the business—to quicken a fellow's paces, and to sharpen him up; because, no sooner does the work grow easy than you get a remove, where you have to quicken your paces just as much again."

Ned. "But, perhaps, some boys can't learn. If they positively are not able, how do they do then?"

Nat. "Oh! as to can't: there's no such thing as can't; fast or slow at first coming, they all get on with the help of the birch. A fellow is ashamed to be always in the lower school—standing up in a class, head and shoulders taller than a parcel of brats.

"Half the things you talk and boast of at your grand Mount Pleasant House—all fudge!—Mount Misery or Mount Milksops we should call it—a sort of 't'other school' that our fellows have all grown out of,—well, half you brag of doing there you wouldn't dare mention at Eton; for one part you would be laughed at, and for the other part kicked, as a set of sneaks and shabby fellows.

"The first notion I formed at Eton was, 'no nonsense'—my tutor stands no nonsense—my dame stands no nonsense—and the fellows stand no nonsense. Thought I to myself, Like it or not, I am in for it: no worse for me than for those small boys I saw cutting about as jolly as chicks; so I must make a back and bear it, and take my chance. The first thing I saw was the fellow next me late for absence, put down in the bills—'Harrison to stay,' was the order. 'What's that?' I inquired—'stay! for what?' 'Switching,' was the reply. Harrison looked very uncomfortable all that lesson; I saw him afterwards, while the rest were at cricket, staying in the school-room, growing more and more white in the gills, till the awful hour of execution arrived. All this staying and funking is as bad as the flogging: so, I thought to myself, I must look a little lively, or perhaps before long it will be 'Walford to stay,' too."

Ned. "But, perhaps, a fellow does not know the time, or some accident happens, and he can't reach the school?"

Nat. "Then my tutor would tell him. I heard him spin this yarn one day—that 'punctuality' and 'duty' are as well worth learning as Latin and Greek; that a calculation of time, three or four times a-day, is worth practising; and as to accidents, a switching is part of the accident, and no doubt it will sharpen him up wonderfully against another time."

We trust we have said enough to make it quite evident that the elder brother and the younger were receiving a very different kind of education. To relate such a history without various feelings and reflections of a serious kind arising in the mind, were obviously impossible; but, as we were unwilling to make a break in the thread of our narrative—spoiling the story for our younger, in order to converse with our elder readers, we have ventured to introduce a separate chapter on the subject of schooling—public and private—which chapter any one may read or skip, as he pleases.

CHAPTER VII.

A FEW WORDS ABOUT ETON AND THE OTHER PUBLIC SCHOOLS, WHICH THE READER MAY SKIP WITHOUT LOSING THE THREAD OF OUR STORY.

The first reflection that arises from the history of Ned Walford at the private school, and Nat Walford at a public one, is, a conviction of the inestimable value of a school like Eton to the wealthier families of England. We say the *wealthier*, because, we repeat, few private teachers will dare to correct a rich man's son; and also because wealth, and a sense of being born to a fortune, as will soon appear, is attended with disadvantages to a boy in heart, head, and habits, that do, indeed, require something very powerful to counteract them. "Save me from my friends!" is a well-known cry. To save a boy from the cruel kindness of his parents is no less an act of mercy; and a public school is now the only place in which a parent has no power to interfere: it is, therefore, the only place in which, from the spell of necessity, the mind of the boy cheerfully acquiesces, and in which alone bad habits can be corrected, because nowhere else is discipline complete.

In a private school the boy always feels there is an appeal and an escape; and treason to his master and falsehood in letters home are the result of the identical measures which, at Eton, would re-act on the boy himself.

The mind of a boy is only partially sound: the same ideas and actions, which seem natural in a boy, would be deemed a mark of insanity in a man. So, it is easy to believe that, in the process of education, certain hints may be derived from the treatment of the insane.

An insane patient can, with difficulty, be cured in any private house. The great principle of cure is to stimulate the patient to self-command. To that end, you must cut off all hope of evasion, all possibility of resistance. This done, it soon appears that there is a natural resignation, from a sense of necessity: irritation and impatience subside; and the tone of temper is improved, and powers of self-control are called forth, to a degree long unknown before. Certainly, the discipline may seem severe to friends anxious only to comfort and console; but the sacrifice of feeling must be made. Perhaps, also, the attendants may be hasty, and measures, unnecessarily harsh, may tempt the relations to interfere. But, of two evils, choose the least: the possibility of interference would ruffle the mind, and, as it were, open the valve just as the strong moral power is exercising an irresistible pressure on the whole machine.

Exactly similar is the discipline of a public school. It is the only establishment in which the boy reads, with undoubting conviction, "Who enters here must give up hope"—hope of any escape, but by strict obedience. The school-law is inexorable; and, since the law won't bend, the will must.

This is the great benefit of a public school: an advantage great, not only in itself at all times, but at the present day a hundred times greater, from comparison with private schools, fettered and demoralised as they are under the prevailing errors of false kindness, and a weak and womanish public opinion—a kind of sentiment perhaps natural enough for woman, tender and devoted as she is to her offspring, and shocked perhaps, at the tales of barbarity, too true of the last generation—but the shame is that so many men should know no better.

As to these private schools, the master is the mere puppet, of which the mother pulls the strings. One man here and there, perhaps, may nobly risk his reputation and his fortune, both of which, a very breath of maternal indignation smarting for her boy may scatter to the winds; but what vigorous measures, what independence of action, can we ordinarily expect when a master cannot move—least, of all, with the son of very rich and influential parents—under fear of utter ruin? Is it not evident that, but for the independent position of our public schools, the higher the rank of the parent, the more hopeless the discipline, the correction, and all worth considering in the education of the son?

Add to the advantage of perfect discipline, as regards Eton (for instance), that its influences are superior to any sphere available for boys. Far, indeed, superior to those of almost every home, where the groom and the gamekeeper, and some smoking-room or lounging-room, in the nearest market-town, form no small part of the associates: and as to academies like Mr. Watson's, if there are but one or two vicious boys, they are wholly uncontrolled by any public school traditions, sentiment of honour, or public opinion, and "the select number of young gentlemen" constitute a small hotbed of vice and every kind of meanness.

Every man who recals the impressions of his early years will admit that his principles, his standard of what was mean and shabby, and his preference of things honourable and of good report, resulted scarcely at all from lectures expressly for his guidance, but almost entirely from the sentiments that prevailed around him. Did we not imbibe them as part of the moral atmosphere, whether more or less healthy, that it was our doom to breathe? "Strict attention to morals and religious principles," which we read in almost every school-prospectus, merely means that the master will do what he can—which, independently of his own good example and sterling inward worth, is not worth talking of. One of the most trustworthy masters of our acquaintance once requested that we would prepare one of his senior pupils for confirmation. He added, "Of course you know enough of the relative position of boys and masters, to be well aware that any serious advice that I can offer will be, in their language, 'all bosh.'" We cannot help observing that our good friend is obliged to continue "Morals and religious principles," as well as "Dancing and drilling," in his prospectus, all the same.

For these reasons we more than ever congratulate ourselves that there is one healthy sphere, at least, for forming the characters of youth—namely, Eton, and the other public schools, properly so called; and we hope and trust that an effort will now be made on the part of the Masters and Fellows of Eton to do full justice to those committed to their charge. However genial the atmosphere, however healthful the clime, for the expansion of the minds and the energies of youth, the homœopathic quantities in which instruction is exhibited, the world has lately been made aware, defy all patience in reflecting minds. Of the *genius loci*—the healthful influences—we have at all times heard enough from the friends of the school; we trust they will henceforth learn to discriminate between the fine old oak that has long weathered the storm, and the evil parasites that sap its strength, and threaten its decay. The question is, Why should an Eton boy be left to little else than atmospheric influences alone?

We are unwilling to dwell on the quotient of one master to forty-five boys, when the fair proportion—to give a relay of fresh, and not jaded and soured men—is one to twelve; but we would simply point out, that while such a disproportion continues, those who join in the popular cry against the dead languages, and Latin and Greek, have decidedly the best of the argument.

No doubt, out of many hundreds, some clever boys will surmount every disadvantage—advancing in spite of the slovenliness of Eton tuition, if not by virtue of it: but, as regards the system itself, classical training and culture, so conducted, deserve not the name. With one forty-fifth part of the energies of one master, there can be no exact knowledge, no step-by-step reasoning or deduction, and no systematic training or development; and as to the formation of taste, the very worst sample of school-boy platitudes will but too readily occur to the mind.

This is not theory, it is fact. Sir John Coleridge has borne testimony to the decline of Eton scholarship. The pupils have increased, as also the profits; but have masters been added in proportion? and even of this poor staff, how many of the existing masters can boast a University degree as high as would ensure an election at any of our Proprietary Schools? Why should not Eton, like Rugby, be able to boast of the best scholars their funds can procure?

We conclude, therefore, by saying, "*Floreat Etona!*"—"May Eton flourish!" and being second to none in our appreciation of the public schools of England, of which Eton—with its rich foundation and its superiority in traditions the most inspiring to youth, and every incitement to noble emulation—certainly ought not to be, as a place of learning, the very last, we trust that we are doing all that in us lies to make the fair flower flourish by—letting in daylight.

CHAPTER VIII.

THE HEIR OF RICHCOURT AND HIS PRIVATE TUTOR—TOM SNIPE.

We return to Ned Walford, at Mr. Watson's academy; more particularly because our recollections are very vivid, not only as to Walford himself, but also as to several others of his school-fellows, who cannot be lost sight of in this history.

Mr. Watson, like many other masters, would exert himself where the boys were eager for instruction: though, to turn a mill that grinds no corn was too severe a trial of his perseverance. Among his best pupils, we particularly remember Tom Harding, John Hackles, and Jameson. We speak of them when they were about sixteen years of age, and all in the same class.

John Hackles had just then divulged, with high glee, that though his father could not afford to put him to College on his own account, an aunt had inquired the lowest sum that would clear every expense; and on his promising to be steady, and not to form a subject for the discussions on college debts, which about every three years enliven the newspapers — the money was forthcoming. John and Tom Harding were great friends. John once said, that what his sister would do in the event of his father's death, and their having to turn out of the Rectory-house, he did not know: she was very weakly, and required wine, slops, and sundry expenses, at all times: indeed adding, in his quaint way, that her lungs were so particular that even the air of some places they were too dainty to breathe; and if he could only squeeze through Oxford, it would be very bad luck if his father — who was pretty hearty in spite of his family cough — did not last till that time; afterwards he could live cosily with his sister, and take pupils.

So John read very hard: he was a very good fellow, indeed; and save that he would sometimes pocket some of the Watson candle-ends to read by in his bedroom, I do not remember a fault in his character. Letters from his sister used to drop in frequently, and after one of these he always seemed to read harder than ever; and, since the end sanctifies the means, while his temples throbbed from over-work, his heart had all the exercise of noble emotion.

John would have been very glad of a little of Ned Walford's money, because some he would have sent to his sickly sister, and some would have paid for books and a private tutor: though, of course, it were a thousand pities to have risked that the yearnings of so generous a nature should have shrunk before the torpedo touch of gold.

Jameson, also a promising fellow, knew he had only his own exertions on which to depend when college days were over, so he also read very perseveringly. But Tom Harding, who came from Liverpool, and whose friends were in flourishing circumstances, used to say, it was no use cultivating the luminous qualities of a man's mind unless you had a substantial body, like a lanthorn, to put it in, and therefore, out of principle, he paid a little more regard to the good of his constitution.

All, however, young as they were, had sense enough to see that Ned Walford's money was, as regarded any good it seemed likely to do him, a very questionable commodity. "If I were sure it would only tempt me to make as great a goose of myself," said John, "I would rather be without it." Though, of course, they were all too young to understand that, counteract it as we may, such is the natural tendency of wealth in early life.

To draw out the powers of the mind to a proper focus; to attune the heart to moral harmony, and to set the compass to the poles of truth; to increase the zest for every pleasure, and to supply an opiate for every pain—and all in the first outset of life—this, indeed, were well worth striving for, though hard to accomplish in an age of gold.

Ned Walford could not help seeing that there was a higher principle at work in John Hackles and his class-fellows than he himself was conscious of. No one of them could equal him in baskets of prog to treat the school, nor in new clothes and pocket-money for indulging every whim and fancy that arose. Still Ned felt, with sundry inward qualms and misgivings, that that was not everything. He could read in the very looks and manners of his school-fellows that money was nothing compared with mind; and when every fellow was talking of the many lines of Homer John had "floored" before breakfast, and almost before any one else was out of his bed, he could not help feeling it quite flat and insipid to display his new whip or fishing-rod; and he was no little chagrined to find that, flatter who would, his only superiority was in mere trifles and externals, and that the self-mastery and energy of John Hackles was cried up by all the school as something wholly different—as an achievement really to be proud of—as if it reflected honour even on the greatest idler in the school.

As Ned Walford was now between sixteen and seventeen years of age, Mrs. Walford was advised that it was time to enter his name on the books of King's College, Oxford. A little examination soon showed that Ned was rather backward in his studies—a discovery that almost invariably results in a change from the school to the private tutor. When this arrangement was whispered among Walford's friends at Mount Pleasant House, in the minds of the more promising and "the reading set," it caused no little envy, or at least longing, and sanguine calculations as to the prodigious quantity of work they would "get through in no time," if they had actually a tutor all to themselves;—"yes, and a clever fellow, too," they would take care to secure; "like that Lecturer of Trinity and Gold Medal-list, lodged at Harbury Court." "Oh!" cried

Harding, "from what I hear, poor Gritty Thompson would be the man; having just won the Latin Prize Poem, and considered safe for a Double First."

"Lucky fellow, indeed, is Walford," said Hackles. "I only wish I stood in his shoes. Why, what good to me is Watson? Our class has regularly used him up. Eddowes detected him in his back-parlour getting up over-night what he doles out to us next morning. Eddowes was sharp enough to espy the literal translation!"

If John Hackles could have raised money enough for a private tutor, there is no doubt that his tutor would have been the best that could be found;—for every penny he would have had his pennyworth. But you cannot have the stimulus of necessity, and the facility of riches, both at the same time.

Lady Macbeth spoke words of a world-wide significance and application when she said, as any Mentor might have told John Hackles,—

> "Nor time nor place
> Did then adhere, and yet you would make both."

Continuing, to the Walfords of society,—

> "They have made themselves, and that their fitness now
> Does unmake you——"

In the race of life, the one can say I have

"a spur to prick the sides of my intent;" the other carries weight—handicapped with the heaviest of all metals. This seems a providential set-off and compensation, by virtue of which we find that these very questionable things called "advantages"—which Bacon, perhaps, would comprise under that most apt term *impedimenta* —bear generally an inverse ratio to the successes of men of mark.

But all this time the movements of the heir of Richcourt had been watched by more parties than one. "Watson has had a pretty good turn at young Walford," said Mr. Franklin, the steward of the estate. "It is high time, what little advantage there is, should be put in the way of some one else, who has something more like a claim or connexion with the Manor and our people. Watson, indeed! What business a man like him had with young Walford at all, I never could see. He is not even one of our county—not a Berkshire man at all; but from quite the other side of England!"

This Mr. Franklin, having no children of his own, paid the usual penalty of being regarded as a kind of relieving-officer in the family to provide for nephews and nieces without end. He used to complain, "if the boys were but steady—if they were only reasonable—would stick to business," or the like, "he would not mind, but——" but, in short, he had the average run of frail mortality among poor relations: for a swarm of expectants take the very grace out of charity, and rarely do seem either a very deserving or a very interesting set of objects.

But the most troublesome of all was his nephew Tom, son of a favourite widowed sister, Mrs. Snipe. Mr. Franklin could not find it in his heart not to maintain his sister, and the sister was equally tender of all the necessities, as well as the scrapes, of Tom: so the uncle's constant irritation was that, while feeding the patient he could not starve the disease,—there was a sucker at the roots of the parent tree in the form of Thomas Snipe, Esq., M.A., of Christchurch College, Oxford.

Every man in Oxford knew Snipe. He had "begun life" at an early age; that is, he had very early been initiated as a looker-on at the clubs, as also at Tattersall's, and all the haunts of betting-men; and, in the popular phrase, when a man sets about *killing* and extinguishing every spark of proper manhood within his breast — burking conscience, and marring moral sense, a traitor to honour and true nobility—with every feature sharpened into cunning instead of expanding and glowing with generous sentiments—that man is said "to have seen *life*."

No young man at Oxford, save one or two, who knew him by the unerring instinct of a kindred spirit, had the least chance with Snipe; simply because, at the age of Oxford life, most young men look in vain to their own hearts and feelings to find anything which can at all shape or shadow forth that sordid nature, which coldly sets to work to design, overreach, and defraud, amidst the easy confidence and hearty good-fellowship of college rooms.

It was Snipe who was seen to ride so hard—passing every one on the road from Ascot, and who reached Peckwater in time to lay heavy bets on the winner of the cup of those who little suspected, for months after, that he had actually been present at the race, and hedged his bets after the event!

It was Tom Snipe, who, in company with Dick Whistler, got up and contrived that ever-memorable race-day at Bicester, with five-guinea sweepstakes, for the horses of Oxford men. Snipe winning the first race, and Dick Whistler the second; and that on horses beyond all doubt borrowed from John Day's racing-stables for the purpose!

So Snipe, being used to live by his wits, and being one of the first of Dr. Keats' scholars, at one time took pupils at Oxford, crammed them knowingly for their degree, aided and abetted in passing papers to the candidates, or sent them in pellets across the schools, and even plotted to intercept examination papers while printing at the Clarendon press.

But there is no place where men like Snipe are more quickly stranded, and left high and dry by the receding tide of men, than at Oxford. Their contemporaries drop off, and to form new leagues with freshmen is not easy. Tom Snipe's ways were known at last;—his name became a by-word as "an old hand." So at Oxford his game was up, and it was high time he should try "to shape his old course in a country new."

He next appeared in London; but there he met others as keen as himself, and his capital was too small to operate to advantage, and he unhappily fell back on his poor mother's little establishment. Something must be thought of—some definite employment; or Mr. Franklin's dear sister would be worried to death. Accordingly, to allow time and opportunity for consideration, he sent Tom an invitation to spend a month at his house, two miles from Richcourt, and forthwith set about devising some pretence for introducing him at the Manor House. He spoke of Tom's talents and scholarship—of which there was no kind of doubt, and by saying nothing of iniquities—which were equally beyond dispute—he comforted his conscience; forgetting the old adage, that one side of the truth is the greatest lie that can be told.

Mr. Franklin soon descried a very fine opening for maintaining his nephew out of the Richcourt estate. Tom was put forward, first of all, to examine Ned Walford. "Really, Mr. Franklin, nothing can be more kind," said Mrs. Walford, "nothing can be more obliging and considerate, than your proposal. Of course I cannot judge of Latin and Greek: but the state of Edward's English history and geography, of which I can judge, I must say, makes me a little anxious."

Well enough it might. Ned's ideas of history were the usual jumble. He knew that some kings died with their heads on, and others with their heads off. Either Charles I. or Charles II.—not quite sure which—was an instance of the latter mode of royal demise—beheaded at *Vaux*hall.

As Mrs. Walford was running on with such complaints of the historical studies of Mount Pleasant House, Tom Snipe was as loudly depreciating the Mount Pleasant Latin and Greek

—saying, that for his part he was no believer in drawing the pure Castalia from such little stagnant pools—and that Mrs. Walford's son was a youth of very good abilities, only he wanted a thorough grounding; still, with tact and experience, much might be done with backward youths. And after all he had effected in slipping in a foundation for one pupil, filling up corners for a second, and training a third "right up to the day that the knowledge was wanted"—to evaporate, of course, directly the eventful day was passed—"he did not doubt but the right sort of tutor, however hard to find, could still make up for the time that had been lost."

Advice of this kind always means, There is only one man in the world who will suit you, and that man is—your humble servant.

While Snipe was thus exciting the fears of the mother, simply that he might be chosen to allay them, he was at the same time complimenting the boy on his talents, and stirring up all his love of pleasure by sporting adventures and scenes both in college and in London life.

The conclusion may be anticipated. Ned Walford was soon lodged in one corner of Tom Snipe's house, taken for the purpose, with two horses in his stable, of which Tom Snipe rode the one quite as often as Ned Walford was mounted on the other.

Sir Buller Tawstock, who had been absent from home, no sooner heard of the intended arrangement with Tom Snipe, than he hurried off to stop it; but too late. The only result was, that to counteract Sir Buller's influence, or any prejudice he might raise against him, Snipe took care to poison the mind of his pupil with all kinds of cautions against allowing himself to be interfered with, or his liberty to be fettered, by "a set of meddling old Fogies."

The very mention of leading-strings, when a youth is impatient to be his own master, is enough to organise an opposition in a moment. So, from that day forth, all that Sir Buller could say against Snipe was set down as spite and disappointment at being exposed, and completely found out, in all his own interested motives. As to the prospect of Ned's ever availing himself at any future time of any judicious advice from Sir Buller, as a man of experience, it might as well have been whistled to the winds.

Cicero said, that two soothsayers could not look each other in the face without laughing: the same may be said of any two men of sordid cunning and dishonest feeling; each reads his own motives in the other's eyes. Sir Buller, though essentially a hollow, a selfish, and a time-serving man, we have no intention of representing as on the same low level as Snipe; still, at heart they were men of the same stamp—"birds of a feather," and of a kindred nature. Accordingly, when once Sir Buller came to remonstrate with Tom, and to "speak a little of his mind," he no sooner opened his lips than, as he happened also to open his eyes, at a single glance he felt his powerlessness. One cold, sneering, impudent look, that peered from beneath Tom Snipe's half-closed grey and sinister eyes, said, as plainly as looks could say, "*Et tu quoque!*"—You are another: "we are both playing the same game, though, of the two, I am rather the more likely to win." One encounter was enough: Sir Buller never tried again; though one observation which he made left a deep and lasting impression on the mind of Mrs. Walford. "I am very sorry the boy has got into the clutches of that man Snipe: I should not be surprised to find that he contrives to stick to him like a leech the longest day he has to live."

All who knew Tom Snipe were very well aware, that a young fellow like Walford would be as good as an annuity to him. In early days Tom had paid for others: he had now fully resolved that others should pay for him: and, as usual, the spendthrift and the "good-natured fellow" bated a little of his high and independent spirit. If there were nothing to be said for Tom—had Tom no redeeming qualities—we should not have introduced him so prominently to public notice. But Tom had once known better days; and, in those days, a better character: for, his honesty served just as long as his money; but when that was gone, he "lived by his wits:" which means, by a kind of privateering and making reprisals on the world that first preyed upon him. For Tom had learnt that, by a certain court and code of honour, there is a conventional "granting of indulgences" to dispense with the eighth commandment on all sporting occasions, and on certain other occasions also: provided your predatory habits are never of a vulgar kind, and, above all other things, never forget that you may offend against anything but—*good taste.*

By the time of which we are speaking, Tom Snipe had been accustomed to take full benefit of this toleration act: still, there was nothing at that time repulsive in Tom's ways. He seemed simply reckless, and indifferent in the article of pay: and, supposing a community of goods to have been the law of the land, no one would have taken any exception to Tom's character, as a free and open-hearted fellow.

We trust, therefore, that our recollections of Tom Snipe will not be deemed too charitable, if we paint him with something less than the blackest colours at the date of his first acquaintance with Edward Walford. Whether, with "the man about town," the conscience does not every day grow duller as the wit grows sharper—and whether the mere boon companion, at another's cost, may not sink into the deep, designing knave, at a later period, is another question.

As to Tom Snipe, just at this time the path of interest, as also the line of taste and inclination, lay side by side with the strict line of duty; insomuch that Tom went about his new employment with such a spirit, that he seemed to have turned over a new leaf, and to be throwing back Sir Buller's words of ill-omen upon himself.

If the pupil did not pass and enter college, the tutor could hardly hope to retain his hold beyond the day of failure. But, when once at Oxford, there was no knowing the various complexities that might require so skilled and wary a master's hand to help him through. Accordingly, Snipe set to work to make up for lost time, and was indefatigable in cramming Ned

Walford up to the mark. Few men could have done it better: for Snipe was, constitutionally, a most incessant talker—as if he could never tire. He was also fond of Latin and Greek; and felt all that interest in his work that a man always does feel, when he is doing that which he is conscious he can do well. Still, it was no easy matter. Tom, as a first-rate Oxford "Coach"—from time immemorial the term for a tutor or a lecture—had found brains for many a man—making all the jargon of Oxford logic as plain as possible. But to supply the place of habits is another thing. To drill and marshal certain raw recruits, in the shape of ill-trained, scattered brains—to make the owner thereof think, instead of guessing; and, from two facts, to see the sequence of a third; and, above all, to master self, and to work with a will, because "any sensible fellow needs must do so," to finish a chapter or to round a corner—all this was just what Nat Walford had learnt at Eton, but just what Ned Walford had not learnt at Mount Pleasant House. In other words, Ned had never learnt to learn; Ned had yet to be taught to teach—himself.

Snipe was well aware of this difficulty, and did all he could to put Ned upon his mettle; lengthening his lessons by inches, and each sitting by minutes, until, at the end of six months, he found himself in a position to go a-head with his pupil; with no want of natural talent to complain of, and with a full year before him for College work.

Nothing could tend to give Ned Walford a higher opinion of his tutor, than the talent and the untiring energy he displayed; nor could anything be more stirring, than a sense that it was done by the spur of good-fellowship, without the least appearance of authority. They were like two boys together; and even pleasant jokes and good-humoured rallying added far more stimulus than all the black looks and lugubrious lectures, which any grey-headed old Don could affect. Still, it was a very nervous operation —a very critical time for Snipe, as the day of examination drew nigh;—building on a sandy foundation being as unsafe in scholarship as in other matters. And after knowledge has been rather bolted than digested, it is wonderful, when an examiner begins his sifting and probing, how a new way of putting an old question will draw out a whole string of nonsense, to the utter confusion of the crammer intellectual.

CHAPTER IX.

NED WALFORD'S FIRST IMPRESSIONS OF COLLEGE LIFE.

THE time came at last, and the tutor of King's College, Oxford, had appointed a day in the Whitsun week for the candidates to make their appearance. This is a very critical season in the annals of King's; being the Election week, in which three or four scholars are annually chosen, from twenty or thirty candidates, to receive an education partially free. And as Ned was looking curiously at a group of youths that appeared little more than big schoolboys, awaiting the opening of the examination-hall, who should run up to him but John Hackles.

"Why, John, who would have thought of seeing you! Have you passed? Are they very strict? Is the examination ——"

"*Passed!* My good fellow, I am flying at higher game. I am up for a Scholarship. This is the third day of the examination. I have made short work of all the papers yet; and I have private information through Hilton, who is Fellow of Baliol—a great friend of a friend of mine—that my papers are among the very best. What turn the examination will take to-day, I do not know; but I have had the best 'Coach' in England for six months—a capital fellow, a curate next parish to ours—who volunteered to read with me for the love of it. And with good luck, by Monday's post, I may have the inexpressible joy of writing home to say,—All's well; Scholar of King's. Hurrah!"

Hackles had little time to say more: for, at that moment, two of the tutors brushed through the throng into the Hall, followed by all the candidates, to continue the examination; and, almost at the same time, one of the College servants ushered Ned Walford, anything but at his ease, into the rooms of the Vice-President.

As Ned went in he met Snipe coming out. Snipe was not the man to throw a chance away: he had been in, ostensibly with most courteous apologies, and a ready-manufactured message, as if duly to represent the family of Richcourt Hall, but, in reality, for the much more sensible purpose of securing an opportunity of a few words of intercession, supposing Ned should prove barely up to par. It was lucky that he did so. All that Mr. Walesby, the Vice-President, was in the habit of requiring at matriculation, was a degree of proficiency at entering, that augured rather a pass than a pluck at the University examinations: and when Ned came down into the quadrangle, Snipe saw by his looks that he had been hearing no flattering tale of himself, but a far more plainly-spoken account than he had ever heard before; and Snipe was not a little cheered at hearing that the Vice-President desired to speak a few more words with him.

Snipe knew the only topic that would avail. He explained in a minute, that the disadvantages of his pupil's early education made even his present proficiency full of hope and promise; and that, with the five months which would intervene before Mr. Walford would enter College, he would undertake to prepare him to the Vice-President's satisfaction.

Thus did Ned Walford just squeeze through: though a flaming account of his performance was sent, post-haste, to Richcourt; and the tenantry were feasted, and the health of the tutor, as well as of the pupil, was enthusiastically drunk, with three times three.

Of all seasons for a visit to Oxford, none compares with the month immediately before the Long Vacation. This is the time for the Newnham parties in the day, and the boat-races in the evening. This is the time, when every College Eleven thinks of challenging every other College Eleven to a match at cricket; when hard-reading men know no other distraction than the notes of the blackbird or the thrush, as they read, with their windows up, at five in the morning; and when men, who read in a milder form, lounge out after breakfast, and lie about the garden, on their backs, with cap half over the eyes and gown nowhere, and read Bulwer or the "Quarterly," till Kirkly calls out to Welbore, "The 'Heavy Ten o'Clock' is up; the 'Aristotle Highflyer' will start directly:" such being the then popular designations — one of the heaviest and the slowest, the other, of the lightest and the sharpest—of all the lectures in King's.

This joyous summer term was far too delightful to Tom Snipe to allow him to take his pupil home directly. Neither had Walford much difficulty in commencing the usual round of breakfasts, luncheons, dinners, and wine-parties, in the halls or rooms of all the leading colleges in Oxford. He was even made free of the buttery in —— one College—we won't tell the name—where, after the boat-race, there used to be an evening conclave, the chairman sitting, like Bacchus, on a beer-barrel, discussing the "bump," while the crew imbibed malt liquor to renovate their moist and trembling limbs.

For this general introduction to College life, it would have been enough for Walford to have known but one Undergraduate in a first-rate, fast set—so readily is a friend's friend invited to breakfast, "wine," or supper. But Brother Nat was already well established with all the Eton men, who were showing forth on the Isis and on Bullingdon the powers they had developed on the Thames and in the Shooting-fields.

Snipe was, of course, not sorry to be relieved of his charge: freshmen were no company for him: least of all, when there were no long evenings to lead to cards. Snipe made his way down to a certain "Hare and Hounds" hostelry in Carfax, in those days kept by one of no slight influence with College men of sporting caste—a man ready at all times to lend or to procure a loan of some hundreds, for the heirs of large estates. He was a jovial, genial character, well known as "Daddy White;" and so much the gentleman in a tradesman's way—knowing so exactly the line between easy-dealing and free, intrusive manners—that he might have made a princely fortune at a place like Oxford, were it not that prudence and keen love of money rarely go hand in hand: and were it not that the spell of honest and ingenuous dealing alone can cement and bind any largely-growing business.

Tom Snipe was well known to Daddy White, and White to Tom Snipe. For, like Snipe, White could sum up a man in a moment, finding him out instinctively—just as a detective reads "business" in the very look of an imposing gentleman of another class. Both Tom and Daddy were betting men; both considered themselves men of advanced and liberal opinions—unshackled by the narrow bounds of—— what we are still so bigoted as to call strict integrity, and a high sense of honour. Both knew intuitively, from the first, that they understood each other, and before long they were quietly seated over a glass of White's best port, in a small room decorated with winners of St. Leger's, the "Age" coach, some of Hogarth's old and dingy pictures; as also Mr. William White's own portrait, flat as if painted with treacle—which used to hang high over the fireplace.

Daddy White brightened up at seeing Snipe. For, Snipe owed him money, and on the principle that "loan oft loses both itself and friend," Daddy did not expect to see Snipe any more: certainly not without some such sudden turn of fortune as realised "virtue made easy;" in which case Snipe never doubted his score would be paid—not more as a matter of honesty, than as common sense. So the conversation commenced as follows:—

"Well, Mr. Snipe—happy to see you again. I always thought I should, if luck turned, some day. What, is the old gentleman dead? Have you taken to yourself a lady of fortune, or what?"

"Not quite that: still, things do look better—better perhaps in your way, as well as mine. You have heard of old Walford, who left that fine estate, to accumulate till—a boy came of age?"

"And you have the bringing of him up—eh?" said Mr. White, in a tone that rang merrily as to the prospects of a youth entrusted to Mr. Snipe's tender care.

"Something like it. He matriculated at King's but yesterday; and a close shave it was, too. They are so particular now-a-days. You remember Count Rat, as we used to call him. Well, I positively remember, long after he came up, he did not know the Old Testament from the New."

This piece of intelligence being more interesting to the scholar than to the tradesman, White next asked,—

"But what sort of an allowance has the young gentleman now?"

"Rather liberal, though limited, for the present; but in about two years he will have all."

"You haven't finished your tutoring, or whatever you call it, yet, I suppose?"

"No, no. Trust me for that. I live close by Richcourt. I intend to keep him as steady as I can; but if he will get into scrapes, I suppose I shall have to help him out."

"I understand."

"He is very easy-going and expensive in his ways. His present income is small, compared with the rent-roll two years hence: so, in all probability, he'll want money accommodation, and all that sort of thing.—You know there's no keeping young fellows out of it."

"I see, I see."

"You need not be in a hurry about my old score. I have sent you one or two good customers already; and now I am about the old place again, I hope to send you more.—You have horses and drags to let as usual, I presume?"

"You must do me the justice to acknowledge, Mr. Snipe, I have always dealt with you like a gentleman."

"Yes, yes; no doubt of it: and perhaps a little longer credit, while I am getting things rather better together, and making up lee-way, won't break the bank of White and Co."

The mind of Mr. Thomas Snipe was very soon relieved on this point. "Don't mention it, Sir," said his obliging creditor; "you and I have done a little business together, and shall do more, I am quite sure.—If you would like to try an idle horse at any time, or the like o' that —I am not particular."

If the exact consideration for this little credit and indulgence were put into plain and pitiless words, as by an excoriating counsel to twelve family gentlemen in a jury-box, it would have looked very ugly;—indeed so ugly, that neither Mr. White nor Mr. Snipe would have thought it just to have anything so monstrous fathered upon him.

Tom would have persuaded himself he meant no harm—he was only keeping up appearances; and—like many a better man than himself—making capital out of the influence of his high and commanding position.

To return to Ned Walford: for the first time in his life, he felt he was nobody. He had passed from a sphere of self-ignorance and of darkness into a land of light and self-knowledge. To his nineteenth year he had breathed an atmosphere of flattery and lies; he was now, for the first time, where his gold was no longer current for any such poison — where the man was everything, the money nothing—and where the first question is, "What can this man do?" And the very last question, "What has he got?"

"Walford—did you say Walford?"—asked one man at a Christchurch breakfast party. "Is this the brother of Walford we knew at Eton—who came up to Baliol only last term? Oh! who doesn't know Nat Walford? What a jolly fellow he is! he pulls a very pretty oar: his sculling's perfect; and, to say nothing of the help he will lend the College boat, won't he make their eleven strong for our next match with Baliol at cricket?"

"What, then," thought Ned, "is Nat to take the wind out of my sails in this way, when he hasn't an acre of land he can call his own, while scores of people down at Richcourt salute me, as retainers and vassals bend before their liege lord?"

However, Nat soon found that the flow of Oxford ideas ran quite another way. For there, every man seemed known, or at least seemed ambitious to be known, for something. One man was sure of a First Class—another was a first-rate speaker at the University Debating Society—another had run well for the Ireland Scholarship, if he didn't get it—another rode in first-rate style across country. And as to the man who could uphold the honour of the College by pulling in the College boat, and being a useful man in the College Eleven, and yet more, by gaining the prize for the English or the Latin Poem, or promising "one more First Class for our College"—every one was ready to drink his health, and award him the precedence he so well deserved.

While these and similar expressions of the prevailing sentiments and the generous emulation of Oxford life are recurring to our minds, we cannot help remembering a cursory remark which must have scattered to the winds Ned's last idea—if any yet remained—of being honoured at Oxford, as at home, for his landed possessions. The conversation was turning on the follies of one Becket, of Exeter College, who paraded his chains and trinkets, when some one remarked, "His pate's as empty as his purse is full: all he is good for is for shabby fellows to live and fatten on."

But, besides manly sports and the academical

honours, Walford found that distinction was won by various pleasant and social qualities also. To tell a good story and amuse a party by lively repartee, for which the vernacular seemed to be "Chaff," was of itself quite the making of some men. There was even a kind of genial, easy good-nature, a "benevolence in little things," all depending on a free, unselfish nature, and a natural opening of the heart to others—this also made some men very popular.

Walford could hardly understand what there was in men of this easy-going temper, or how and why they were such general favourites. It was beyond Ned's philosophy to descry that this world is made up of an heterogeneous mixture.—Society all force and fire, all talent, would be a state of wear and fret, or railway speed, trying and painful in the extreme; whereas these calm and quiet natures serve as a very pillow of repose: or, as Shakespeare would say,—in the very "whirlwind" of our contentions they "beget a calmness that gives all things smoothness."

In plain words, Ned had almost arrived at a conviction that he should not so much enjoy Oxford; he felt so different—as little complimented by the voice within, as by any voice without—in short, he began to feel that Oxford men must consider him a very slow fellow as yet: but then, perhaps, all freshmen seemed slow, and felt queer at first; though it did appear that his brother Nat had come up a "jolly fellow" all at once, and took up his place in the most enviable society from the very first day. How could these things be?

Born as good, and entering life with as fair a promise as his twin-brother Nat, you had but to look in their faces to perceive how wide the difference—how open and expansive one, how cramped and stunted was the other. Ned's better sympathies and more noble parts had no fair scope—dwarfed out of all healthy growth and expansion.

However, the evil is not wholly irreparable at the age of entering College: and of far more worth than all Oxford Latin, Greek, and logic, is that γνῶθι σεαυτὸν—that self-knowledge,—that finding one's own level, place, and bearings, which University experience is so well suited to impart.

On the Monday following, which happened to be a great day in the history of "Sir Edward King, Knight, our founder"—for whom, as he lay in marble on his back, with the Lady Elizabeth, his wife, on her back too, in the College chapel, we used to offer up our thanks, as the most bountiful of benefactors—Ned Walford came sauntering into College. He had altogether forgotten that anything dearest to the sanguine heart of his friend John Hackles was that day to be decided, till he saw John, with some of the late candidates and one or two other friends in animated talk around him—looking whether glad or sorry, Walford could not tell; but he rather thought John's eyes appeared glazed and red. This seemed strange to Walford; for, during the whole of Walford's life, his hopes and wishes had been met half way: so he had never known what it was to set his whole heart and soul on anything that might or might not come to pass.

Just as Ned had come up to Hackles, some casual word about "happy fellow"—"beat them all in a canter," recalled Ned to a recollection of the existing state of things. At the same moment John, who was talking husky—his heart being undecided between a muffled and a merry peal—sprang forward, but too glad to make a plausible escape from comparative strangers—took Walford by the arm, and yearning to find vent for his pent-up emotions, hurried him off through the inner quad, past the iron gates, and hardly found words to speak till he had reached the black yew-trees half down the garden. There, throwing himself down on the grass, and giving Walford a pull to sit down beside him, he exclaimed,—

"Oh, dear me! It seems like a dream! I can't realise it—a Scholar of King's! And the first on the list!—What a blessing!—what a relief for the present!—what a promise for the future! Every Scholar of King's, they say, can get a First Class if he pleases; and if so, his fortune's made—think of that, Ned, for a needy fellow like me!"

Walford wished him joy, of course; but he had no such experience as could enable him to taste the joy he wished his friend, or to realise the relief the overstrained Hackles felt in every nerve and fibre of the brain,—when John continued,—

"What shall I do for that kind fellow, Kirton, and for all his many hours of reading?—To him I owe it all. Stay—but when is the early post? What will they say at home? Ah! Ned, you little know what it is to have your brain strung up tighter and tighter;—your memory on the stretch, and your whole heart set on one great object, like life and death to you, and then to feel the burden off,—the bow unbent, and the heart-strings twanging and vibrating from the recoil, as though they would never rest."

Here was another phase of Oxford life, and by no means an unimproving picture for Walford to contemplate. No doubt Ned thought, if all the world were born to landed estates, or at least had their infant names as regularly entered on the books of the Three per Cents as they are on the parish register, it would be a decided improvement in the ways of Providence. Still it seemed that men could achieve fortune, and honours too, who were not born to find both ready heaped upon them. Ned had heard many a case of ruined Collegians and long-credit tradesmen, and his first idea of Oxford, derived from exceptional and other exaggerated instances, was that of a place where money flew on all sides, and all spent money first, and thought about how it was to be paid afterwards. Yet, here was an instance—and we could tell him there were many such, though not so likely to fall in the way of men like Walford,—an instance that met him at the very outset of his University career, of a noble-hearted youth, gratefully snatching at any casual instruction, pursuing learning in the midst of difficulties, and finding in his very exigencies a spur and stimulus sharper far than all the books and tutors, and the supposed unqualified advantages, which the affluence of Richcourt could command.

There is nothing in which the world is more commonly deceived than in that one word—advantages. Tutors may pour in knowledge, but it is with knowledge as it is with money—only they who have worked hard for it know the use of it.

"The advantages of the rising generation are very great—so many books; everything explained—everything made easy." We confess we cannot see this. Facilities often prove a hindrance. The mind is like a manufactory; the facts are only like the raw materials, which require a certain process before they are turned into the available form of knowledge, properly so called. The mill may be clogged by too much grits; and, as we never remember the time at which the machinery intellectual could not command quite as many materials as it could possibly convert or digest, where can be the advantage of adding more? Surely, we only load and encumber—we only distract and dissipate—the mind.

These thoughts, however, have too little to do with Ned Walford's state of mind, as he lay in the garden of King's. Still, Ned could not help feeling that John Hackles, to the end of his term in College, must stand immeasurably before himself—admitted, as he had been, on sufferance, and all but plucked on the first day he made his appearance in the University! His brother Nat had also a considerable start, and a decided advantage over him. Why, Nat had "reaped golden opinions of all kinds of men." You could see how popular he was the moment he entered a wine-party—just as if the evening could not be fairly begun till Nat Walford had taken his seat among them.

As soon as Ned had made these reflections, and dealt thus honestly with his own mind, he was already on the high road to some little improvement—though the many pliant years that had been cruelly misapplied were hard, indeed, wholly to retrieve.

CHAPTER X.

HOW MAN IS BORN TO TROUBLE; AND MUCH MORE—WOMAN.

The poet says, "Man was born to suffer"—no doubt, woman was. It may be that these charming creatures are endowed with a moral chemistry, enabling them to extract sweets from bitters, and to feel a thrill of pleasure amidst the throbs of pain: but certain it is, that woman's life commonly affords no slight opportunities for exercising such amiable instincts, if nature did really intend them such endowments.

This hard fate of woman-kind is not peculiar to the present generation. About two thousand years ago, according to Euripides, a lady's lot was very little better. When the Argonauts went in quest of the golden fleece, it is a mistake to say, with some writers, that this is a mere poetical description of some bargee sheep-stealers on a marauding expedition: it seems more like a ship-load of gentlemen (instead of ladies) going out to India on a matrimonial speculation: for, certain it is, that one Mr. Jason succeeded in eloping with a rich Miss Medea, a lady of handsome fortune. Well —this Miss Medea, now Mrs. Jason—feeling herself, in course of time, cruelly ill-used, philosophised as follows. She said,—

"Of all living creatures, I really believe we women have the hardest lot. If we don't positively out-bid and buy a husband—like a lady of fortune—we have small chance of any at all: and when we have one, it's all a lottery how he will turn out. If he is all that is desirable, I grant life is delightful; but rather than be linked to a bad one, I would rather die. As to applying to the Divorce Court, it is so damaging to your character. No; we must sit and pine at home, though the horrid men can go out to their amusements and their *club*."* And then she comes to the hardest part of all, having "to look to,"—"to have all one's hopes and interests centered," "on one mortal being only."†

This "looking to one mortal being only," this hard fate of having one troublesome inconstant

* Πρὸς ἥλικας τραπείς. † Πρὸς μίαν ψυχὴν βλέπειν.

being the very pivot of our fortunes, and the centre of our hopes and fears—entwined, as it were, round the very fibres of our hearts, which throb at the mercy of these heedless, thoughtless creatures—this is the fate of widows as well as wives, provided they have "the affliction of an only son."—A favourite son and heir of all, like Ned, proved much the same to the fond and devoted Mrs. Walford.

And now her anxieties were to commence. For, having addressed a letter to the Vice-President of King's College, ostensibly requesting to be certified as to the time of her son's residence, but not without a secret hope of receiving some complimentary assurances as to the promise of her son, she received a letter, characterised by that peculiar mixture of kindness and plain-speaking for which the Vice-President was remarkable.

Mr. Walesby said he thought it only right to repeat, that every exertion must be made to qualify her son for taking full advantage of College lectures, as also for going through his academical course with credit. He implied, that there were various indications of that "no father," of which Mrs. Walford had informed him; and said, in other terms, that since from our fathers we have had the discipline of life, and from our mothers the kindness and the consolations, her son seemed, as usual, to have had too much of the latter sort of blessing, altogether unqualified by the correctives of the former.

However uneasy these remarks made the mother for a time, still, when Ned came home—already metamorphosed by all the newest Oxford fashions—he did seem so much improved, so much more manly, and in every respect so interesting, that a glow of satisfaction and delight came over the delighted mother; and all the group of cares and dark forebodings fled, as usual, before the beams of present happiness.

Pope says, in truthful and harmonious numbers,—

> "God from all creatures hides the book of fate."

Supposing Life like a three-volume novel, we may try in vain to read the last part first—not one leaf can we turn over in advance: tic, tic, tic, goes the solemn clock of Time—the same unsympathetic pace for every one. However breathless our impatience, not an Act can we skip in the Drama, nor dispense with the formality of hours or minutes, whether in the winter or the summer of our fortunes: but out of the mass, black with sorrow in the background, Providence so mercifully doles out the bitter portion for thc day—that our greatest troubles, as the world measures them, are by no means the seasons of our greatest unhappiness.

But the book of fate is a closed volume also in another respect. While our eyes are gladdened by our own pleasant pages, we little think of the black chapter that has at the same time opened to some other person: and should we chance to hear it, we might be puzzled indeed to trace the yet disjointed links, if warned that there was also a subtle chain by which the throbbings of that stranger's heart would one day quicken the pulses of our own.

Mrs. Walford, we know, was a kind-hearted, charitable person; but when, in the village at the end of the park, she was sure that every lying-in woman had the loan of the customary bag and her quantum of caudle and small groceries, and every old granny had coals and other comforts—she felt at ease, and her heart glowed with a sense of temporary satisfaction, "that the world was so happy just at present." Perhaps this is as it should be. Some persons try very hard—or at least talk as if they did—but all to no purpose, to sympathise with all the world at once. They are not, perhaps, aware that the heart is so tuned and tempered, that it will not thump very violently without some regard to time and space. It virtually says, "I have nothing to do with you—you are out of my district." For instance: when Dame Tucker came up to the house, to say she wanted some stuff in a bottle, because her Tommy's pinafore had been on fire, and caught his lips, and nose, and eye-brows, Mrs. Walford was far more excited than if she had heard of the burning of Moscow.

Still, however fairly Mrs. Walford was entitled to make the most of her own share and seasons of heart's-ease while it lasted; however naturally engrossed with her own hopes and fears, and motherly hallucinations, amidst the affluence of benignant Fortune,—a scene of quite a different kind was being enacted in a very humble apartment in the town of Westwood, in the same county, which it is now time to relate.

"Is this where Mr. Hengen, the station-master, lives?"

This question, in a soft and sympathising voice, was asked of a kind of maid-of-all-work, by Dr. Batson, a physician, who had long retired from all practice but that charitable kind which gentlemen of his profession are too well trained in active benevolence ever entirely to give up.

"Yes, Sir; he does *live* here, and that's as

much as ever he does. His cough is dreadful. I can't sleep o' nights for hearing of it."

At the same time, the Doctor was admitted into a narrow passage, with yet narrower stairs rising almost perpendicularly before him, as the servant opened the narrow green door; and, not till this door was closed again, could he turn sideways into a little parlour, where he remained for "Miss Hengen" to be called to see him.

The little parlour was not much bigger than a full-sized table-cloth. Still it was quite a fashionable drawing-room in miniature—tidies over every seat; mats under everything on the table; ornaments, however cheap and showy, far more than in proportion to the furniture, while about two penn'orth of fancy shavings, as dingy and poverty-stricken as everything else in the room, helped to vindicate the gentility even of the grate. A very few moments were enough for this little survey, and then Miss Hengen came softly into the room.

Miss Hengen was a fine, elegant-looking young woman, but at that time, cold and impassive; reminding one almost of the statuesque appearance of a stereoscopic likeness. Still, when she spoke, there was a sharpness and decision in her phrases which impressed you more with the powers of her mind, than with the suavity of her manner. But, almost immediately understanding who it was, she melted into a degree of cordiality, all the more pleasing from the contrast. She took the Doctor's hand, and interrupted him in the midst of his apologies for volunteering a visit with,—"Yes, yes; very, very kind! Such a surprise, too!—a blessing indeed, to find a little loving-kindness lurking in the by-corners of this world."—With this world-weary and misanthropic comment on the Doctor's visit, she proceeded to lead him upstairs, and, shutting the door after him, left him alone in her father's little chamber.

As the door opened, so small was the room, it hid the patient and half the bed. But the Doctor had no sooner cleared himself of the door, than one glance at the sunken eye, the hollow, livid cheeks, and the lips that hardly covered the dry and projecting teeth, told him that the patient was far gone in consumption.

"The Rector was here this morning," said the sick man, in a painful whisper. "He called at Mrs. Rayworth's on his way, and begged those grapes for me;—a good, kind man is our Rector—well meaning—very: but, with all the comfort of his prayers, some conversation he drew me into raked up all my troubles, quickening the memories of things that never should have been—so, ever since, I have been very uncomfortable—vain regrets, remorse, and all my old anxieties, have once more fastened on my mind."

The Parson had asked—though poor Hengen was too full of the troubles of this world to take the question as relating to a world to come—"whether Mr. Hengen had anything on his mind."

The Doctor, with all his long experience with frail mortality, would have been far more tender of consequences. He would have known, that men who live by their labour must, with failing strength, have empty cupboards, and untold miseries of other kinds; and the dying station-master had a great deal upon his mind—he had two grown-up daughters, wholly unprovided for. It was also well known to all acquainted with his history, that, in a long career of idleness and frivolity, he had early "sowed the wind" of folly, and was reaping "the whirlwind" of lacerated feelings and agonised affections in later life. At the period of Dr. Batson's visit, the heart-wound for a day or two had ceased to throb: perhaps he had dozed all thought away; but any casual question like the Rector's would make the worm that dieth not rear its head and gnaw again.

There are some few positions in life in this nineteenth century, almost invariably filled by persons who were never intended for anything of the kind: as, for instance, to be a school-master is generally "the accident of an accident;" and to keep a turnpike, holds the same place in humble life; while a little higher in the scale, to "order your coals," or "sell you wine," or to be "private and confidential secretary to an elderly gentleman of high estate;" these all are spheres of action, if not of idleness, supposed to require no "special training or qualification." To these must be added—especially now that "something under Government" requires at least the education of a charity boy—"something to do upon a railway." No doubt the number of steady men promoted to fill the higher offices in railway life is daily on the increase; still, in the course of a hundred miles we are—or at least we used to be—whirled by no small number of broken-down gentlemen or disappointed men. At this moment there rises before our mind the soured and enduring looks of one or two, evidently doomed, for the sins of their youth, to hard and irksome labours for the term of their natural lives.

Poor Mr. Hengen's was a case of this kind; and if we fit together bits of Mr. Hengen's history as he related it to others, as well as to the Doctor, at different times, it would run as follows; and we know not for how many railway officials the same story might not, with a little change of names and incidents, be made to serve.

CHAPTER XI.

THE DYING STATION-MASTER'S HISTORY.

"I HAVE not a relation in the world but my two dear girls; and if from the time I was a youth I had never had a relation, but had been thrown entirely on my own resources, it had been far better for me. The truth is, in early days I was buoyed up with false expectations; I was tricked with delusive views of things, till I was nearly thirty years of age. By that time I had squandered my own little inheritance—however little then, it would have seemed large, indeed, just now—on mere amusements, and as pocket-money; for, between the home of my own mother in early life, and the home of my wife's mother a little later—rent, taxes, and housekeeping seemed, like the sunshine and the shower,—too much things of course to say 'Thank you' for.

"In the course of this time I had talked of all kinds of professions, but followed none; though I soon felt that public opinion and the feelings of society were more and more against me, as also that I was uncomfortably living amidst a general expectation that, of course, I should do something soon—which kind of general presumption at length resulted in very uncomplimentary hints and marks of contempt at the idle life I was living at the time then present. This was too evident to escape notice, even among some of the younger, and certainly among all the middle-aged people; but as to the old and intimate friends of the family, they did not care to mince the matter in the least, but sorely nettled me, by speaking out and giving way to certain very ominous remarks—remarks, of which I never saw the exact truth till far too late—namely, that this state of things could not last for ever; and one old gentleman, yet more significantly said, 'Now mark my words, young man, some fine morning you will find yourself *left high and dry*, and live to curse the cruel kindness of your relations: for I have lived quite long enough in the world to see that, dying without Wills, and all the caprices of fortune, are so common as to seem a natural visitation upon those who depend on resources not their own.'

"The old man added something more, about there being in the human mind an innate resentment against idleness; indeed, that men who take an honest and industrious part in the great workshop of this busy world, are out of all patience at seeing others coolly reaping what they did not sow—and 'Served them right,' was the first exclamation, whenever they were *stranded*, and left to work out the hard problem of life for themselves.

"Before I was thirty-one years of age all this was verified to the letter; the very words my tormentors had used, formed the most truthful picture of all that happened. My wife's mother died—bequeathing, or intending to bequeath, her daughter fifteen thousand pounds Consols, besides a residue not worth much. But the said fifteen thousand pounds were in trust—the deceased had only a life-interest, with what is called 'power of appointment,' or of bequeathing it by Will—which power, if she failed to execute, it was directed that the money should be paid over to another member of the family.

"I never shall forget the quiet sneer, the air of triumph, and the cold satisfaction, scarcely concealed beneath the thinnest veil of courtesy and business-manners, when I applied to the trustee to arrange to transfer this tempting fifteen thousand pounds to my name in the Bank of England.

"'Certainly,' was the provoking reply; 'but first, you must show me your authority to receive it.'

"'Nothing can be easier. Here is the probate of my mother-in-law's will, bequeathing all her property to my wife. Surely, nothing can be plainer than that?'

"'I have simply to say, that none of what was legally the property of your late mother-in-law is in my keeping.'

"'What! are there not fifteen thousand pounds Consols in your keeping?'

"'Yes; but the capital never was held in trust for the deceased: only the dividends—a life interest—which dies with her.'

"'Then what becomes of the capital?'

"'The capital I hold in trust for your wife's cousin, unless your mother-in-law should otherwise appoint; that is, bequeath it differently.'

"'Bequeath it differently!' I cried, in an agony of consternation and passion. 'She has left every farthing—"real and personal, wheresoever and what kind soever"—to my wife.'

"'Yes; all *her* property. There is the distinction. This was not hers. The Will has no mention of this fifteen thousand pounds Consols. Therefore, it is not yours. But the deceased had a life-interest in the money in question, and a power of appointment. Show me that she bequeathed this particular fifteen thousand pounds in Consols to your wife, and you shall have it. But—you saw that gentleman, Mr. Elways, the solicitor, who left the room as you came in?'

"'I think I did pass some one on the stairs.'

"'Well, that gentleman had just come to give me notice on behalf of his client, of what, indeed, I well knew before, that the tenant for life being dead, and her Will being no execution of the power to appoint, the money must forthwith be paid over to him.'

"You would hardly believe it; but, as the story spread among high and low—fast as tales of sudden fortunes, gained or lost, always spread—satisfaction smiled in every countenance. Certainly, many expressed pity for my poor wife; but there was evidently no pity for me. The prediction had proved too true. 'Served him right,' was the prevailing feeling: and since the lucky man was known as a striving, hard-working fellow, who had fought his way manfully at every step, with no one to look to but himself, his virtues were played off against me, and his praises sung in so very aggravating a way in every house I entered, that I could hardly bear to show my face; and resolved to realise on the little furniture and small residue which alone I could claim, and to leave as soon as I could.

"So now I literally was 'stranded,'—'left high and dry,' was the very term for me. The tide of fortune had ebbed. I was left like a waif upon the sands; and as to friends, I might as well have been in the middle of Salisbury Plain.—Scarcely one person called at the house, unless he wanted something, for the whole month I was preparing to leave!

"While a man has still a fund on which to draw, however low his little capital may be sinking, he does not feel the full misery of distress. But six months sufficed to show me the frightful pace at which money flies, when every article of meat, drink, and clothing, every shovel-full of coals, and every inch of candle, is wasting and consuming the limited store which, alone, stands between reduced gentlefolk in their cheap lodging, and the beggar who crouches on the doorstep, or shivers under the arch of the bridge.

"My fears and anxieties were now painfully excited. My wife had, at that time, one daughter, and was within two months of giving birth to the second. Each child may be a blessing, where born to plenty; but, from my heart, I pity the delicate woman, who has nothing but privation in prospect as a solace in the hour of her trial.

"I was now driven almost to despair, and living in a back-street, in the town of Marlington, in the midst of a population all depending on their own labour to keep the wolf of hunger from the door.

"It would make your heart ache to hear all that I endured, while a gradual revolution was going on in my mind and feelings, and while hard necessity was grinding and bending my high neck and proud spirit to realise the necessity of working for my daily bread; and even then, to find work was no easy matter. For a clerk's place, I was told, I must learn to write better: for the part of master, I had not the knowledge or the capital—for the part of man, I was not handy—and, as one said, 'should be thinking too much of myself, and be above my work.'—Nothing could be thought of but a railway: many an official had been engaged without knowledge or experience, so, why not I?

"When this destination was accepted as my lot, I felt acutely the degradation of canvassing for the interest of the very men I used to treat lightly, and affected to despise; but dire want and hunger goaded me on. Meat had become scanty, and a glass of beer almost a delicacy unknown. I was literally starved, and my system reduced into submission; and no one, who has not felt the same, could believe how I trembled with anxiety the day I waited at the office of the railway secretary to know my fate: so intensely did I crave, as the least of two evils, the liberty to stamp tickets at a guinea a-week—well knowing that I should pass my days at that mere wooden box, which is called the 'Blacklane Station;' exchanging no ideas but with porters and guards; and ever acutely sensitive, and dreading to be recognised by some one who had known me in other days.

"My wife earned nearly as much as I did, partly by her needle and partly by educating the children of thriving tradespeople at no great distance. And at length we learnt to pick up crumbs of comfort, and to make the most of a little sunshine between the showers, like other people: and really it seems to me as if there were happiness enough in this life, overlooked and wasted by the rich and prosperous, to cheer hundreds who toil for their daily bread.

"Time went on, and we mutually comforted each other through every sorrow, till things began to mend. In course of time, I was promoted from station to station; and I must not forget to tell you that the same plain-speaking old gentleman that predicted my downfall slapped me on the back very unexpectedly one morning, and said,—

"'Cheer up, my good friend. It's a pleasure to help those who help themselves. I greet you now as a brave and proper sort of fellow: you are putting your back to the burden, and bearing your part in life as best you can, though bad is the best. So, let us consider: how can I help you?—what can I do?'

"The name of this friend in need, you, Doctor, have, no doubt, often heard. It was Mr. Hardaway, the Contractor; one of those men who, by luck as well as labour, begin with no more than a pickaxe in their hand and a bundle on their back, and end with a fortune. The worst of it is, that they are apt ever after to make the mistake of thinking and of talking as if every other man could do the same."

"Very true," said his friend; "this is a mistake, indeed. All depends upon the mainspring inside us: and God has put it into one man much stiffer than into another.—But, go on with your interesting history."

"Well; the first thing Mr. Hardaway did,

was to take my wife and children to his house for change of air, though I was dull and sad, indeed, without them; and ere long he made interest with our Secretary, which resulted in a salary of two hundred pounds a-year at the station where you so long have known me.

"But the more of one thing, the less of another, is the way of this world—I really believe that the place never agreed with either of us. But, good air is a kind of luxury that the sons of toil can never go in quest of. And you well remember that bitter hour when I had just one day allowed me to lay my dear Emma in the grave, and returned with heavy heart to stamp away at tickets, or prepare way-bills, and guard against collisions: for, one mistake might have turned me penniless upon the world!

"Since that cruel loss five years have passed away, and every day my daughters—the elder in particular—have been to me a source of constant uneasiness; so many are the hours they have been left to their own devices, with no one to guide them. It is a sad privation to have no pure and noble influence within-doors, to counteract the hollow and the heartless ways and sentiments but too rife in a neighbourhood such as this. For, the severest trial to a reduced gentleman is the reflection, that his children can rarely ever play in the same gardens, or meet in the same walks, as the children who are reared with refinement and good example."

Such were the chief points in poor Hengen's history. We all know that, especially in dear times, living is expensive: but thousands have never been so situated as to realise the fact that it is sometimes quite beyond the limits of a man's income to afford to live at all. This was too true as regarded the hard lot of the broken-down Station-master. The cutting easterly wind on the platform was like daggers to his lungs. He had just battled with it over one more quarter-day, and then took to his bed, and became the painful picture of mortality described at the time of Dr. Batson's visit.

But our history is concerned rather with Mr. Hengen's daughters than with himself.

"I was remarking," said Mr. Hengen, "that the Rector asked me if I had anything on my mind. There is something more than usual in my anxieties as a parent, because there are points by no means ordinary in the character of my two dear girls. The elder, Hannah, is a very strong-minded girl—extraordinary in many respects, and devoted to her sister Alice. She has performed quite a mother's part towards

Alice, having educated and brought her up, more like a parent than an elder sister. Indeed, there was a period in the life of Hannah when, had it not been for this occupation, and the diversion of mind and feeling which it caused, the unhappy girl would, I really believe, have gone distracted.

"For, Hannah was engaged to be married to one of those fascinating villains, whom we all have known at some time or other: the result I cannot exactly mention, having promised her that, though one or two persons were cognisant of it, no living soul besides should ever hear it from me. This promise was a weakness, for which I have often blamed myself—uncertain whether a very unpleasant report might not have spread, and whether the honour of my family might not have been compromised by my withholding explanation. But, be that as it may, ever since that sad affair, a kind of misanthropy has taken deep hold upon her: all that should be love in her nature has soured into hatred: though, to say the truth, she always was cold, silent, and reserved. Few could understand her: she made her fond mother very anxious: she chose her own friends: had ways, and schemes, and designs of a most curious kind. In short, had Hannah been born in troublous times, she is just the character to have laid deep plans and to have threaded crooked paths, and so reached her objects by a boldness of adventure wholly unknown to other women.

"That Hannah will watch over and protect her young sister as long as she can, I am quite sure; but what is most on my mind is, that there is a degree of violence in Hannah that alarms people—a force of character that no employer, no mistress, could withstand. Nothing can be more unfavourable for gaining her own livelihood. And this is the more provoking, because no one can be more agreeable, when she wishes to ingratiate herself."

The Doctor knew what the father meant. Hannah's frown was like a thunder-cloud; but her smile as soft and glowing as the morning sun.

"Then," he continued, "Alice is lost without her sister: impulsive, sensitive, and sympathetic in the extreme, she may be led any way, and—I am painfully afraid—misled, too, in a world like this."

Dr. Batson listened to this description of the two orphans—for orphans they were evidently on the very verge of becoming—with no slight misgiving at the heart; so truly did this character of Hannah coincide with his own observation. It also coincided with one or two little incidents, strongly savouring of deceit and cunning, which had become known in the neighbourhood.

CHAPTER XII.

A SLIGHT INITIATION INTO THE WAYS OF THIS WICKED WORLD.

BUT we must leave the Hengen family for the present. We must return to Ned Walford, and consider how Tom Snipe proceeded to prepare him for Oxford.

Snipe's position was peculiar. His duty lay one way, and his interest another; for, the sooner Ned was assisted through his academical course, the sooner Snipe would find his "occupation gone."

We can hardly suppose, therefore, that Snipe should see any great necessity for despatch. Indeed, he could, with a clear conscience, advise Mrs. Walford that it would be desirable that Ned should not enter College quite as soon as at first intended. So, he was readily allowed to arrange with the Vice-President of King's that his pupil should have full time for his studies in the country, and should not "require rooms," or enter on residence, till after Christmas.

And now, every day, Mrs. Walford began to perceive that a wonderful change had taken place in dearest Ned, so long the very pivot of her existence and the idol of her heart. Every hour tended to reveal a fact, which is one of the phenomena in the natural philosophy of growing lads—that she had rivals in his affections; that what she fondly mistook for the charming simplicity and the confiding spirit of boyhood, had sunk to zero. There seemed now to be always something the mother was not to know; while various shrugs and signs of independence were meant to say, in dumb show, Ask no questions.

The experienced reader will at once perceive that the mother, as usual, had been raising aërial castles, always of the florid architecture, in which to dwell and guide her son for ever; and now she felt she should be one too many. She had been weaving for her boy a suit of gossamer robes, and was awaking to the fact that he had entirely outgrown them. And, even as the hen that has hatched ducks is horrified at the discovery that they have a liking for the pond, so is it with the mother when she first realises the difference between the love and devotion of her nature, and the concentrated selfishness of an overgrown boy.

Ned was now a fine, strong young man, looking older than he really was; but rather too rural and unpolished for the refined taste of Mrs. Walford. She also perceived that, in the absence of other objects of attraction, the society of a very second-rate order of young ladies in the neighbouring town, with "far too many visits to be prudent" to the daughters of his late tutor — the Misses Watson — were exercising a very dangerous influence.

On this theme, no one could talk more virtuously, no one could evince a more delicate sense of propriety, than Tom Snipe. He fell exactly into Mrs. Walford's way of thinking; he fully agreed in the wisdom of introducing the Heir of Richcourt at once into society that was worthy of his regard: so, on the principle of providing a safe channel for the stream you cannot stop, an arrangement was made for Mrs. Walford and family to winter at the fashionable town of Wanton.

We need not describe the exact latitude and longitude of the town of Wanton on the map of England. It is enough to observe that there are only two or three towns of this peculiar kind, from the Land's End to John o'Groats;

and though it is well to have a specimen of everything in this world, still we reckon it among the wisest dispensations of Providence that there are not more. For, Wanton was a fashionable town. Fully to understand such a town, a man should first of all live in one of those hives of industry, yclept the manufacturing towns of England. There, every man you meet wears a brow "sicklied o'er with the pale cast of thought." He is walking a business-like pace, absorbed in his own enterprises; and every man going and coming conveys the idea of one busy commonwealth, in which one and all are solely bent on their severally allotted parts. As to style and deportment, they have no time or notion of anything of the kind; and there is scarcely one man in the town who would pass muster at Wanton, inasmuch as it evidently wants a great deal of leisure to make a gentleman of the Wanton type. For the correct air and style, it is almost indispensable that he shall have nothing in his head to mar the vacuity of his expression—no object of pursuit to hurry him out of the lounging loiter of his movements.

The inhabitants of Wanton were, for the most part, persons of great ideas and small fortunes. There were retired Indians enough to illustrate every case in the most complete treatise on bilious derangements. There were half-pay officers, living in a state of oscillation between papers and pool; and some rather substantial-looking characters, who sunned themselves regularly at certain library doors, or other haunts, each after his kind: any unphilosophical observer would have thought that these men had nothing to do; but by degrees they learnt to spread their little nothings over time enough to astonish any busy man;—add to which, Providence almost invariably accommodates idle men with a little employment; for, when eating and drinking are obliged to constitute not only the means of life, but the sum and substance, and serious business of it, their inner man soon ceases to go right of itself, and then, what between a fit of indigestion at one time, or an attack of the gout at another, many a man has filled up some of the listless void caused by lack of a regular profession.

Well, Wanton was a place of this kind, where, having no call of exertion from without, nearly all the people were pretty well occupied with things within—their ailments, nerves, and constitutions.

But people cannot live without excitement of some kind; so, while the class aforesaid chiefly sought a stimulus in dinners, balls, and parties, another section, who called this worldly and profane, found the same stimulus in prayer-meetings, with a favourite minister to chat, expound, and chat again. Those people at the town of Wanton practised, under a very celebrated minister, a kind of religion for which it were hard to find a name. It was something between Terrorism and Morbidism. Had any traveller met such a sect in Crim Tartary, he would have concluded they were devotees of some dismal heathen deity, to be propitiated only with sighs and groans, pale faces, and "solemncholy" looks.—Instead of carrying religion into every act of life, and living like the nobler and spiritualised order of human creatures, they tried, and tried in vain, to merge all life into—what they called religion.

This party was generally hard and unsympathising, absorbed and centred in the Ruffles' clique and faction: their chief worship consisting in finding "a soul of evil in things good," depreciating all creation, and superstitiously mystifying their brains, clouding their minds, and stinting their affections, until they degenerated in a very low type of intellectual and moral existence. Mr. Ruffles' congregation had one cast of countenance, as well as one muffled tone and one set of words. They wore, out of principle, a sad expression, as if they never enjoyed anything—always making a wry face at the world for fear of seeming worldly. Yet people are not the less sensual for being sour, and may live in a state of very demoralising dissipation, without ever going to anything stronger than a tea-party.

This at least was the tendency, and with many, the effect; though, as some constitutions resist the most virulent malaria, so some genial, generous hearts at Wanton would expand, in spite of all that could be done to cramp and to contract them—though their uncomfortable tenets did very much to qualify their innocent enjoyments. Such was the unpleasant struggle between feelings which were right and healthful, and principles which were absurd, that the doctrine of Mr. Ruffles produced in the breast of Mrs. Walford.

Mr. Ruffles had a very forcible delivery, and a very strong way of putting things: he was perfectly honest and sincere, though a man of rather narrow mind—far too narrow to comprehend how wonderfully the Gospel is adapted to regulate and purify, without disturbing the successive stages, in the development of human society. With him, balls and parties, as well as hunts, races, plays, novel-reading, and every kind of amusement or diversion, were not things to be regulated, but were unhesitatingly classed with all sin and wickedness. That they were providential alleviations for weary limbs, aching hearts, and fretted brains—that they were safety-valves for pent-up spirits—toys for full-grown children, to keep them out of worse—all this he could not understand.

We must admit, however, that in course of time, Mr. Ruffles' belief in his own doctrine was considerably shaken; because, on the principle of "the lower the Church the larger the family," in course of time he was blessed with some very refractory sons, and some equally self-willed daughters. From this time a change came over the mind of Mr. Ruffles, for he then found that his doctrine positively would not work. However worldly it might be, Mrs. Ruffles could not endure the idea that such fine girls as her daughters should look as lank and stinted as they would look if with dresses as primitive as the Ruffles pattern. Then, the girls themselves would come down-stairs on a Sunday morning, as also to the tea-and-negus prayer-meetings, looking no more indifferent to the opinion of this world than other young ladies.

On this point Mrs. Ruffles was not to be convinced. She was positively reason-proof.

One glance at her dear girls — one thrill of maternal instinct — and a general impression that the whole world was not all mad together, caused Mrs. Ruffles to take up a position, flanked by her four fine girls, from which no power of words could move her; till, at last, the Rector found it very hard to preserve the severity of his doctrine in full view of his own family pew.

Meanwhile his sons' love of pleasure broke out in all kinds of illicit ways, simply because the buoyant spirits of youth were denied the vent that Providence intended as a natural diversion — a diversion all the more safe and innocent, because before the public eye, and not selfish and solitary, but in genial sympathy with their fellow-creatures. The consequence was, that the Ruffles doctrine was observed to grow milder and milder as the young Ruffles grew bigger and bigger; and when, at last, after the most impracticable teaching of the nothingness of worldly things, a Ruffles memorial was projected, and his regard for his growing family actually tempted him to reply to the memorial committee, that in no form would it be as acceptable as in money, people began to find that he took a more common-sense view of things necessary for this mortal state. Mr. Ruffles suffered no little in public opinion. Some of his oldest supporters, as they claimed to be—that is, some who had longest cheered him through many a visionary harangue, with rustling dresses and sympathising eyes, bitterly complained when the idol of their worship proved a man of like interests with themselves.

All Wanton remembers old Sir Wootton Cave—tobacco, snuff, and spirituous liquors were "the chief of his diet;"—he, of course, was delighted to cry "Hypocrite!" as an apology for his own evil ways. But Mr. Ruffles was no hypocrite; he was a good man: only, he had been going on under a mistake. Instead of purifying the waters, he had been fighting against the stream; and when nature, rife and powerful within, putting forth all her elastic energies, burst the cobweb bonds and scattered his doctrine to the winds, what wonder if the fond father did greet any new theory to reconcile what it was quite evident he could not possibly resist?

But we are chiefly concerned with the Ruffles doctrine, as affecting the mind of Mrs. Walford and her son.

As to Mrs. Walford, how to profit by the Ruffles' ministry, and to look after her son at the same time, she found a difficulty indeed. To the sinful vanities of the much-forbidden balls Mrs.

Walford went, at first, purely on account of her son; but soon she felt all the more guilty, because, drawn into the whirl of excitement, she was inwardly conscious of a worldly desire to dress as becomingly, and to look as much to advantage, as other ladies.

As to Ned Walford, the effect of the Ruffles doctrine was simply this:—It manufactured new sins, sure to be committed; sins which, though imaginary, made him all the less scrupulous to add real sins to what, he deemed, his already black and desperate account. We have much sympathy with poor Ned, because a very large number of preachers, either innocently or unguardedly, have conveyed to our minds the same impression; namely, that the next world depends on certain conditions, which no mortal man ever can fulfil, in a world like this.

The consequence is, that a youth naturally resigns himself to a dreamy state of mind, putting all such uncomfortable thoughts out of his head; and instead of hailing the Gospel as the light in darkness and the rule of life, he is quite prepared to welcome the theory of the first idle fellow, who declares that a devout and earnest course is utterly impracticable, and therefore mere "cant" and superstition altogether. And Ned Walford is not the only young man who has, practically, believed nothing by being required to believe too much; not the only one who has been supposed to abjure the Gospel, when all he abjured was a version, so far garbled, that it were more truly Christian to hope of the Allwise far better things.

It will readily be conjectured, therefore, that the Wanton society was divided into two parties —those who called themselves the "serious," and those whom they called the "worldly." Mrs. Walford's tastes and religious intuitions inclined her to the former: and the very fact of her taking sittings at Mr. Ruffles' church caused not a few to call; and thus, as Master Nat very humorously expressed it, "Melancholy marked her for her own." Indeed, a lady of Mrs. Walford's standing in society was no little acquisition to this set. For, it was comparatively easy for Mr. Ruffles to persuade his congregation to shun the paths of fashion—there being, with the generality, small chance of their receiving an invitation within that charmed and charming circle.

In Wanton society the upper strata were High Church, the secondary series were Low Church, and the tertiary deposit, Dissenters: and since ambition and worldly-mindedness, though banished under one form, will creep in under another, Mr. Ruffles' congregation were no little desirous to have the honour of Mrs. Walford at their prayer-meetings.

But no sooner had Mrs. Walford joined this privileged coterie, than she found it was a convenient stepping-stone to raise vulgar people considerably above their proper level. Their "religious" freedom and "pious" impertinence were insufferable; and Mrs. Walford's taste soon rebelled as strongly as her sympathies against the narrow and contracted character of her forward visitors. No sooner did she disclose that she had accepted an invitation to the ball of her old friend, Lady Wytham, than she was answered by looks so repulsive, and remarks so pharisaical, that she had little scruple in breaking off the connexion at once.

If making a beginning is half the battle, certainly, at a place like Wanton, the first party commits you to the giddy whirl at once. Heathen nations are not alone remarkable for worshipping "the rising sun." There is something in the very idea of the rich and prosperous that has a charm and an attraction even for those who have not the remotest interest in their possessions.

It is wonderful how the eyes of every hearer sparkle, and how pleasurable it feels to tell that any young man is born to a fortune, or that such a young lady is an heiress—a ward in Chancery—or coming of age, with thirty (always *thirty*) thousand pounds. So naturally does there arise a flow of lively, longing sentiments, exciting a delightful tumult in the breast.

As Mrs. Walford walked into the Wanton ball-room on her son's arm, it was not long before thoughts, hopes, castle-building, and calculations of various kinds, had supplied entertainment for ladies as well as gentlemen, young and old.

To say that all the young ladies formed designs upon the heir of Richcourt might be natural for those who know little of the true character of those of whom they speak. Young ladies are rarely mercenary; and we doubt if there was one lady in Wanton who would have valued at a farthing all the wealth of the Indies, in comparison with the heart that should fondly realise the golden vision—for, no doubt, they had all indulged such ecstatic waking-dreams—of "blessing and being blessed," and pouring forth the treasures of a devoted nature on one truly responsive to her love.

That Wanton was quite as full of sordid match-making mothers as some pretend, we are equally disposed to question. The truth, fairly and honourably stated, we believe to be more nearly this:—Our sons, for the most part, have all the inheritance: they also can, alone, earn the means of subsistence. A lady's fortune and a lady's profession, sphere of usefulness, and independence, too often depend on marriage alone. If so, what mother can be indifferent to a daughter's prospects? And as to setting their minds upon rich young men,—character, no doubt, might be more carefully considered than it is; but middle-aged people have generally arrived at a conviction that it is in vain to wait for any better fish than are swimming in the sea; and, scrutinise as they will, the family and the fortune of the suitor are, for the most part, the chief points which lie within the sphere of parental foresight. So, surely, the days of chivalry are past, when men indulge in heartless reflections on a lady, as she proudly sails into the ball-room, for no worse offence than a natural yearning for the happiness of "that fine young creature," the care of her life and the pride of a mother's heart.

Still, without suspecting sordid motives, where was the mamma who could help feeling something like an "Only suppose it were to be?" Who has not experienced how, when once he gives reins to a sanguine imagination, away it gallops, dragging him off, Mazeppa-like, into the wildest and most romantic situations, and calling up, from the vasty depths of his heart, the spirits of ambition, love of money, or any other, ready in a moment to do his bidding? And who, waking in a moment from his rapid day-dream, has not tried to think of something else; though, rub out the gorgeous picture as we will, its outlines are ever ready to re-appear on the tablets of the mind, and mingle with every other scene we try to sketch thereon?

So, there is no denying that the mammas of Wanton did—of course, "with the purest of motives"—lend a ready ear, and "devour up your discourse," whenever you talked of Richcourt Manor—aye, and perhaps they tenanted the Hall with elegant shadows of their own dear girls, and saw unborn babies on un-foaled donkeys, in panniers, of which the osiers had yet to grow, gracing some patrician avenue—with happy visits in prospect for the old people, too!

With the young ladies it was, at all events, a little adventure to have danced with Mr. Walford: so, many things tended to make Ned sensible that he had received much attention; to feel no little flattered, and on good terms with himself, so as not to be sorry to be invited out again.

This desire was easy to gratify; indeed, very much easier that he had any idea of: for, next day, as he was walking with a friend down Queen Street—the fashionable promenade of the town — he met three other young men, lounging along in the usual way, when the following conversation revealed in a moment how very exclusive was Wanton society, how highly prized was its hospitality; and, in short, it explained the way the Wantonians kept pace with the fashion and filled their rooms.

A. "Where are you going to-night? Victimised as yet, eh?"

B. "Now I know this man has something shabby to propose by his very question."

A. "Shabby! no I haven't. I have no less than three cards here, so you may choose for yourself."

C. "Pray don't let him impose upon you. Look at my tickets first. Here 's one in the Crescent for to-night; for Tuesday I can take you to Mrs. Mowall's; and Friday I know I shall be asked to find some fellows for the Lawsons'."

After no little badinage, pretending to quiz and depreciate either the rooms of one and the expected supper of another, and talking of the "squeeze of old Mother White," or the "stewing proposed by old Mother Black," a selection is made with the greatest condescension, and in the course of the afternoon A. pays a visit to the lady who had given him the commission, and duly informs her that she may calculate on a very fair sprinkling of beaux.

We need not say what was the entertainment at a fashionable Wanton party after such means had been made to fill it. What did it matter if any one did get no further than the landing-place? the lady had made "a return," and that was enough. All kinds of stories were told, though few could be more absurd than the truth;—Laced dresses rubbed to shreds, ladies' ankles kicked, and satin shoes trodden to pieces; and such grotesque pictures of dancing—men whirling and driving each his lady through a mob of muslin, with a most antagonistic expression of countenance—these scenes certainly could not be exaggerated, as regarded those who got into the room, but these were generally the favoured few. A place outside, where you could still enjoy that indescribable company-sensation arising from stifling air, best clothes, and vanity combined—this, with real Wantonians, was counted something still. In a word, there is no saying how far on the road to folly—each improving a little upon the silliness of his neighbour—human nature out of lunatic asylums may, step by step, be led to go.

It was here that Mr. Ruffles would expatiate triumphantly indeed, because here he had truly the best of the argument. Considering the influence he possessed, and considering also that he manfully spoke out and called things by their proper names, sensible persons the more regretted that he never could understand that in resisting recreation, amusement, society, and the diversions of the day, he was fighting against the laws of nature. The consequence was, that he brought ridicule upon the course he tried to serve; whereas, had he brought the powers of his party to bear upon the abuses alone—extravagance, dissipation of mind, and turning night into day—he might "have done the State some service."

If Mrs. Walford ever set her mind on the advantage of initiating her son into ladies' society, this object, after one week at Wanton, was already attained.

Ned was promenading with the ladies, and invited by the mothers, at all hours and under all pretences—perhaps a little more than his mother desired. But the attractions, luckily, were so many, that one neutralised another; and Snipe did not fail to fill his mind with sordid suspicions, and to pique him with being regarded as a dupe and a pigeon by all the old women in the place.

But Ned Walford soon found himself among a new set of gentlemen as well as ladies. The patronage and the countenance of an older man, himself the most popular and knowing character of the day, is irresistible with a young man like Ned. In almost every neighbourhood there is some such character—one who, by a jovial humour and a pleasant manner, seems to be free of every cellar, and to command the key-note of every heart.

Dick Cheston was a man of this kind—a "perfect gentleman when he pleased;" and so attractive, both to young and old, that if he only seated himself by the side of Mrs. Walford for ten minutes, it would set her talking about the pleasant evening she had enjoyed for a month: while many a young lady, though Dick was above fifty years of age, had rather talk and laugh with him, than with half the young men in the room.

Dick Cheston's success and popularity were really surprising. He had done strange deeds, enough to ruin the characters of six ordinary men; but everybody had an excuse, everybody made allowance for the thoughtless Dick Cheston. No one could believe he was not much better than he appeared. Here they were right. A man rather soft in the head, however strong in the heart, is sure to submit his principles to too strong a strain. And a man who begins as "nobody's enemy but his own," will not go far without considerable danger to his neighbour also.

When once a man takes so fatal a step as to accept hard cash from a friend—not to help a sick wife and family at a difficulty, but simply to carry him on in a career of pleasure—from that day you may count the decline and fall of all that marks the proper man. Dick had long since turned the critical corner—though not without the questionable excuse that many were the friends on whom he had lavished money—before he had been reduced to Mrs. Cheston's settlement, and what little he "could pick up by his wits."

It had now become habitual with Dick to levy black-mail on all sides; and as the generation of his own contemporaries were nearly tired out, Dick took care to recruit his tributaries from the ranks of the rising generation. His knowledge of horses, dogs, game-preserving, wine, guns, racing, and the ways of the world generally, were well worth paying for, as Cheston was a perfect sportsman: so, there were few country-seats of the sporting members of the aristocracy at which Dick Cheston was not, from time to time, a welcome guest.

A man of large fortune—to say nothing of his being kindly and hospitably disposed—soon finds, especially if he has few literary or other resources within himself, that he cannot exist without society around him; and he is often obliged to hire persons to break the loneliness of a country-house, as also to amuse his company in dull winter days. Dick was upon the list of no small number of such men, and was not the less in their employment because paid rather in kind than in coin; though, with one or two of his more generous friends, a cheque in Dick's dressing-case was sometimes left, to keep him afloat with fees, fares, and turnpikes.

The secret of Dick's popularity—and this is true of most other popular men—was his perfect good-nature, warm heart, and frank and ingenuous character. What! with all the failings already set down against him? And why not? These better qualities surround a man, as with an atmosphere of amiability, every hour of the day; while the stiffer virtues, perhaps, are not called out on active service above once a quarter: for, fair-weather honesty, like company-manners, answers every purpose in quiet times.

Snipe saw the fatal ascendancy of Cheston, but could not stop it. There is something repulsive, we know not how, about a selfish and designing man. His words may be specious, but his tones are hollow, and there is a look that mars the credit of his tongue. And Cheston was fast supplanting the influence of Snipe. Cheston's name was ever on Ned's lip; Cheston was quoted upon all occasions: till, so overwhelming was his influence, that Snipe thought it scarcely prudent to say much against him; more especially as Cheston had cast a knowing look at Snipe, which plainly seemed to say, "I have seen your sort before to-day: be careful, or I'll clip your wings for ever."

In one respect Dick Cheston was very useful: he encouraged Walford in hunting and shooting, and thus caused a diversion to female snares. He had no daughters of his own to provide for: he had, therefore, no inducement to forbear enforcing a theory which, with him as a sportsman, was reasonable enough—namely, that till a young man has "had his fling," married and marred are convertible terms.

CHAPTER XIII.

FIRST IMPRESSIONS OF COLLEGE.

It was now time that Ned Walford should enter College. The nearer it drew to the first day of term, the less he liked the thoughts of it. The stern and serious look of the Vice-President, as he appeared while criticising some very Anglicised Latin writing, and the difficulty that gentleman had made about letting him in, would naturally feel very strange to the Heir of Richcourt, whom every one had been running after and flattering all through the various stages of nursery, school, private tutor, and all.

And "how would the Vice-President receive him, when he reported himself at College? What would he advise—what inquiries would he make—what would he say about this—what had he himself better answer about some other matter?"

Such were the questions, all founded on his own great importance, which rushed into Walford's mind as he put on his new cap and gown, to make his appearance at Mr. Walesby's rooms.

How many times, in the course of our lives, do we make up our minds, and stand, as it were, in battle array, ready for a defence which is never wanted, or racking our brains for an answer to no one's thoughts but our own! Just as Æneas, that gay deceiver, in the Shades below, was primed with a whole string of excuses to make to poor Dido, about that cruel breach-of-promise case, when, after all, she cut him dead, and turned upon her heel, without troubling him for one of them.

Mr. Walesby was just as far from entering into all the minutiæ of the particular case of Ned Walford.

As Walford entered the room, Mr. Walesby, who had to give audience to half the College that morning, was standing, shaking two men by the hands at the same time, and making the same words, full of pleasantry and good-humour, serve for both, and ended one minute's hasty discourse by saying,—

"But I will tell you what you can do for me. Let me introduce 'Mr. Walford.' Now explain to him all about the Lecture-board: but mind, Norman; no more of your hoaxes, or you and I shall quarrel. And, Mr. Walford, as to the rooms, you can have in the first instance —— Here, Robert" (addressing an old, trusty College servant), "you will know what rooms —— and the lectures, they do not commence till the day after to-morrow. Good morning, Mr. Walford! I hope your father's quite well."

Before Ned could explain that his father died before he was born, he found himself backed out of the room, in company with Norman and Rickworth, both laughing heartily at some joke which Walford could not understand. This lasted about a minute: when Rickworth, who, like Norman, had a lively sense of the ridiculous, said to Walford,—

"In handing you over to the tender mercies of Norman, Walesby did well and wisely to 'bar jokes;' for, the way this man has imposed upon some well-meaning freshmen, is positively a cruelty to think of."

"But Mr. Walesby seems to have found him out," observed Walford.

The explanation was this:—Norman was just one of those men who appear, in a tutor's eyes, the very flower of innocence and cream of perfection.

Mr. Walesby could not at first detect that there was more mischief, as well as dry humour in Norman, than in any five men in the College: so Norman was, on all occasions, the man most commonly requested by the tutors of King's to act *proxenos*, or receiver-general to freshmen—services for which, at last, as he found them tedious, Norman thought it quite fair to reward himself by a little fun at their expense. At length, Mr. Walesby remarked to Rickworth one morning, when he had invited him to breakfast, that the manners of the rising generation seemed very free and easy. One and all of them were coming up to shake hands on every occasion, and one of them had actually invited the Vice-President to breakfast: but, to crown all, one youth, who had been showing Norman a hundred newly-engraved cards, was forthwith set upon leaving one with the Vice-Chancellor, Heads of Colleges, and Professors, according to a list of dignitaries in Norman's handwriting. But, unfortunately, this credulous youth proved to be Mr. Walesby's own nephew, who thus detected Norman in being a corrupter of modern manners and perverter of the prevailing etiquette.

Mr. Walesby endeavoured to look serious, when he taxed Norman with imposing on every freshman he undertook to initiate; but strove, in vain, to end his admonition without a smile.

When Rickworth had parted from them, Norman took Walford to the Hall, ran his finger down the lecture lists, and found Walford's name down with "the Slow Ten o'Clock (Coach)," otherwise called "The Heavy Euripides;" for, lectures were commonly called "Coaches" — "fast" or "slow," as the case might be.

Walford hereupon put a sifting question,— "Whether there were supposed to be any gradations in these arrangements?"

"Why, to say the truth," replied Norman, with mock solemnity, "in this august seat of learning you will observe, in course of time, that there are various stages of intellectual development among the literary gentlemen, and this class marks—an early stage."

"You expect no academical distinctions from the members of this class, perhaps?"

"On the contrary; several are highly distinguished. One man had as many as three plucks to his own share: and, no doubt, he would have had more, but the College authorities interfered."

"Rickworth, I see, is in an Aristotle Class."

"Yes; Rickworth is a man of varied talent.

He is one of the 'Scholars;' but Walesby does not approve of his goings on. Imagine our Vice-President getting hold of one of Rickworth's cards of invitation, and reading to his horror those astounding words,—'Rats and porter at two P.M.—N.B. Every gentleman to bring his own terrier.'"

"And what did Mr. Walesby think of that?"

"Why, Walesby is a rare instance of a man who sees things as they are. No one is more fully aware that invention, originality, and imagination, are essential for winning prizes, and keeping up the honour of the College. All these erratic qualities meet in Rickworth; and Walesby, no doubt, read at a glance character—yes, decided character—in the 'Rat-and-porter' invitation then before him. His idea is, that Rickworth can't be expected to be as steady as if he were stupid; well knowing that fast trains are most apt to run off the line. In other words, many men only do not go wrong, because there is in them hardly any 'go' at all."

Never were two College chums more unlike than Norman and Rickworth. Just walk with us round the garden. It is a fine sunny morning—a saint's day—and, therefore, there are no lectures; and some of the men, not having quite made up their minds what they shall do with themselves, with a whole day to dispose of, are sauntering about the walks; while friendly and rather entertaining inquiries resound at a little distance, as men are calling to each other from window to window. There sits Norman in spectacles, on a camp-stool, sketching the President's house—always with a cat upon the chimney. See, he is surrounded by men who keep up a running fire of sharp-shooting repartee, while Norman gravely reads them a lecture, in mock heroics, upon High Art.

"And where is Rickworth? *He* is the most devil-me-care fellow possible," cried Churton, one of the senior scholars. "Woollaston agrees with me that the Latin prize poem he has finished, all but some thirty lines, is sure to win:* yet not another line can we induce him to write. The day after to-morrow is the last day allowed: so, we have locked him up, with pen, ink, and paper, and declared that he shall not come out till he has finished it.—And now we are off, at twelve o'clock to-day, to hear Weston examined *vivâ voce*. Here is a certain first class for King's, no doubt. Walesby has

* The Latin prize poem thus finished *did* win.—J. P.

inquired about Weston's paper work, and, of course, won't tell: but it is easy to read by his looks that all goes swimmingly."

Here we have a glimpse of the two best sets in King's—the scholars and hard-reading men, such as Churton and Woollaston, and the general-information men like Norman—men who read Classics enough to enjoy the beauties, or, perhaps, to encourage their sense of the ridiculous. Norman's discoveries in History and Mythology were curious indeed:—"the first great man of antiquity who had a woman's name was Polyphemus (*Polly famous*); Ceres agitated the Corn-law question; Bacchus, the spirit-duties. Apollo, in the first lines of the *Iliad*, represented an ignorant military doctor, "who sent many a lusty fellow to his long account, a little faster than he would have gone otherwise;" and as to Diogenes asking Alexander to stand from between him and the sun, it simply means that he presented a petition, that while he lived in his tub he might not be charged tax for the bung-hole."

Norman's set, therefore, formed a useful gradation between the reading men and men like Walford, the idle and good for nothing; and Cyril Jackson, the famous Dean of Christchurch, once said he should not desire all reading men in his College;—"No," he said, "we want some idle men, to make diversion for the studious."

Rickworth belonged to both sets—both scholar and *dilettante.* He also—witness, ye rats and terriers!—fraternised with the sporting set, too. Rickworth's room was quite a study—curious for any contemplative man to behold. Greek plays, Aristotle, and all the *apparatus criticus* thereto belonging, marked a mind that could grapple with the giant spirits of ages past, while the same worthies were surmounted with boxing-gloves and single-sticks; and on the branching horns of a stag over the fire-place were spurs pendant, a hunting-whip, and small key-bugle.

Mr. Walesby, once in our presence, spoke to Woollaston about the erratic doings of his friend Rickworth. He urged that, for the honour of the scholars of King's—a select society, always characterised by propriety of conduct—they ought to endeavour to keep Rickworth within bounds. Woollaston replied, that really so strong was the excitement in Rickworth's mercurial temperament, that you could not deal with him as with ordinary mortals. Mr. Walesby shook his head despairingly, saying, that "great wit to madness was allied." Indeed, he had been informed that Rickworth's reading was all done by night. He was too excitable to settle down by day: and perhaps the foils and boxing-gloves were almost indispensable, in his case, to carry off the buoyancy of his superfluous spirits.

Besides these "sets"—such was the usual term—Walford found that King's College had, among others, its Boating set and its Cricket set. The enthusiasm that prevailed for the honour of the College Boat was surprising—insomuch that Mr. Walesby designated them "the Hydro-maniacs." Waddington was the Captain of the Boat, and kept an eye on the make and shape, and thews and sinews, of every freshman, to decide whether he was worth pressing into the service. Walford of Baliol was so good an oar, that Waddington was sanguine of finding an ally in the brother at King's: but Ned not only could not row, but there was no "gumption" in him—he did not seem a likely sort to do the boat good service.

Waddington used to say, that rowing with a man, like racing with a horse, wanted pluck as well as muscle: it was common enough, he said, to find a man who would put forth all his strength; but, when you came to a struggle, you wanted more. Every old Oxonian of the Isis remembers what it used to be to feel about the bridges, yclept "the Gut," ready to drop from exhaustion—mouth parched, heart thumping, ears saluted with deafening cheers,—"Now you're gaining!" "Now you're into her!"—all the time he would feel it a mercy to stop: but "pull and die" is the feeling; and a man of the right sort would no more "throw up" his oar in a race, than lose his colours on the field of battle.

These being the qualifications for the boat, it required no great penetration to perceive that Walford's energies had never been used to the severer tests in boyhood, and therefore could hardly be trusted now.

Walford's cricketing was also moderate. *Nil sine labore*, that nothing is to be had without working for it, is a law of nature. No golden key unlocks the stores of mind, of heart, or of any treasures in the proper man. It is true now, as in the days of Horace, that in manly sports no one must hope to come up to the mark, who has not been well fagged as a boy. And, though we would walk a long mile to see any bully, young or old, have his just deserts, still we cannot descry unmixed evil in the bumptious little urchin, who, pleading the privileges of the aristocracy, when told to make himself useful to his elders, was answered, "Then here's one kick for your lordship and another for yourself."

We always pitied Walford: so manifestly did the curse of gold blight all his youth. Not his the training of the bold and daring spirit that, reckless of self, and merged heart and soul in the generous cause, rushes madly into the thickest of the fray, where ten are battling about the foot-ball—clears himself away, and just saves the goal—the ball soaring high in air, as if exulting in triumph at his prowess.—Not his the training of the Cricket Field, when all stand, breathless in anxiety, to save each hardly-fought run, when the telegraph is running up near the point of "Game"—when, animated with a spirit far from self, each youthful breast is thrilling with a generous desire of victory, for victory's sake.—No: but, unhappily, all the supposed care and anxious watching of his health and safety—of the particular bias of his mind or disposition—this all had tended to centre his emotions all in self—starving the eagle energies of the man to the cowering of the domestic fowl—and to send him forth into life stunted, slow, and spiritless—in effect, good for no one of the higher purposes in this mortal life.

Nowhere in life does a man so surely sink

down and down to his proper level as in a College. The intellectual sets, of whom we spake, saw at a glance Walford was not the man for them. Norman, always kind and affable, asked him to his rooms—just once—to meet his brother Nat; but that done, Norman, like all his friends, let Ned pass as a non-entity from one term to another. Rickworth would ask him in at luncheon, when the gloves were in requisition: but Walford soon felt quite unequal to the ruder civilities of the sporting set: so, of course, he must take up with the only society in the College with whom he could feel at all at ease—a kind of foppish, dressy set of men—spoilt children like himself; who, by horses, and tandems, and "spreads" various, virtually purchased that society which men like John Hackles enjoyed, far better in its kind, by virtue of their own social qualifications alone.

When in society I hear heavy complaints of the temptations of Oxford—of the debts and difficulties, and "the wicked tradesmen, all conspiring to lead unhappy youth astray," I am never much at a loss to understand the true position of the case. Every mother's son would appear to be mis-led by some one else: so, where the evil impulse first comes from, is a puzzle!

In a College like King's there are various sets of society, all more or less improving to a youth; but so long as the Ned Walfords are reared in folly and self-indulgence out of Oxford, so long will there be a reckless set in every College; and we have said enough to show how naturally, by their own inertia and gravitation, they sink to the bottom, and so come together to form no very improving society.

This particular set in King's, at the time of which we are speaking, were called the Ek-lectoi, being a Greek word borrowed to imply a very select and pretentious clique of young fellows, with more money than mind—men who kept each other in countenance by affecting to despise all that stern stuff in human nature, and all that fierce quality in which they were themselves so pitifully deficient. All the reading men they voted slow—as aspiring to be Dons: as to the Boating set and the Cricket set, "they quite felt for them," as committed to what was "a deal too much trouble." To recline lazily on a mattrass of leaves, in a punt, and to smoke, or pretend to read a novel, while punted up the Cherwell—a shameless piece of girlishness too common since—this they claimed as their own invention; while their tandems, and occasionally four-horse drags, were things of which they boasted, as if they alone upheld the honour and respectability of the College—simply by driving over to Henley, eating 'sparagus, and driving back again!

We have always observed, that the dupe of to-day has a natural tendency to become the sharper of to-morrow. When generous feeling proves unrequited—when a man has again and again found his liberal estimate of another's character a delusion and a snare, and when a cold and heartless sneer is all the response he gets from those of whom—good, easy man!—he had taken for granted far better things—the reflection too often arises that high principle is quite Quixotic, and that the standard adopted is too high for the wear and tear of "this tough world."

It will therefore be easily understood, that there were sharps as well as flats in the set of the Ek-lectoi, otherwise called "Le Croix's set," for he was at the head of it—the set which Walford very soon joined.

Le Croix saw, with a master's eye, that Walford would be an acquisition. Le Croix's principles and politics will appear at a glance, from the following conversation with his "Scout"—brief for the servant—at Oxford, called "Bedmaker;" at Cambridge, "Gyp."

"Please, Sir, you want some more glasses."

"No, John, I don't. That is quite a mistake of yours."

"Please, Sir, I'm always a-borrowing, and—"

"Then go on borrowing; you can't do a wiser, or a more economical thing."

"But, please, Sir, those I borrow of are come at last to be as short of glass as you are. I keep telling their servants, Sir, that they must try and persuade Mr. Watkins—he is one that has been lending, Sir,—and Mr. Kirwan, and Mr. Woodley too, Sir—they are the only gentlemen in your staircase—to persuade them to buy more glass; but they say, they do get 'pitched into so uncommon' for mentioning such a thing, they won't say no more."

"But there are four freshmen this very term —eh?"

"Mr. Walford is one, Sir, that I wait on."

"Very well, then; that settles the difficulty. You take care and indoctrinate him with the quantum of glass: let him turn half of Apsley Pellatt's factory into his cupboards. He must have, as a *gentleman*—put an emphasis on that word 'gentleman,'—that's the name to conjure up a spirit with a freshman. These freshmen, you are old enough to know, John, are all rather ambitious; so, no doubt, your Mr. Walford, or whatever he calls himself, will feel it quite an honour to find me in glass to the end of my time in College,—I am sure he will. But, while I think of it, let me ask you,—Does Mr. Walford bring his own wine up with him?"

"I think I saw a hamper, Sir."

"Exactly; and remember that you duly inform him that this is quite a correct thing to do, and that of gentlemen in our set we expect as much—no Oxford black-strap goes down here."

"Please, Sir, if it's about your time for a wine-party, you would let me know, Sir?"

"My time for a wine-party, indeed! What, with these said fine promising freshmen? No, no, John: I have kept things going pretty well, I think. I have done my part—I was *young* once. You understand——"

Exit John, who after some thirty years' experience in King's, understood the ways of young and old too well for a man like Le Croix to trouble himself with the least disguise. All who remember old John Billings will testify that his respect for Le Croix's politics must have been greatly raised by the presence of mind then exemplified.

Le Croix and his set were the very men to appear great in the eyes of Walford. Le Croix was well known to be connected with more than one branch of the aristocracy. He could talk without affectation of the vacation he spent at his cousin's, Lord St. John's; or at the Hall of his brother-in-law, the Marquis of Donallin. He was also known to visit as much at Christchurch as at King's; and "Tufts" various dined with him at the Gentlemen Commoners' table in the course of the term.

Le Croix was not long in learning who Walford was, and the wide range of his prospects. Neither was Le Croix long in informing his Christchurch friends that, although Walford's estate had been to nurse for some twenty years, the owner was still a long way from years of discretion.

Of course, the society in Christchurch had the same tendency to precipitate its grosser and heavier elements to the bottom, which we have noticed in the society of King's. There was also the same indisposition in any other class of men to fraternise with a man like Le Croix. This was the Gambling set of Christchurch—a set carefully watched by the College authorities, and broken up from time to time by wholesale expulsion: but still, such rank weeds are ever apt to grow again in such a soil. For, so long as the rich men of England recruit a College with spoilt children, having more money at command, and more time, too, than they know what to do with,—so long gambling, like other forms of idle excitement, will continually re-appear.

To an observing tutor like Mr. Walesby, every set in a College, and the habits of every man, are as well known as to the undergraduates themselves. Full well did that excellent tutor know the distinctive character which each set in King's clearly implied. To be much seen with Norman or Rickworth implied something entertaining in a man—some originality and inward resources. The Boating and Cricket sets, he shrewdly calculated, had enough to think of to keep them out of mischief most days in the week: but the mere lounging apathy of Le Croix's set he deemed the most dangerous of all.

Mr. Walesby was very sorry to find Walford in the very circle which was his dire aversion. He had characterised Walford as open and ingenuous, and one who, with eligible companions, would do well. But it is amongst the sorest trials and disappointments of a College tutor of feeling mind, to see youths like Walford, quite capable of the right path, yet hurried down the wrong, all owing to errors too late to counteract.

"Le Croix has introduced Walford to his

Christchurch friends, I suspect," said Mr. Walesby to the Dean, while over their wine in the Common Room. "I see by the porter's book, that they both came in together, and both within a minute of twelve o'clock; and twice, later still. That looks like high play. I have my suspicions."

"I wish we had some pretence for getting rid of Le Croix, altogether. But I think Mr. Walesby appears to be rather too indulgent in his view of that young man."

This was said by the Dean, a young man of about six-and-twenty years of age.

"By the time Mr. Dean has observed men and manners as I have, with some thirty years of College life, perhaps he will learn to be a little more tolerant too," was the reply.

"You must explain, Mr. Walesby."

"My meaning is, that our College has never been without these Le Croixs. Of characters so commonly bred in the country, we must of course expect to have some representatives at Oxford. As spoilt children, reared in self-indulgence, with no self-command, no resources or well-attempered genial nature to recommend them to the improving influences of our best sets—such men must sink among the worst. Le Croix, at first, was promising enough; as much so as Walford appears to be: but, unhappily, the Walford of to-day will degenerate into the Le Croix of twelve terms hence."

"Walford has a brother at Baliol; they speak well of him, as one of the best men in the College."

"I am well aware he has such a brother. I have seen them together; the likeness is very remarkable: but though they are as like as two peas in countenance, the one brother has all the rigidity and marked lines of character, while the other looks soft and unstrung. There is no mistaking which is "the eldest son." The one has roughed it at a public school; the other has sold the birthright of manliness for the pap and porridge of that, of all things the most cruel in its results in after-life—'private education,' 'the limited number,' and 'all the indulgence of home.'"

"If we could send Walford away for a year, might it not be a kindness to him?"

"That depends where he would spend that year; he will find men to flatter and to live upon him anywhere. No. College is the only place in which a young man of his fortune feels any restraint at all. Be sure that every day he passes here, that youth must feel his own inferiority; he cannot hear the quadrangle ringing with shouts for College victories, whether in the

Schools, on Bullingdon, or the Isis, without an improving consciousness that life in earnest—to do, to suffer, and to conquer—has more true satisfaction than his present courses."

"Then you consider we owe a duty to the idle as well as to the industrious?"

"Most undoubtedly do I think so. 'Pity the sorrows of the poor *rich*,' is the burden of my song. If for the city Arabs we provide Ragged Schools, shall we have no sympathy for the victims of cruel kindness, too? Walford has learnt a lesson since he has been here; I can see ingenuous shame rising on his cheek. I can perceive in lecture when a man day after day leaves the room discontented and disgusted with himself, after twitching for an hour at the performance of those whom he tries in vain to think his inferiors."

Mr. Walesby's opinion of Walford's feelings was true to the life. We have reason to know this, because every man likes to confide in some one: every man yearns for a kind of Confessor—a friend before whom to disburden, and to tell the secret of his own disgust—his own un-rest.

The honest nature of plain, hard-working John Hackles, was quite of the kind to invite the confidence of Walford; and Walford, when occasionally thrown upon his own resources for an evening, would stroll into the rooms of Hackles. It was quite of the nature of a private and an in-door intimacy. It was perfectly well understood between them that, beyond a friendly nod of recognition, they were no company for each other in the High Street or the Christchurch Walk: the one would lose caste with men of style; the other, with men of sense. Indeed, while making this observation, we feel sure that every Oxford man will remember how smoothly and sensibly, without the least offence on the one side or compromise on the other, a social understanding of this kind could prevail between the rich or fashionable, and plain, striving, reading men, who could, with difficulty, afford the bare fees and College "battels."

Walford confessed to Hackles that, though he could not complain of Oxford on the whole, yet he found things different from what he expected. He spoke well of Norman, of Rickworth, and some of their friends.

Hackles knew what he meant. The explanation was too plain to be mistaken;—that the only pleasant, genial, and unaffected men that were in the College, declined Walford's society:

money alone would procure but the company of fools!

Then the discouraging truth came out—intelligible enough to the shrewd John Hackles, though only very innocently implied by the perplexed, but disgusted Ned Walford; namely, that he felt nobody in Oxford: for, mere externals are nowhere held so cheap.

In Oxford society the Le Croixs and the Ned Walfords may exist, but they do not preponderate: and, true as it may be that wealth wins everywhere, yet nowhere is the veil so thin—nowhere is it so difficult for the silly dupe to conceal from himself the unpalatable truth, that no man cares for him one day longer than he provides "spreads" in-doors or tandems out.

Over a quiet cup of tea, in Hackles' room, Ned, unknown and unsuspected by his stylish and fashionable "set," would lounge on the sofa—John reading and thumbing his lexicon all the while, and putting in a word about once in five minutes—and in these sober hours Ned would enjoy the true pleasures of friendship, with mutual confidence, with sincerity, and respect. Ned was now breathing a healthful and a genial atmosphere; and the conviction would gradually steal over him, that "honest John"

—save and except in the cut of his coat—was, as Norman once expressed it, worth as many Le Croixs as could stand between Carfax and Magdalene tower.

So, Walford's eyes were gradually opening to the fact, that life had higher pleasures, and the heart owned nobler transports, of a kind which no wealthy father ever could bequeath, and which gold could never buy. On all sides—in the class-rooms, the schools, the merry-meeting, or the sports of the field—Ned could not help marking men, whose fame he emulated and whose prowess he admired. Here were prizes worth his winning: but then came the humbling conviction, that not Richcourt Manor—not all the fawning and flattery which had greeted him from the cradle—could avail him here.

The society of Brother Nat had now become anything but enjoyable. Nat's success was a reproach to Ned: neither was it easy for the younger brother, at all times, to conceal certain feelings of self-satisfaction, which, to the acute sensibilities of the elder, seemed to say, "Great as you are at Richcourt Manor, you must acknowledge my precedence here."

Hackles used to speak hopefully of Walford, and to say that there was more real goodness in him than had yet been drawn out. In the days of our youth we cannot help looking hopefully on such men. We think, "If they would only do this," or, "If they would only avoid that practice"—points of wisdom on which they have already so cordially agreed with us, as a matter of principle—"all would be well." We forget, that where Habit is so strong, Resolution must be weak—establishing "one law in the mind, and another law in the members;" or, as Norman, with all the simulated gravity of the Johnsonian philosophy expressed it, "Why, Sir, that young man's self-control and mastery are very much of the nature of a certain limited monarchy—limited by the constant rising of a lawless mob—yes, a very mob of unruly passions, moonshine notions, and asinine imaginations!"

All this was so far true, that Brother Nat was frequently coming to Hackles, to ask how it was that the men of King's could allow Ned to make such a fool of himself. One day Nat had been chosen as one of the University Eleven against the Marylebone Cricket Club, in their annual visit to Oxford—we allude to the days when Mr. Aislaby, whose flannel cricket-jacket has been likened to the breadth of a mainsail—used *immani corpore* to act Choregus to the

Marylebone Eleven. The match was played with no decided advantage on either side, the first day: and so Nat and his friends were sanguine in the extreme of the result of the second innings, when Sir Wootten Burns disappointed them all, with an excuse that they had an engagement in London which the threatening state of the weather would make it folly to break; and so the whole party cleared off by the twelve-o'clock coach! Such conduct seemed very mysterious at the time: but soon the explanation was whispered around, that Sir Wootten had good cause to take himself off before the reflections of the morning were brought to bear on the operations of the night before. Sir Wootten had been to the rooms of C. R., of Christchurch—Le Croix and Walford being two of the party—and had ended with laying the youngsters under contribution for several hundreds at Vingt-un!

About this time an election of Fellows took place at King's, resulting in adding to the number of Walford's tutors, and of those placed in authority over him—one whose presence at the high-table, and whose superior rank in Oxford society, tended still further to confound Walford's notions of the greatness of the man of many acres, and the littleness of the man who had none.

All the University had heard the name of Thompson of St. Vitus's—one of the most insignificant Colleges in Oxford—a College so far secondary, that the very name of a St. Vitus' man sounded low as "Whitechapel" to any one in the set of Walford and Le Croix.

Walford had often heard, without heeding, the name of Thompson, the winner of the great University Scholarship; the winner also of a Prize Poem and the Latin Exhibition, besides other prizes and honours; and ending with the honour of the best First Class of the Term. Of a man so highly distinguished, Walford could not help hearing, at least, the name and achievements, however indifferent he might generally be to the literary news of the day.

The election was over, when Mr. Walesby, meeting Walford in the garden, observed, "We have had the honour of electing a gentleman of your county, Mr. Walford—Mr. Thompson of St. Vitus's. He is a great acquisition, particularly now, by the loss of Mr. Kenyon, we want another Lecturer, without loss of time. He appears to know something of your family. He said one of the two Walfords was once his pupil; but he was not quite sure whether you were the same."

"Humph! that's very cool of him, certainly!" said Walford to himself.

This happened in the Whitsuntide vacation; after which, as Walford went up to the late Mr. Kenyon's lecture-room, and took his seat with about a dozen others, he found the identical "Gritty Thompson," once usher of Mr. Watson's school, already installed as Lecturer—standing quietly and composedly, with his eyes upon his book, while the class was assembling; and then turning round, as Walford happened to be nearest to him, he said, "I will trouble you to begin:" looking at him quite in the Oxford fashion, as if he were a statue, and as if Mr. Thompson had never seen him before in his life.

From this time Walford was, of course, bound to "cap" Mr Thompson, and quite to forget the subordinate position of his earlier days.

"What!" said Walford to Norman, "are they really aware that Thompson's father is a small miller, and that he has carried a sack of flour on his own shoulders?"

"Thompson has admitted as much to one of the Dons, a friend of a friend of mine," replied Norman; "but Oxford owns the aristocracy of mind and of worth.—Were his manners boorish he would not be here: but, the intellectual taste and deep sense of the beautiful, which Thompson's academical course attests, make men comparatively indifferent to those less certain criteria by which men judge (and perhaps wisely, as a rule) in general society."

It is no easy matter for "worth by poverty depressed" to set its foot upon the ladder academical; but once there, no one can limit the prospect of advancement. We could name, at this moment, cases in which the highest honours of the lawn and the ermine have been awarded to men who eked out with a Scholarship the small fund which their friends with difficulty contrived to scrape together. Indeed our two Universities serve, in a wonderful manner, to bridge over the wide gulf which otherwise — as regards a sphere and prizes intellectual — would separate between the rich and poor.

Behold, there, the son of a saddler in a country town — he is admitted as a free boy to the B. Grammar School, — as head boy he is chosen to deliver the annual speech to the mayor. His talents excite admiration; a small sum is advanced to send him to College. By College prizes, by a tutorship or fellowship, he makes a purse, while he also makes friends and useful connexions, — goes off to London, and at once starts even — ay, and with the spur of necessity in his sides — starts with a better chance by far than the richest or the noblest in the land!

The private history of the first men at the Bar, as also in the Church, and the highest places in both Universities, at the present hour, would be a singular illustration of this remark.

CHAPTER XIV.

WHAT BECAME OF HANNAH AND OF ALICE HENGEN.

We must now revert to two characters, already introduced to the notice and the sympathy of the reader—to Hannah Hengen and her sister Alice, whom we left standing by the death-bed of their fond and broken-hearted father.

Harsh and violent as was the character of Hannah, and wounded and lacerated as her feelings had been, after the cruel trial to which we have before alluded—she was fondness and tenderness itself as regarded her younger sister Alice.

Some said that Alice had been solemnly committed to her care by her dying mother; painfully conscious as that mother must have been of the failing health, as well as the precarious income, of the father. Such solemn changes have their weight, no doubt; but duties are never as well performed—a sacred charge is never as well preserved—as when much has been done and suffered, till the finer tendrils of the heart have had time to grow and cluster around the object of it. And it was partly in this way that the soul of Hannah was knit unto the soul of Alice.

Hannah had nursed the delicate child through a long illness; had seen her as it were dead, and traced and identified with her own fond care every flickering of glowing life. Hannah had found in Alice a vent for her yearning affections—a sphere for those surging energies that, in her as in many another woman doomed never to be read aright by the drawling monotony of this world, might wisely and tenderly receive a safe direction, but never a control. Hour after hour would that restless spirit find repose, while working and reading with her sister in her little room: and if this were so before the—yes, *the* great heart-blow of her life fell upon her—yet, more endearing did the much-loved child daily grow, when, knowing all but uttering nothing, she would betray her conscious sorrow only by nestling the more closely to her sister's side, and reflecting the pearly sadness of her sister's eyes in the softer sympathy of her own.

Can we then be surprised to hear, that at the father's death, Hannah's dearly-bought wisdom in this world's ways made her look fearfully and fiercely into the dark future? As her eye rested thoughtfully on Alice, can we doubt that she discerned snares in her beauty, and danger in that confiding spirit, which made her all the more dear and devoted to herself?

But this was no time for weaving—as who does not?—the plan and pattern of a life; whether shot with gold and purple, or one dead hue of sable colour. No, it was time for action. It remained to realise and bring their little store into the smallest compass and the most convenient form; and to hasten their departure before the coming quarter-day. Their little home, with all its memories, and all the silent witness it had borne to the hopes and fears of ten years past, was already bespoken by the new station-master, entering on his new office as full of sanguine hopes as they had been; and doomed no doubt to his own little budget of cares and trials, before his appointed course was run.

Well, poor people cannot sit down and indulge in floods of unavailing tears. Hannah and Alice Hengen at once found themselves in a position to realise that touch of nature in the *Antiquary*, where, after the drowning of poor

Steenie Mucklebackit, the father is found by Oldbuck repairing the fatal boat, and says, "It's weel with you gentles, that can sit in the house with handkerchers at your e'en when ye lose a friend: but the like of us maun to our work again, if our hearts were beating as hard as my hammer."

But there is something mysterious and almost awful in contemplating how, with the ocean of this life, one wave follows another with the same ruthless, angry roar, whether to sweep away the senseless sea-weed or to dash two living creatures, clasped in each other's arms, high on some inhospitable shore.—Alice was of importance inappreciable in the eyes of Hannah, but to the landlord of the house, coldly looking at his fixtures, and to the clerks who came to receive the father's books relating to the railway, they were simply "the party going out;" while all thoughts shot past them and seemed to give them the go-by, being, as usual, wholly taken up with "the party coming in."

"*Man never continueth in one stay.*" Trials should be counted as changes—as stages in our development—and so many "removes" from class to class, each higher and more improving in the severe school of life. The time must come to knock the cradle from the noble vessel, and launch it for a venture upon unknown seas. So the stage of self-guidance and self-dependence, to Hannah and Alice Hengen, as to many another orphan, had come at last.

However, if our troubles in this life are unexpected, their alleviations are often equally so; and God put it into the heart of a kind old widow, who saw Mr. Hengen's death in the newspaper, to give the two sisters a little breathing-time, by inviting them for a while to her house.

This good lady was Mrs. Hardaway—Her husband, the Contractor, whom we have already introduced, had been at this time about two years dead.

We need hardly say that the invitation was most thankfully accepted, and the two sisters most kindly received; and, naturally, some little time was allowed to elapse before any allusion was made to the necessity of finding situations or employment for their eventual support: though this view of the question, of course, presented itself at last. For, to help persons to help themselves, is the greatest effort that charity, in our experience, was ever known to make—the friend in need that changes rags into silk and satin, and the cottage into a mansion, existing in fairy-tale alone.

While the sisters were considering what assistance Mrs. Hardaway might intend, or what provision she might have in store for them, the mind of the inexperienced Alice could not help indulging hopes in proportion to the boundless wealth reputed to have been dug by the Great Contractor from many a tunnel or railway-cutting.

But Hannah's less romantic intuitions led her instantly to declare to the sanguine Alice that such golden visions never would be realised. Nor was it long before Mrs. Hardaway's eminently practical turn of mind made her call her two guests into her little room; where, looking up — as Alice afterwards innocently described the expression of her countenance — "quite different" through her spectacles, she said it was now "high time to talk of business." — What were their views? — what situations were they thinking of? — what were they fit for?

Almost every one is aware that, as regards men, one who is only "brought up to be a gentleman," can hardly hope to earn a decent livelihood; but few consider that special qualifications, of a useful and a marketable kind, are no less indispensable for a lady: but Mrs. Hardaway, by the striving, thrifty habits of her younger days, could hardly suppose that any young woman should ever dream of expecting board and wages of a mistress unless she had practical knowledge and realised experience to offer in return.

"People won't pay much for gentility now-a-days," said this shrewd observer; "least-wise we never found it so."

Hannah, rather nettled at this remark, could with difficulty prevent saying, somewhat significantly, "She supposed not" seeing that, though age always confers a semblance of respectability, Mr. Hardaway rose from a carpenter's bench, and Mrs. Hardaway was a plasterer's daughter.

However, Hannah succeeded in choking down her rising spirit, and quietly suggested that she might be useful in Housekeeping. Whereupon the old lady ran on with something between a commentary and a leading examination about pounds and half-pounds, and "so much a-head all round the family;" and ended by saying, as one way of implying that Hannah knew nothing about it—"However, live and learn is the way of the world; and I should think, Hannah, you would be one to stand no nonsense with a parcel of impudent servant-girls, at all events. That part of the business you seem a likely sort to do first-rate."—Mrs. Hardaway then turned more directly to the case of Alice, and suggested something in the way of a nursery-governess.

Alice rather drew back at this, and asked if, under the name of "companion," something more eligible might not be found?

"Why, as to that, child, there is no accounting for taste. Only, you must consider, when a body is well and hearty, one does not want a companion very often; and if a body is frail and feasy, why then I wish you joy of waiting about and putting up with them."

This we give as a sufficient sample of the little Committee on Ways and Means held between the two orphan sisters and their worldly-wise adviser and plain-spoken friend. Their conference, no doubt, resulted in setting before the eyes of Hannah and of Alice such bleak, and bare, and wintry views of life, as made their next step feel as one cold plunge. The world was sadly changed: life was no longer friendship, hospitality, or courtesy of any kind: it had come to a hard state of exchange and barter—give and take; and the most withering aspect in which you can look at human nature is from the money side.

After much inquiry among her friends, Mrs. Hardaway succeeded in providing both the sisters with situations. One morning she informed them, with the greatest satisfaction, that she had something to announce—namely, that she had succeeded!—expecting, no doubt, the pleasure of lighting up a gleam of sunshine in the faces of both her penniless guests. Great was her disappointment "at the unreasonableness of people," as she expressed it, to find that they received the award very much in the spirit of the pauper, who did not seem above half hearty and grateful enough when the overseer handed him the ticket to break stones.

"It never was so in *my* younger days," said Mrs. Hardaway; "for then, a good place was jumped at by a girl—like the beginning of a fortune."

Mrs. Hardaway did not consider that it was only among those, born and bred to labour, that we see—what, to all others, is so hard to understand—as much delight in finding work, as others feel in spending money.

The old lady was soon softened by perceiving—what, at first, she never thought of—one peculiar drop of bitterness in the orphans' cup.

In all the touching stories that bring the horrors of slavery, even in its mildest form, home to the heart, there is none which we feel more acutely than where two loving sisters are described as bought and sold to different masters, and cruelly doomed for ever, hopelessly to part—If only together, they could endure anything; if simply blessed with each other's company, every burthen would be lighter, and every sorrow less. This tie grows stronger, as others fail. We feel—aye, feel acutely—that at this moment we hear one of such sisters say, "In mercy, do not part us: she is all the world to me."

"And must we be very far asunder?" asked Alice, sorrowfully, when Mrs. Hardaway had explained her plans for their support.

"Yes," said the good woman, the tears now rushing to her eyes. "I am afraid you must—far as Woodstock is from London. But you'll soon forget it; you'll soon be used to it; you can write and hear of each other: and then—it isn't as if the world stood still—no, things never remain long just as they are. All sorts of things turn up. Why, one of you might marry—aye, why not both?—likely lasses as any I know of. So, cheer up; and that, you know, will set all to rights at once."

Besides the pain of parting—which Hannah's sterner nature could more composedly endure—Hannah had one deep and abiding thought as to her sister's welfare, in which we well may sympathise.

"Alice is young and unsuspecting," said Hannah. "She goes forth into the world with the two most fatal of all nature's gifts to unprotected woman—a lovely form—a soft and yearning heart!"

At the end of the morning explanations, and all the reasonings of the timid Alice on the one hand, and of the far-sighted Hannah on the other, Mrs. Hardaway, as she folded up her letters, observed, rather emphatically, that "she had now done all she could:" as much as to say that, whether they accepted or refused the situations proposed, the visit was at an end.

The two sisters felt that their little store would soon come to an end, too: so, with all that peculiar energy which pressing necessity is soon found to inspire, they began to enter into the detail, and make the little plans for—"going out into the world."

With this detail we need not trouble ourselves. It is sufficient for the present to say, that Hannah undertook the situation of companion to an elderly lady in London.

Alice, with whom we are more immediately concerned, went as a companion, and to make herself generally useful, to Mrs. Winter, the far-famed landlady of the "Stag Inn" at Woodstock.

CHAPTER XV.

GOING OUT IN THE WORLD.

No doubt, the acts and inventions of the present day—as, for instance, to see the steam-engines pant and pump, in lieu of hearts that used to throb and beat, while their boilers do the perspiration of five thousand men at once—all this, upon the balance, must be confessed to be a merciful provision to feed the hungry and clothe the naked, far beyond the unassisted powers of laborious man.

But what we gain in the realities of life we lose in the romance—what we gain in the substantials we lose in the lights and shades—in all that lends a pleasing variety of character—as also in the interesting and the picturesque. See yonder shaft of brick, gurgling forth its black volumes of smoke, that blights vegetation far and near. What though we are assured it marks the incessant whirring of a thousand spindles, cheapening Molly's cap by twopence a-yard, still I cannot help remembering when, as a child, I could peep into a cottage window, and watch old Susannah Mason do, what seemed such marvels, on her patchwork cushion. This was one little pleasure of my childhood: another, was to watch the stage-coaches; to race by their side, or look at the passengers—queer-looking figures they were, some of them, after travelling all night. Besides this, once a-week came by the ponderous waggon, drawn by eight horses; and all these horses had bells; and sometimes there was quite a little colony of travellers, who always looked so snug and comfortable in the straw behind.

In all this there was variety. It left lasting impressions, and hung my youthful mind with pictures—pictures that at this distance of time yet remain, and such as I should be very sorry to change with any child whose imagination has starved on men and things, bearing one monotonous and ugly regulation cut. Now-a-days, costumes are gone; suits of certain sizes alone remain, as if men and women were cast in moulds, or shaped by circumstances, with no fancy to please, but dressed by contract or by slop-work. Many are the distinct and gipsy-like varieties we miss—as if the poetry of life were done into prose—all lost, and gone for ever!

Among other characters, we have lost the very queen of the realms of comfort — the landlady of our country inns. Almost the last, as the best, representative of her race, was Mrs. Winter—of course, a widow; for "the bar" has generally proved as destructive of the gentlemen as it has proved conservative of the ladies. "Ever since I buried my dear husband," has been, from time immemorial, a standing epoch in mine hostess's chronology. At one time, four of the most extensive coach-hotels in England, with Ann Nelson at the head, were personated by women, and those women widows. No wonder, therefore, that good Mrs. Winter was a widow too. But though a lone, by no means an "unprotected female," was this good woman. No one could take her own part better; and few had more and stancher friends. That Mrs. Winter's fame and individuality had taken up their lodgement in the minds of no small part of the county may be judged from this—that by means of clandestine communication with the maker of her neat gowns, caps, and white pocketed aprons, a sporting gentleman, whose countenance happened to bear some resemblance to hers, costumed as "Mrs. Winter," was once a highly popular character at the Wanton fancy ball!

Yes, Mrs. Winter was a character worth remembering—pity 'tis she died before the days of photographs—one oil-painting, looking rather as if drawn by the black slime of leeches crawling over the canvas, which used to hang in her back-parlour, alone preserves her likeness. Yet was she most truly sovereign in her own house; indeed, in this respect, she admitted, she could do as well without her husband as with him. She reigned by moral means. Who could resist or disobey, above all, when, looking round, she said,—"I throw myself on the good feeling of you, gentlemen, to support me, and uphold the credit of my house, as a poor, unprotected female?" (loud laughter); a petition that she offered up whenever high words in the coffee-room threatened to lead to serious consequences, or a case before the magistrates.

On this point we have a vivid recollection, that once at our race-time an uproar in the coffee-room of the "Blackford Arms," after repeated remonstrances from Mrs. Winter, roused the old lady to a sense of the proprieties of time and place.

"I must, for the honour of my house, put an end to this," said she. "Who is it? Let me know whose fault it is."

"That is the noisy and the offending gentleman," was the reply of one of the party, with affected gravity; at the same time naming no less notable a person than Mr. Thomas Spring!

"Come along, then! come along, sir! indeed you must" (taking the ex-champion of England by the arm). "Boots shall see you safe to bed, if you please, sir: otherwise you must leave my house directly."

With these words, the good-natured fellow, putting on as much as possible the sheepish look of a naughty boy, and amidst roars of laughter, allowed himself to be led out of the room. Of course there were many to intercede: so they soon came to a compromise; and Mrs. Winter's heroism was the subject of unanimous applause.

Well, such was Mrs. Winter in the days of her glory; but one sad day the news came that the Great Unnecessary Railway Bill was carried, and soon after a Committee sat to consider the compensation to be paid for levelling the famous "Blackford Arms" Hotel to the ground, and turning poor Mrs. Winter from her little realm.

The whole story were long to tell. That

these vile railways should be tolerated, first of all threatening to whirl away an honest woman's best customers clean past her door, at the tantalising rate of forty miles an hour, and, after all, to turn her, neck and crop, from her tenement; — this did, indeed, seem like adding insult to injury: so, she sat to work to see how much she could make them pay for it. Some said, the burden of her life-long song was altered in a day. Before, there had been a succession of hard times, and a profit to be made by nothing; but now it was sworn that there was a tremendous profit upon everything, and a very mine of wealth was passing from her hands. Well do we remember the amusement afforded in court when Sir William Follett enumerated, with scarcely a smile, the profits of bottles of wine when done into glasses of negus, and the financial results of calves' heads when converted into mock-turtle soup.

After netting a tolerable sum for all she lost, and all she should have gained, good will, inconvenience and all, Mrs. Winter was promised the support of her friends if she would undertake the "Stag" at Woodstock; and of these friends the name was legion, and drawn from all ranks and orders of society. Mrs. Winter used to tell of the days when the first families in the land regularly passed a night with her on the way to town. To some it was quite another home. Lord West had always the green room, and the Marquis of Eastwood the blue; and even certain bins in the cellar and closets in the bedrooms were sacred to the use of families of the same distinction. Add to this, sickness and even death had often overtaken noble guests while at Mrs. Winter's house; on which occasions, all the sympathies of her kind, motherly nature, gushed warm and generous from her heart—a kind of comforts which, as they could never be charged in the bill, raised the good woman to the rank of a friend of the afflicted family ever after.

It was amusing to hear Mrs. Winter's stories of the families who had invited her to their country seats, and had insisted, in spite of all she could say, that she should make one—and, we may be sure, not the least entertaining—whoever formed the company then gracing their hospitable board. Indeed, Mrs. Winter's recollections of men and manners, and yet more of ladies and ladies' maids, were a treat to hear, especially when told in her own quaint way. As spectators of the drama of this life, few persons had been more behind the scenes. If no man is a hero to his valet-de-chambre, no lady is more than a common mortal to her waiting-maid: and, the gossip at a servants' table, especially at an inn, where servants often bear their ladies' names and titles, running entirely on the families from whom they derive their own brief distinction, would furnish a chronicle the most curious in the land; and it was in such family histories in which Mrs. Winter was most deeply read. Few nine-days' wonders from the school of scandal took Mrs. Winter by surprise; she "had heard enough before;" she "had put one and one together;" and, reasoning from old causes to novel consequences, she "expected nothing else." Yet could she never be entrapped into a witness-box; the moment the lawyers came for evidence, no one was so stolid or unobserving as Mrs. Winter; indeed "her stupidity was quite provoking."

But we must return to Alice Hengen, already having parted from her anxious sister, dried her eyes as she travelled along, and having by this time reached the Firmington change of horses, two stages from Woodstock.

"There must be a young lady to go by me," said Joseph Hyde, the famous coachman of the Oxford road, to the clerk of the booking-office—"comes from Ullingford way, I expect."

"All right, coachman. The lady's in the house."

As Joseph Hyde walked in and touched his hat, half respectfully, as to a stranger, but not without a slight air of familiarity as to one who, he considered, was coming as a kind of fellow-servant, he was rather struck with the timid and distant manner of his new acquaintance.

As Alice asked, with a painfully tremulous voice, if he would convey her to Mrs. Winter's, at Woodstock, Coachman replied:—

"Lud bless your honest heart! Don't be afraid, Miss. Ah! but I remember now, you arn't used to be out in the world they tell me, and this is your first situation. But, cheer up, you'll soon be used to it; and as to our Mistress, there is not a worthier soul in any roadside house in England. Her tongue is the worst part of her; not to say but she's civil enough—most in general—and then she has alway an excellent heart. Well, then, she told me to mind and see after you all comfortable like. But please, Miss, wouldn't you like to have a drop of something hot this cold day?"

Alice became a little reassured by the hearty manner of Joseph Hyde; though every word tended more and more to make her realise service and servitude, and to make her doubtful as to what her future lot would be. But these doubts and anxieties were soon to be solved; for, two hours brought her to the door of the "Stag Inn," and ushered her into the presence of Mrs. Winter, who, as she held out her hand, exclaimed,

"Lord love your little soul!—and is this who it is? Why, what could my old friend Mrs. Hardaway have been thinking of to send me the like of you—and in the way of all these Oxford Collegers! Well, to be sure! But, then, perhaps you are not more pretty than you are proper; and if so, she thinks we shall drive a roaring trade!"

Alice, hardly knowing whether this talk, as yet so unintelligible, was of good or evil omen, as regarded her eligibility for the situation at the "Stag," made an attempt at some natural reply; when Mrs. Winter went on soliloquising:—

"Well, I always have said, Business is business, and charity is charity; but a soft heart never does in money-making: but there now, Mrs. Hardaway has gone and mixed it up together! Who would ever have thought that, after all the years I kept the Blackford Arms, and dealt with all sorts of the very queerest of customers, Mrs. Winter should ever have been so weak! However, now it is done ——.

Never you mind, my dear (turning to Alice): have a good heart: we shall be the best of friends — I am sure we shall; only, you do whatever I tell you, and keep out of those false Oxford gents' everlasting wheedling ways."

In this last caution, Mrs. Winter's eye for business proved rather a check on the heartiness of her expression: for, every one who kept a wayside inn within an easy drive of Oxford, knew full well that the fame of a pretty barmaid was almost a fortune to any house. Certainly Mrs. Winter was too good a woman to throw a young girl into danger's way: still, as she said, "business is business," and the good looks of her helper and companion, no doubt were anything but a disqualification; and Alice had soon the comfort of feeling that she had made no unfavourable impression, but would commence her new duties with a mistress very kindly disposed, and already prepossessed in her favour.

CHAPTER XVI.

WAYS DELIGHTFUL BUT DANGEROUS.

IF there is any time in a man's life when he is romantic, sentimental, and likely to do a foolish thing, involving, as Milton says,

> "Innumerable
> Disturbances on earth through female snares,
> And straight conjunction with this sex,"

it is just about the time that is usually spent at Oxford; and it happens most fortunately, that there, all conspires to counteract this "softening of the brain," by calling into action the manly energies: and nót least by removing the fair enchanters far away. This is more especially true of Oxford; for, at Cambridge the town is not so completely merged in the University: but at Oxford there is, or used to be, but the smallest sprinkling of the ladies we can conceive practicable—exceptions there must be, of course.

We do know one elderly gentleman who ventured to take up to Oxford a very beautiful young lady; but no doubt she was rarely seen but in one of those nunneries yclept "the private gardens," which, in one or two instances, remain under privileged lock and key.

Almost all the ladies who, in the whole term of a three-years' residence at Oxford, ever met our eye, appeared as strange, and as much out of their proper element at Oxford, as an old College Don seems in the country. It quite took you by surprise, and made you stare, to meet a lady: and you could hardly get over a certain contraband sensation, or be reconciled to the correctness of their being where they were. And when the friend you were walking with did nudge you, and say, "Here they are, Mr. and Mrs. President"—or, "Mr. and Mrs. Principal"—for such were their usual designations—they did not give you the idea of man and wife, or inspire the slightest connubial sentiment; it was more like a kind of statutable arrangement. And as to female attractions, to mere boys as we were, a woman at all on the other side of thirty seemed shelved and superannuated.

The College Fellows, we know, were bound down in heavy penalties not to marry till their fellowships had led to livings—very cruel and tantalising!—like putting away the toy till the child is too old to care so much about it. So they could not have had much sympathy with these tantalising instances of conjugal monopoly—about twenty married ladies in a society of about some hundreds of would-be married men!

But the value of ladies, in a moral and a humanising point of view, is best learnt by the absence of them. Throw men together as bachelors in London chambers, or men in barracks, and they degenerate very fast. Without the presence of woman, we cannot talk of having a home or fireside. Hence, smoking, billiards, and heartless excitement, to kill time in divers ways, become too often the rule of a reckless and ill-spent life. At Oxford, the family circle and domestic life are lost sight of for shorter periods: and happily so: many a wild and dissipated character has appeared to us visibly softened and checked in his downward course when first he returned from home—yes, from *home*—after the long vacation.

Now the truth must be told, for the honour of the ladies, that no sooner does the Commemoration and the usual gathering of mothers, sisters, and ladies fair appear, than everything else gives place to the thrilling sentiments that the very sight of parasols, muslin, and pretty feet, electrically inspire. To be invited to a breakfast or luncheon with ladies in College-rooms is a compliment indeed; and as to the drive to Woodstock, or the boating picnic down to Newnham, arranged to fall in with the racing eight-oars on our return,—these are treats for which the very Cricket-grounds are deserted.

All this we sketch as a mere reminder to old Oxonians of pleasures past, and also as a proof that sentimental feelings do exist, though under high pressure, ready to find vent on the slightest provocation. Shall we confess the fact, that Ned Walford was only one of many scores who were always ready to drive a dozen miles, with no better object than to order luncheon as a pretext for chatting with a pretty girl, and to drive the same dozen miles back to College?

Woodstock, of course, is one of the common resorts of riding and of driving men. And when there every idle man, whether he knows a Teniers from a Titian or not, is led a kind of pace that enables his eye to rest on nothing in particular, through all the rooms of Blenheim; and hears the old monotonous lecture from the housekeeper about the Duke of Marlborough and his white dog that followed him in all his campaigns, and now figures in his pictures. When this dismal ceremony has been undergone, for self and casual visitors from the country too often to be any more endurable, then to buy driving-gloves, and other leathern wares, seems as much part of going to Woodstock as eating the far-famed cakes is part of going to Banbury.

But Ned Walford had always one lounge more; namely, to go into the "Stag" and have a talk with Mrs. Winter.

Mrs. Winter had known Walford from a boy, and his father before him. Amused as Ned was with many of the old lady's recollections, still, in the presenee of some friend who happened to share his "buggy" or his tandem, he sometimes found her vivid reminiscences of the past rather inconvenient. For, Mrs. Winter could not think of any other name than "Master Edward," and what was worse, she remembered points in his parental history that might possibly reveal that there had been a time in the memory of living men when Richcourt Manor had no connexion with the name of Walford.

Walford, therefore, very naturally preferred to pay Mrs. Winter a visit when no one else was with him: but, just now, Walford had another reason for having the chat in the back-parlour all to himself—he had exchanged glances with Alice Hengen!

There are many points of view from which ladies are most killing—most captivating.

There is the early morning, the more natural and the domestic point of view. Here we fancy that we see them as they are.—So far it is true that nothing less than simplicity of manner, glowing health, and natural charms beyond all cosmetics, with easy and composed good-nature, and the semblance, at least, of being the favourite sister or the loving daughter—nothing less can justify the father or the brother from inviting a friend to a quiet dinner, to pass the night, and return to town with him next morning.

Then there is the ball-room point of view; when the false glare of lights and many an artificial aid of ornament conspire, with music and the poetry of motion, to lend enchantment to the scene. But this is the most ingenious of all ways to see ladies as they are—not.

But there is a character of female charms, for which the most killing of all is the pathetic point of view—the pale, yet calmly interesting; the patient and the enduring—striking the softer notes of pity akin to love within the breast.

The very sight of Alice Hengen inspired awe and reverence in the heart of Edward Walford. She casually met his eye, looked down, and passed away upon her lowly errand, and left him. She was in every look and movement so out of character with the glasses, the labelled bottles, and all the furniture of the bar, that she inspired him with curiosity and interest—such a boon to an idle man—to find out who and what she was.

Walford knew just enough of Virgil to remember the peculiar interest excited in the breast of Æneas, when he saw, by the very walk of a lady, that she was of more than mortal mould; probably he would have understood "*incessu patuit Dea*" as, "moving in the upper circles."

Walford knew the weak side of the Duenna. And Mrs. Winter was bound, as she laudably felt, in honour and decent feeling, as well as in interest for the credit of her house, to keep a watchful eye "on those mischievous young Oxford Collegers"—of whom Mrs. Winter had been known to remark, that although some of them came along looking as mild and as proper as if they might be trusted to give lessons in a lady's academy, for her part "she would trust them no further than she could heave a bull by the tail." Mrs. Winter's virtues and proper feelings, like those of the world at large, played all the better for running with the stream of her interest, and making good for the "Stag Inn," Woodstock. And, the great problem to be solved in the profitable introduction of the lure of beauty in the way of business, consists in so contriving that the fluttering little creature, though ever venturing near the candle, shall never singe her gaudy wings.

As Alice had entered upon her menial duties shortly before the long vacation, she had time to feel comparatively settled, and also to make no slight impression on the prosperous glovers of Woodstock, before she was seen by Edward Walford.

Walford was not satisfied by a passing glance. Unaccustomed as he was from the very cradle to be denied any toy which money could purchase, he never doubted that any one under the care of Mrs. Winter could soon be enticed again into his presence.

And as this was a game at which the idle can always beat the industrious, Walford was by no means wanting in address; and so he soon set to work to draw the old lady into some of her long stories. As to flattery, Mrs. Winter had heard so much of it, that it came quite natural to her; and a pleasant suggestion of change of air to see the fowls, and pigs, and dairy of Richcourt, and to give Mrs. Walford for a while her sage opinion and experience of things in general—this soon sufficed to open the heart of Mrs. Winter, and to make him free of all the secrets of her soul.

Of course, the history of Alice Hengen soon was told—that she was a real lady, come down in the world, being the chief burden of the tale.

Mrs. Winter complained, there never was such a mistake as that of having to do with gentlefolks in the way of business—they not only didn't know the ways of the world, but that actually "they had such maggots in their heads, that it seemed as if they were never to learn it—indeed, that lately some very well-to-do men of business had been, evening after evening, to the bar, more than they were ever used to do, all to keep company with her pretty young woman;" and, said Mrs. Winter, with an emphasis, "Would you believe it, Sir, for all that she has not a penny to bless herself if I should die to-morrow—when I'm sure no one else would put up with her gentility and nothing besides—she looks cold enough to freeze them all! It's no use my talking to her—they do say always that pride must have a fall; and she does herself—let alone the business of the 'Stag'—harm, where she might do good."

If Mrs. Winter had held a general retainer to do all she could to light up a flame and stir up an interest in the mind of an idle man like Walford, she could not possibly have said anything more directly to the purpose.—Here was the dramatic incident of a fair lady in distress, beset by boors as suitors, from whom she turned in fierce disdain, and only awaiting the casual visit of a modern knight-errant to rescue her from the bonds of poverty and restore her to herself again.

Alice Hengen soon entered the room in obedience to a summons from Mrs. Winter, who soon found some pretence for indulging Walford's curiosity. Walford was so far impressed with the sable emblems of her sorrow, as well as by her quiet demeanour, that he instinctively hesitated to address her, till Mrs. Winter had made some friendly remark to serve as an introduction. This done, Walford found something to say—some kind inquiry to make—in a tone so feeling and so deferential as to touch a chord which had not vibrated during all the time Alice had been in the ruder regions of Woodstock.

Whether it was for better or for worse to

this poor orphan girl that a chord of tender feeling, so long mute and quiescent, had now been made to thrill, is a question it would puzzle philosophy to solve.

A man will coldly weigh his pains against his pleasures, strike a balance, and say, "Would that it had never been!" But not so woman. To woman it is in vain to utter lugubrious warnings, how her heart may ache with pain; she would venture all on a certain note of sympathetic joy.

A man will live — there are thousands upon thousands of such men who are content to live—a life of so many meals a-day, of wild excitement, drowning thought, "with none to bless us, none whom we can bless;" but woman, if she cannot live the life of the heart—if she cannot hold enshrined one object of more than mortal worship, cares little to live at all. Deprive woman of this longing, lingering hope, and life to her is bleak and blank; and when of this hope she is seemingly bereft, as Alice was, by one dreary prospect of penury or toil—it is wonderful how slight a thing will kindle the spark yet smouldering in her bosom, and set every pulse of feeling once more beating and throbbing, till the old heart-struggle has been again, and the same emotions, after writhing within the aching bosom, have battled themselves to rest.

Till this day, poor Alice thought she was resigned. Before Walford's visit, the fluttering emotions of her bosom had known some weeks' repose; but now they had all taken wing again, and the tumult and the ruffling had begun as bad, or worse, than ever.

In modern times the temptation, the trial, and the struggle between the birthright and the mess of pottage, seem to apply to hapless woman alone. Birthright, did we say? Let us call it Heart-right. It is not only that by a match of convenience woman is linked to one for whom she little cares; the cruel pang is, that by one and the same repulsive act she shuts herself off for ever from the most distant hope of one to love — and all have one — real or ideal, it is the same. No woman is so wanting in charms or so destitute of charmers but she carries within her breast a certain type — she "bodies forth" and turns to shape a certain form or vision of one unseen; aye, and how often does she leap to a fond conclusion, and identify with this mental picture one of very slight resemblance after all!

Then comes the trial, to be once and for ever disenchanted of the fond illusion; and, instead of the hero of her romance, to compound for some plain, prosaic, and unsentimental specimen with whom to jog along the dry and rutty road of life, as far as possible from those romantic passes and enchanted bowers which entered so largely into all her life-long imagery of the happy state.

Alice might have been toned down to the sober colours of a Mrs. Glover, had she been a few miles further from the haunts of men of other mould. There is a strange assimilating power at work in this world. He who "tempers the wind to the shorn lamb," mercifully blunts the edge of those feelings which, while they are vehicles of pleasure in one state of life, would only grate and jar and torture us in another. So, Alice Hengen was insensibly undergoing a change in her standard of taste—taking, like other creatures in creation, the hue and complexion of the objects which lie around. At last her feelings might have been comparatively acclimatised to the meridian of Woodstock, when, unhappily, the sight of Ned Walford undid it all.

Soon, Alice Hengen was the talk of Oxford; and since in Oxford, as in other places, men always want some object for which to ride, a small matter turns the horse's head this road, rather than the other. So, Mrs. Winter soon perceived that there was a lively run of custom to the "Stag." This was a discovery doubly welcome; it flattered her pride to be able to boast, that wherever Mrs. Winter showed her time-honoured head in the inn-keeping line, there custom was sure to follow; and already the "Fleece Hotel," though with much older connexion, was almost distanced in the race.

But this made Alice Hengen, "the proud, the distant, the stuck-up barmaid," the talk of angry, jealous, slighted Woodstockians too. The bait of beauty was nowhere better understood than in that famous market-town; and as to Oxford, Alice was discussed at every wine-party, and many a man boasted of the little conversation that had passed between him and the pretty barmaid. At last it was observed that Walford of King's, contrary to his usual custom, had begun to order his horse, and ride out alone. Where did he go? What was he after? "No good, I am sure," said Rickworth, at a party; when, all in a moment, there was one shout of derisive merriment and banter, when some man exclaimed—"I have met Walford twice on the road to Woodstock."

The secret soon was out;—"That soft fellow, Walford, was really captivated by Alice Hengen!"

CHAPTER XVII.

NED WALFORD BECOMES FAMOUS IN MORE WAYS THAN ONE.

ONE idea had taken possession of Ned Walford's mind. With Walford, as with other idle, lounging, and resourceless men, Satan finds "the room swept and garnished," and inviting him to take possession. The point most devoutly to be wished for every youth is, that his mind should ardently and enthusiastically be set upon something not positively evil. After that, we will talk about things more or less worthy of the energies of a proper man.

We fully coincide with the late Sir Robert Peel, when he told the students in Glasgow, that the noblest precept ever given to a young man was that grand line in Homer, which we venture to translate quite literally, for the benefit not only of the ladies, but also of those gentlemen—their name is legion—who left off Greek just before they could construe two words of anything. *Αἴεν ἀριστεύειν*, says Homer:—Let every man aspire to be first, whatever it is—*καὶ ὑπείροχον ἔμμεναι ἄλλων*; and always to try to be "top-sawyer."

No doubt it is for some such wise purpose that Providence has strewed this world's school for children of a larger growth with toys, and games, and follies of all kinds—even all kinds of moonshine projects, in this point of view, have a value; they are something for the world to think of, and something to do.

It seems most erroneously to be taken as granted, that in this world wisdom or good sense, and propriety of conduct, are the ordinary state of things, and that foolish and mischievous practices are the exception. But all men have not seen things in this complimentary point of view. Horace speaks of philosophers who maintained that all the world was mad—that men might differ in their delusions, but all had one weak corner of the brain. Our ingenious friend, Norman, used stoutly to maintain that this world was partly the Millbank or the Penitentiary, and partly the Bedlam or the Lunatic Asylum, maintained for the general benefit, and the clearance of those "more worlds than one," discovered in modern times. At all events, we appear to be ruled and managed by a system of diversions, delusions, and impositions, as if we were a very childish set of beings—being tempted by one thing as a bait, to make us do another for our eventual benefit.

On this principle, at Oxford, the mimic contests on the river, or the cricket-field, serve a far more nobler end than to the unreflecting may appear. The value of such ambition—call it foolish, unprofitable, or childish, if you please—is only to be estimated from its absence, or its loss. We can never forget how much we desired some such spirit of emulation, however trifling the object, in the case of Walford. "There was the place where" this spirit "was not;" and there was a void which must needs be filled up with visits to the "Stag," and habits ruinous to himself and others.

Oxford is a little world—a section of the wide, wide world; and all the debts and extravagance of which we read are attributable to the same failings at College as in later life. Men will vie and compete in something; and those who have nothing to boast of but their money will, for want of anything better, compete with money and trashy display—bidding high for the very semblance of that distinction and applause which they lack the qualities, honourably, to command.

Walford's money, therefore, flew apace; and since few persons are so old, or their mental calculations so far rectified by experience, but every Christmas they have reason to marvel "how very fast money does go," no wonder that one of "those" proverbially "thoughtless young men" felt, in course of time, that perennial running from a hundred springs by which so many at last are seen to founder.

What Oxonian does not remember—and too often to his cruel cost—the readiness with which his scout catches at half orders, merely suggested by a chum lounging heedlessly on your sofa, and starts off to set in train a breakfast or a supper—or, perhaps, to pack a hamper for a Newnham party—it being the interest of the said scout, as well as of the confectioner, to make the selection the most extravagant of which its nature will admit!

Walford's rooms—methinks we see him now—were the daily cover at which tailors, saddlers, horse-dealers, dog-sellers, and cadgers various, were ever beating up for game. Fancy patterns from Messrs. Stitcham's leather pocket-book, day after day, might be seen streaming, yards long, from the table to the floor. Fancy dressing-gowns for his own, and fancy woollens for his horse's morning dishabille, opened new sources of ruinous variety. The perfumer, with his gilded scent-bottles and his ivory brushes, would next assail him at the head; or the vendor of kangaroo leather, or some such inventions, would carry on the sapping and mining at his heels.

But dress is limited. Your drawers, in time, will fill—with this extravagance, however long the rope, there is an end somewhere: but when once Mr. Pinner, who ministers indifferently to our Mediævalism, with marble angels and mimic fonts, and also to our puppyism, by dressing-cases, despatch-boxes, and follies, "changing with the varying hour"—when once he joined the number of Walford's complimentary advisers, and revealed to him the glad tidings and discovery that "Mr. Walford was a gentleman already noted for his excellent taste,"—suddenly a new light broke in upon him, that here was a new line in which he could compete, and compete with no slight advantages, because, by money alone, he could distance all the College in the race.

From that time Walford's profusion knew no limits. Men are caught by flattery, even as trout are caught by tickling. The Prince of Denmark is not the only man who was poisoned through the ear, his senses first being laid asleep. Praise a man's taste for wine, or pictures; say he is a judge of horses, hounds, or sports of any kind, and you will find that nothing is too trifling to be made to minister to his vanity.—No man is indifferent to another's good opinion, and flattery is a suggestion of that good opinion: a man who would resist it in courts, might imbibe it in a cottage—the huntsman, the gamekeeper, or the jockey, hitting the soft, unguarded corner, that their betters might fail to find.

Ned Walford, therefore, may be excused for believing what many a wiser man before him, with as little reason, had believed. More especially, as men who drank his wine, rode his horses, and even borrowed his money, would naturally warm into a good genial glow, and seemed rather hearty in what they said. Perhaps such men came at last almost to believe what they had been used to utter. The worship of gold is not always lip-worship and hypocritical. No: gold dazzles and blinds men; till in their hearts they really venerate the man who scatters it.

Walford's scout, like other servants, was

never as well pleased as when his master's money flew on all sides. Walford's chums also caught the "yellow fever;" and Walford's rooms, by degrees, became a lounge for men superior to mere toadyism—men who came, because others came, to taste new wines, eat new perigords, and see new things. It is in this way that, in course of time, wealth will command the company even of those who are utterly unconscious of any unworthy motive. Walford grew happy, as if all the College admired his doings, and launched still deeper into Mr. Pinner's books—buying more than one picture, simply because Norman had put on his spectacles and discovered something very creditable in the selection of the last.

There are several things in this world without which a man would hardly care to live; and one of these things is Admiration—or sympathy and approbation, at the very least. Addison says, "that no man is so insignificant but he contrives to be surrounded at times with a little clique of his acquaintances, who echo his sayings, or listen complacently to his opinions." Ned Walford at length had wormed himself into just such a position; and it was very natural that, to Walford, this particular clique counted as "the world." What "the world" says or expects, always means the opinion of our clique, which, be it a wider or a smaller circle, is still a wonderfully small section of the peoples, nations, and languages of this habitable earth.

Since this position Walford had only achieved by money, or money's worth, it followed that it cost a continual outlay to keep it up. Such birds flock around us no longer than they are fed with some kind of periodicity. Stop the golden stream—cut off the supplies—and they migrate all in a flock together.

All this had gone on about two years; and the climax of all expense was when Walford at length—that is, after one pluck—passed his Little Go. No man of Walford's standing will readily forget the circumstances of that most mortifying Pluck, or the splendour of the Pass party—given to barges full of undergraduates, their friends, and friends' friends, by many degrees removed—one beautiful summer's day, near the Island at Newnham.

As to the Pluck, we really pitied Walford: we do not say he did not deserve it: no Oxford man will ever believe that a mistake is made on that side, though mistakes are made on the side of mercy; for some do pass who deserve a pluck. Still, Walford would have been one of that lucky number, had it not been for a sinister influence at work.

In those days there was a kind of University Jack-of-all-trades, well known as "Bones of Lincoln." His pedigree was believed to be nothing to boast of; and at the slightest allusion to his early history, Mr. Walesby and his contemporaries would ominously shake their heads: whence arose the common saying, that "Bones could ill stand any examination, either as to his relatives or his antecedents."

However, at the time of which we are speaking, Bones was said to have "sown his wild oats;" which commonly means, that a man has become a little more proper and careful of appearances. For a wife and family, like any other incumbrance, will steady a man; and Bones had married at a very early age. And now Bones was obliged to work. So Bones canvassed for as many pupils as there were hours between breakfast and dinner. Bones made Long-Vacation parties to pay for Mrs. Bones and the four little Boneses to the sea-side. Bones monopolised as many small offices in the University as would gladden the most determined pluralist —the office of "Little Go" Examiner being among the number of his appointments.

To be an Examiner and to take pupils are

two employments which work well together. For, though a man cannot examine his own pupils with a very good grace, still he is supposed to know all the mysteries of the place, and to have a casting vote and commanding influence when Pass or Pluck becomes the question.

Walford, therefore, soon saw the wisdom of securing the services of Mr. Bones. But Tom Snipe, all this time residing in "the Turl," and never backward in rendering his pupil the assistance for which he so handsomely paid, urged that to employ Mr. Bones was quite unnecessary; and, indeed, hardly complimentary to himself: still Walford argued that it was well worth his while to have a friend at Court, and, therefore, insisted on booking a place by "Bones' Patent Safety Coach," as the expression was.

Mr. Bones, also, as well as Mrs. Bones, saw no little advantage in so promising a pupil as the Heir of Richcourt: for, the little Boneses had by this time become tall and pretty; and already three out of the four were off their hands—all married to old pupils. The contrivance was to have the drawing-room next the study, with the door always a-jar when the pupil was coming out. The result was easy to surmise. Every man for whom the trap was set slipped in, just to clear his head of all the jargon of Propositions and of Predicables; and—since the mornings, as regards matchmaking, beat the evenings hollow—the Miss Boneses paired off apace.

Walford spent many a morning on that dangerous ground; but, partly because the only remaining Miss Bones was by no means the prettiest, and partly from the countervailing spell in the region of Woodstock, the day of the Examination—and therefore, if he passed, the end of his lectures—would arrive before Mrs. Bones had secured the object so devoutly to be wished. We confess, therefore, that when we heard of Walford's being plucked, fully believing that Mr. Bones' conscience was sufficiently elastic to let him through, we were among the number of those who set down Walford's misfortunes as a simple *ruse* to give the young lady a little more time to try her winning arts upon so eligible a young man.

However, the *ruse* did not answer; for, on the principle of "an old poacher making the best gamekeeper," Tom Snipe was soon on the alert. He proceeded to administer comfort to the aggrieved and disappointed mother: he persuaded her that Ned had not had fair play; though, perhaps, he did want those finishing touches, with which he had before been so successful when he prepared him for College: and the result was, that the influence of the resident tutor was now better established than ever: it almost seemed as if Mr. Snipe, and no one else, could teach her dear, ill-used boy.

Of course, there were some who remembered Snipe's former character; but the generation of his contemporaries had, for the most part, passed away. The few who survived were contented to hope that he had mended his ways; for, Time is a wonderful softener of all those harsh feelings which arise rather for the wrongs of others than our own. Snipe's reputation had also the usual benefit of that inclination to mind one's own business, and not to say what it is troublesome to prove.

For all these reasons, Snipe started once more in the University—with no great prejudice against him—as a man who knew life, and was a thorough sportsman, and therefore must be expected to be rather a sharp practitioner; though with as much honesty, after all, as, in the case of so good a judge of horse-flesh and handicaps, could be reasonably supposed to have stood the wear and tear of London life.

Snipe immediately set about vilifying Mr. Bones, and ridiculing all the parental devices of Mrs. Bones also. Neither did he hesitate to say, that Mr. Bones was the son of a College butler. The veritable John Trott was still alive; and what was worse, that this most objectionable piece of paternity did positively insist upon visiting his dutiful son periodically, to the intense disgust and confusion of this otherwise select and fashionable family—who, one and all, would be but too glad, as in classic story, to boil down their progenitor, or do anything else, with the chance of bringing him out a little more fresh and fashionable than he had the unreasonableness to appear.

The effect of all this jest and banter on the mind of Walford, was no little favoured by what was too good a joke not to be heard on all sides —the stinging sarcasm "that Kitty Bones had plucked Walford of King's." Tom Snipe suggested that, no doubt, Miss Kitty would henceforth be conciliated—like another Mrs. Clarke at the Horse Guards—by every man who had no scholarship to spare for "Little Go" examinations!

No sooner did Snipe appear on the stage than Mr. Bones saw his game was up. Bones, though not altogether a bad fellow, had just that laxity of principle which enabled him to look Snipe in the face with a meaning smile, as much as to say, "You are not only a knave, but you can't meet my eye and even pretend you are not." Still, though Bones hinted to every man who came to his lectures, that Snipe was a bad one, every King's man knew full well that Bones had himself no virtue to spare; and since Snipe had already made himself agreeable and popular, all reflections upon his character were laughed away with the old remark, that "Two of a trade can never agree."

There never was a man more qualified to take youngsters in than Tom Snipe. A man may be a great knave, and yet a very genial, social, and good-natured fellow. He may have come into the world with a good flow of spirits, and a large stock of what Aristotle calls "natural virtue." Besides, in most cases of moral insanity, there are long, lucid intervals, and it does not follow that the mind is always darkened with one deep-designing scowl. We have known more than one man of Snipe's class seemingly so anomalous—men who would cordially pass the bottle, though they never paid for the wine; and not the less happy in seeing ten hungry fellows at Ascot eating lobster-salad and drinking champagne at their expense, because they meant to win their money all round before they got home.

Just such a man was Snipe. He would spend his money like a gentleman, albeit he got it like a sharper. And in the opinions we form of others, a little goodness goes a long way. We could mention a remarkable instance of this. Once, in the course of a ride, we stopped near a fair to look at a swindler, who was robbing the country people with the thimble-rig, and observed one man in green coat and top-boots, who seemed evidently an accomplice. At that moment our horse trod his shoe half off, pricked his foot, and plunged dangerously. The supposed accomplice rushed forward to our assistance, so like a good-hearted fellow that we felt quite as if we had done him injustice. Yet, after all, that man was one of the gang; only, as in the case of Snipe, his natural instincts of humanity were not all choked by the growth of rank and evil weeds.

Snipe never coldly designed to lead Walford into ruinous expense—only, seeing him that way inclined, he had no idea of stopping him—well knowing that his fish were always to be caught in troubled water. Indeed, men far more honest than Snipe always like to see money fly. They like even to hear of money—large legacies, splendid fortunes; or to talk of "My wealthy friend—rolling in riches—lucky fellow!" and the like. These are terms and these are topics at which all ears open, and all eyes sparkle with delight.

If Snipe did like to see money fly, it was not long before Snipe was likely to be gratified: for Tom had formed a little class of Walford and three of his friends—all men of fortune and wide influence for a future day—and surprised them all with the self-evident construction he could put on Logic, and the way in which he could slope and smooth the rugged steeps of classical learning, too.

Snipe went frequently to the Schools, as a looker-on, listening to the questions—knowing full well that few examiners can vary the series of their questions beyond the limits of three or four chosen circles, easy enough for a clever fellow like Snipe to detect. The consequence was, that when Snipe's pupils went into the schools, half the questions proved quite like their daily work, and Tom Snipe's name was cried up as beating Bones, and all the noted "Crammers," into fits.

Snipe's star was now in the ascendant. To be a sportsman, a man of the world, and a scholar, at the same time, always causes a man to be cried up as twice the sportsman, and three times the scholar that he really is.

Youngsters like to be listened to, to be sympathised with, and to feel that they are interesting to "an old hand:" and Snipe was "an old hand," in more senses than one. To "know life" in the little world of Oxford, was boast enough for many; but to talk of Tattersall's as naturally as of John Sheard's stables—to talk of the Thames matches, or Lord's, instead of the Isis and Cowley Marsh, with all the gossip of Crockford's or Pratt's—all this placed Snipe on high and undisputed vantage ground: so Snipe's compliments were felt a compliment indeed. Snipe knew this full well; and since they liked it, his mind became a mint, whose spurious coinage passed current for drinking wine, riding the horses, and winning the money of no small number of the undergraduates of Oxford, in or about the year 18—.

And now Walford and his friends had "passed,"—an event that created no small sensation in King's, at all events.

The Oxford tradesmen, and even the scouts, enter into the spirit of the thing, as well as the undergraduates. The scouts have especial reason for so doing; wine-parties, and perquisites numerous, depending on the one event: and sometimes leaving College, rooms vacant, change of masters, and the same glass, china, kettle, or bellows to sell over again—all depending on the other issue.—Our own copper kettle, with name on the handle, was recognised after twenty years! Oh! could it speak as well as sing, what a varied tale of fun and frolic it would tell,—not least of the doings of Walford himself!

"Through, Sir? Passed, Sir? Yes, of course, Sir," said old Hedges, who had risen through all the gradations of lamp-boy, scout, bell-ringer, letter-man, dean's servant, and common-room man.

"Only wanted a little confidence, Sir, in your own abilities. Let 's see, Sir; it was the Logic that floored you last time—wasn't it, Sir?"

"What! did you hear that?"

"Heard it! yes, Sir; and a pretty deal else I hear, as I say nothing at all about, Sir; and my opinion is, Sir, that you had as good a right to have passed last time, Sir, as any other gentleman; but——" And more Hedges would have said, only Walford had by this time the customary bottle of wine ready, and not liking to risk any allusion to the sinister influence of Kitty Bones, cut short the dialogue at once.

And now, by one consent, they voted Tom Snipe an ovation; and Walford readily adopted a hint that Snipe threw out, and instead of drinking hot wine in a hot room in the dog-days, he preferred a cold collation at Newnham, —invitations unlimited, provided his friend's friends were enumerated in time for old King Cole to prepare. Every man to find his own way to that beautiful lawn sloping down to the Isis, where so many a careless, happy day has been spent—idle, seemingly, but by no means fruitless; for 'tis to these joyous hours that memory flies back, borrowing a gleam of sunshine from the past, to relieve the thickening clouds of later life.

Every experienced housekeeper will soon reflect, that to prepare for a party of a hundred hungry men, and thirsty too, five miles from home, is no such easy matter. But at Oxford, all this in Walford's day was easy enough. The mere fiat of Walford of King's—time, place, and numbers specified—was all that was required; so, since the preparation for a happy day is always part—and sometimes *all*—of the happiness expected, away galloped Walford and his friends to the Magdalene Cricket-ground, to consult the oracle in the form of old King Cole.

What Oxonian of some twenty years since can possibly have forgotten old King Cole?—who does not remember him basking in the sunshine in front of the cricket tent, with such rotundity of form, that his watch-chain and huge bunch of seals seemed to plumb a perpendicular to fall half a foot clear of his toes.

There is always some man at Oxford who—every inch a tradesman, and never for one moment forgetting his position—is at the same time a privileged man, and lives on the most easy terms with all the gownsmen. Just such a man was old King Cole, who victualled all our cricket tents to perfection; acted secretary to the University Club, and passed every summer-day under canvas, with plenary powers to arrange and marshal everything. It was old King Cole who chartered the coach and planned the starting, and the breakfast on the road, when first Oxford played Cambridge at Lord's. It was old King Cole who was—quite accidentally, of course—outside the examination school with C. W. of Christchurch, keeping up the spirits of that most diffident and nervous of scholars, while waiting to be called in; which attention was all good-fellowship, though Cole did win a ten-pound bet upon the first class: for, as to bets, Cole, in a small way, kept a bank like another Crockford, always ready to bet crowns, or sovereigns—one, five, or ten, on any event—whether honours academical, a match at cricket, a "bump" upon the river, or the winner of the Derby.

No sooner had Walford asked Cole if his victualling yard was fully equal to the occasion than he replied :—

"A hundred gentlemen at Newnham, Sir! Nothing easier. Hock, claret, champagne—the best of all sorts, sir: only let me know your pleasure. But then, since it is intended for a Pass party, Mr. Walford, I suppose you will leave all that to me. The rent-roll of Richcourt—eh, Sir?—won't feel the difference."

It was soon agreed that Davis's barge, with tables on deck and an awning, should be the order of the day. And when the day came, it seemed made for the occasion—the azure sky, the summer stillness—all conspired to show forth those beauties of the Isis and of Newnham which linger in the memory of every old Oxonian. The reeds bent gently to the stream; the lazy chub were drawing down the flies in the little circles their fat snouts had made. The powerful rush of Sandford Lasher, as usual, was audible far and near, guilty of the sudden death of more than one fine fellow, before its marble column spoke warnings from the fate of Gaisford and of Phillimore. As to the company, it was like a holiday flotilla—the barge carried a band of music to enliven the scene, which passed and repassed the College eight-oars, and numerous skiffs—one skiff bore Norman, spectacles and all, rowed by Rickworth, who hung about the barge, to allow of Norman's well-known sallies and repartees. Many boats were there to see the fun—boats that bore men who, though not invited, were generally hailed by some one from the barge to stop and have a glass, before they went home on that sultry day. "You need not be particular, Mr. Walford," said Cole; "I have a pretty good store, besides a nine-gallon cask of claret, on board, in case of accidents."

The end of all was, that Walford that day kept open house, and regaled all the boats—those not a few—which, attracted by the fame of "Walford's spread," had come, because others came, to see the fun and join in the spirts and races, or the scrimmage afterwards.

CHAPTER XVIII.

A MATTER OF BUSINESS, OF BY NO MEANS AN UNCOMMON KIND.

NED WALFORD was by this time launched on a sea of debt and extravagance. Oxford tradesmen, like other tradesmen, know whom they trust. Like other tradesmen, neither better nor worse, they know that ready money, pulled sovereign by sovereign from the purse, checks the sanguine humour, clips the wings of fancy, and brings a kind of prudential chill all over a customer: whereas, while choice and tempting articles are simply set aside as selected, with a polite bow, young gentlemen, as well as young ladies, feel shopping quite a charming afternoon's recreation.

Sydney Smith said, that so light did all pains and penalties in the distance appear to an offender, safe for the present, that he believed you might find many a man who would take a five-pound note in possession to agree to the most agonising state of things twenty years after date. On the same principle—of the distance smoothing off sharp edges to the view—to Walford, as to many another thoughtless youth, ten guineas added to his former bill did not seem much more than ten shillings paid down in ready money.

We remember the case of more than one Oxford man, whose debts seemed to show that he had never paid a bill all the time he was at College. This was very like Walford's case. "Then, how did his allowance go?" The whole allowance went in turnpikes, odd shillings, travelling, inns, and dinners out of Oxford—not to mention bets and gambling debts, which are called, by an anomalous courtesy, "debts of honour."

It is not every one who considers that dealing upon credit is literally having substance for shadow — something for nothing — while the credit lasts: and, since all going out and nothing coming in is a drain on a tradesman's resources that cannot go on for ever, several of the tradesmen honoured with Ned Walford's liberal orders began, over a social glass of wine, to form themselves into a little committee of ways and means.

The sum and substance of their consultations was to this effect:—

That it was a thousand pities to run the slightest risk of checking the golden stream that must one day flow from such a customer as Mr. Walford of King's—his intentions were so good, his estates so ample, and the certainty of being paid to the uttermost farthing beyond all question.

"He stands heavy charges," interposed one cynical gentleman to Mr. Fearn, the tailor, with a sly allusion to the ingenuity of his small accounts—"linings, facings, patent button-holes, spring bands—in short, as many extras as have ever been invented—eh, my good friend?"

"We all know credit must be paid for: but, joking apart, no charges at all like respectable business can pay for four years' credit."

"True, true!" said Fripp the horse-dealer: "and the question is, whether a man can stand the strain all one way for four long years, for the advantage of a running account of large orders and high prices, booked at the time present."

"I am sorry to say so," said a grey-headed old picture-seller; "but this kind of business, however profitable, has been carried far enough.

Only the question is, Who is to begin the run upon the Walford Bank? Because, you see, Mr. Walford's is a very strong connexion—all the rich young men in Christchurch will hear the story soon enough, and begin to feel for themselves."

"Yes; and as to the name of a dun, the very rumour that Smith is short of money, or that Jones is likely to call in his debts, we all know the upshot of that sort of report—we all know the small fry who will publish it to our discredit, and then——"

"And then we might as well shut up shop and begin the long vacation at once, for any customers that we shall have within our doors."

"But have you made any sort of cast, to see which way the land lies?"

"Oh, yes. I asked a little assistance to meet a bill—pleading a long account, and all that—last week, of Mr. Le Croix."

"Mr. Le Croix is rather an old hand; rather wide-awake, I think—eh?"

"Yes; and he said, 'Why, Mr. Munton, you have come to the wrong house. You want to make up a certain sum, don't you? Very well, Walford is your man; he comes of age in a few months—you understand?'"

"But whom shall we introduce him to?

(*what money-lender?*) Hughes is pretty full, I think; but Daddy White is a likely man."

"Yes; White 's our man. Mr. Snipe is sent up to take care of Mr. Walford! (a laugh all round.) Well, really, that is too cruel; but since Mr. Snipe owes me a small account, that I have let lie fallow for a long time, I will just ask his advice, and see how we can smooth off the edges in this ugly business of ours."

It will now be understood that Walford was not far from being initiated into one of the oldest means of "raising the wind," by selling the crop before it is sown, and burdening the morrow with the troubles of the day.

It was not long before old King Cole came to Walford one morning, ostensibly quite in a complimentary mood, to talk over the great and brilliant success of the Newnham party; but in reality he came to explain that a Newnham party was rather different from other orders with which gentlemen favoured him—that there was "so much marketing in it," flocks of ducks, and whole gardens of peas, a regiment of lobsters, and a vast sacrifice of lambs, all of which involved money out of pocket; and, therefore, happy as he was to book wine and club dinners against any man in Oxford, in this case, as was usual with all gentlemen who entertained in a large way, a cheque would oblige.

This roused Walford as from a reverie. He had too much of the instinct of a gentleman not to respond to the appeal for ready money for eatables supplied wholesale. He would not for the world have the honour of his much-vaunted Newnham party dashed by the slightest reflection on his ability to pay—more especially because that party had become famous indeed.

Walford's "spread at Newnham" was a by-word for all that was magnificent. You could not eat an ice at Hunter's but that prince of caterers would speak admiringly of the extensive order beating everything, with the solitary exception of the Marquis of Waterford's, in all his experience.—The cads about the boat-houses, and every College scout, spoke of it as something to remember the Term by.—Even the wiser sort of men greeted Walford as a good-natured fool: for there is always some kind of admiration for a man who has made himself a name, however strangely that distinction has been attained.

Still, Walford had no money at command: he therefore asked King Cole, after some little self-complimentary talk, to call at the end of the week; and then hurried off to consult Le

Croix as to how that sort of thing was commonly arranged.

Le Croix's first thought was, "If Cole does not get some money out of Walford, he will very likely come dunning me; for, my account is becoming rather beyond the limits of even old King Cole's most exemplary endurance."

The consultation, therefore, between Walford and Le Croix was curious, but not unique. Had Walford looked searchingly into the depths of Le Croix's sunken eyes and overhanging brow—above all, had he watched that feature, most indicative of all that surges in the heart or hatches in the head—the mouth—with lips that linger, first half open, and then are quietly compressed in thought—then Walford might have seen that Le Croix was in no position to act adviser—his whole soul being centered and all his wits engaged in providing for his own emergencies alone.

Le Croix spoke a little cautiously at first, for fear it should prove that Walford was aware of his having so kindly passed his duns on to him: but, at length, Walford's easy, unsuspecting nature, restored confidence in Le Croix, who then began to indoctrinate Walford with some of the more elementary principles of *finance*.

"Daddy White," he said, "was the best man to deal with; because, when he 'did a bill,' though he deducted about ten pounds out of fifty pounds, to make sure of the interest at first starting, still he never expected a man to take the change in anything but cash."

"In anything but cash! What do you mean?"

"I see you are very young in these affairs. Pollingdon of Brazenose, for instance, applied to a London money-lender — he found him out by his advertisement of 'Minors accommodated,' in *Bell's Life* — and for a two-hundred-pound bill he actually received but eighty pounds in cash: and he had all the rest in Princesses, Duchesses, and Countesses — or a warrant to receive the same in a muddy yard in the City Road."

Walford opened his eyes, as if Le Croix were mad.—This quiet, matter-of-course way of conveying ideas completely new, was intended to make Walford stare, in bewildering confusion first, and the more to admire the speaker's familiarity with business afterwards.

"Really, I am in earnest—I am not exaggerating—only these titles of honour, you may not happen to know, mark the various sorts and sizes of slate-tiles—and it was by a discount, not in money but in kind, that this old offender 'did' Pollingdon's bill."

"But, what a nuisance! What did he do with the tiles?"

"In all these cases the money-lender tells you he can, with all the ease imaginable, find you a man who will buy the goods for ready cash—only the hundred pounds worth of goods, whether tiles, bricks, wine, or guano, prove rather a drug upon the market when you want to sell them. You are sure to hear some such old story as this:—'Why, Sir, the truth is, had you only come last week, I could have offered every penny at which our good friend has very honourably valued them—indeed, they are cheap at the money—but, couldn't you wait for a turn in the market a couple of months?' Of course, ready money alone will do; and you feel the goods in your hands are valueless:—and if this customer fails, you know not how to sell at all. The result is, that you accept half price; and so, by these indirect and crooked ways, the swindler obtains—what, in plain words, he could not even mention — about fifty per cent for his accommodation!"

Walford soon understood that money was raised by "bills," and bills wanted good names.

Mr. White always preferring three names to two, and four or five names were better still.

Walford also learnt, that the only way to be obliged by the "name" of another was to show an equally obliging disposition on your part, and to lend your name to him for a similar purpose—"a mere matter of form—because, of course, every honourable fellow takes up his own bill."

The result was, that Le Croix, Walford, and Bond of New Inn Hall, then recently removed from Christchurch, to avoid an inquiry into a gambling transaction, accommodated each other by an "acceptance" for five hundred pounds each. The legal effect being, that any one of the parties was equally liable for all three bills, or for the whole fifteen hundred pounds.

Whether this step on the part of Walford was more or less prudent, any young man would have maintained that it concerned no one but himself. No—certainly not—it could hurt no one but himself.

But, not less in the book of life than in the book of Scripture, can we read the emphatic truth, "No man liveth to himself." It is not so easy to sever the mysterious links of this world, and to hurt one's self, without, at the same time, hurting some one else besides. Some suspicion of this money-raising transaction arose at Richcourt Hall, perhaps, rather before it was actually completed.

Time had been passing rather quietly with Mrs. Walford. Her son had retrieved his former failure in the schools. The *éclat* of his Pass party at Newnham, and all the kind things said by the tenantry — always feasted on the occasion of good news received — had all tended to turn fears into hopes, and to throw over the dark colours of the past the cheerful hue of an agreeable present.

Mrs. Walford's equanimity had been still further established by the exhilarating sunshine of a beautiful morning in June, and a consciousness of her daily duties and devotions having been duly performed. Dinner had been ordered; some little tiffs and jealousies, threatening a rupture between the hater of spiders and the lover of perquisites, had been timely prevented by a stroke of diplomacy—perhaps as great in its way as that by which a Palmerston would earn a European reputation. Add to this, Mrs. Walford had traced the crumbs from yesterday's table safely into the red pitcher of old Betty Bramble, in spite of the blighting and sinister aspect with which the very sight of a pensioner would cloud the countenances of the offended establishment.

For the time, therefore, Mrs. Walford was composed and happy; at least, she enjoyed as good a lull as any fond and anxious mother can expect: though all the time, her thoughts were no sooner absent from the said red pitcher, and those who did not want to fill it, than they were present with her son at Oxford.

One hour after, the scene was wholly—aye, sadly—most sadly—changed. The same good lady might have been seen pale, distracted, miserable—her brain throbbing, and her kind heart beating—food, rest, pleasure, enjoyment, all had lost their charm and power; cruel revolution had taken place in every nerve and feeling.

It will readily be conjectured, that the cause of all this pain and misery lay in the identical youth, whose folly was to "hurt nobody but himself."

"No man liveth to himself." Wonderfully are we linked together. The human lyre is an instrument of many strings; any one of them at the mercy of the meddling and the fussy, no less than of the malicious, to make it jar upon our feelings, and send a sympathetic pang through the heart.

But how had the fond mother so soon heard of her son's new step in the paths of folly?

There is nothing for nothing in this world; the trouble for which a man can make no charge, he too often takes out in the form of fussiness and self-importance. Sir Buller Tawstock, one of the trustees under old Mr. Walford's will, was a man of this kind. He talked of the manor as confidently and imperatively as if it were his own, and ventured on many other things of an obtrusive kind: all tending to mar Mrs. Walford's enjoyment of the property, and to keep up that unpleasant sensation of life in leading-strings, under which many a lady has writhed as in galling fetters, from the time that she has lost her husband.

Mrs. Walford was made to feel—yes, feel—that she could give no permission to fish in the famous Richcourt trout-stream without reference to Sir Buller Tawstock. Sir Buller Tawstock again stepped forward whenever a tourist requested to avoid the Lanaway hill, and enjoy two miles of rhododendra on his way to Canfield. In short, Sir Buller Tawstock was a name that grated on the good lady's ear; he was the fly in her ointment—the grit in her machinery, and like some tiny irritant in a nerve, that keeps up an intermitting fever throughout a whole existence; and many a time she had vowed to deny him the house and all communication. But reflection showed the ties that held her back. To quarrel with a country neighbour, whom you pass daily in narrow lanes, and meet Sunday after Sunday at the village church, to say nothing of the dinner circle—is a serious matter. These are among the drawbacks of country life. There was also a cowardly kind of threat—sure to strike terror into a lady—"I will throw it all into Chancery;" to which Sir Buller was not slow in having recourse: law, actions, and above all Chancery, being dreaded as so many forms of slow torture that had survived even to this humane generation.

No wonder, therefore, that Mrs. Walford uttered a suppressed sigh, as if her day's tranquillity were at an end, when she heard Sir Buller talking in a very excited manner to old Richard, now hobbling after him with a stick, on his way up the avenue to pay her a visit.

And what was it all about?

Mr. Keenley, the principal solicitor and town-clerk of Willingworth, had received a letter from a solicitor in Oxford to institute inquiries as to the rents and annual value of the Manor of Richcourt: and a very innocent inquiry, too, in one point of view. He might have an idle curiosity; he might want to buy up the estate; and he might, in fact, have no object at all: but, on the contrary, the inquiry might—especially as it came from Oxford—be significant of something very different: and all inquiries about our property give us a cold chill. We should not wish our worst enemy a more uncomfortable day or two than would follow the sight of two mysterious gentlemen reconnoitering their estate, questioning their tenants, and, perhaps, applying to search for the certificate of the baptism and the register of the marriage.

Mrs. Walford was never quite free from fear and anxiety about her son Edward, "he was so easily misled"—"so thoughtless—so self-confident and self-willed: and every one had heard of the follies and temptations of Oxford." Only, there is a time when gnawing cares, like crying children, are hushed to sleep—there is a time when the black flock of ravening, cawing visitors, are silent in the furrows; but, all of a sudden, the clamorous sentinel—just such was Sir Buller—croaks the signal of alarm, and immediately the air is darkened with the sable wings of a whole rookery in a flutter of terror: and just such was the darkening flutter in Mrs. Walford's scared and frighted breast.

"Mischief was brewing"—thus did Sir

Buller make his running commentary on existing appearances: "Mischief of some kind—that was very certain—of that there could be no kind of doubt—the exact form and shape in which the boy's folly would be bodied forth, time alone could show. Most probably he was raising money on the estate, or committing himself with money-lenders—nothing more likely. If so, he (Sir Buller) must of course throw up his trust, place the estate in Chancery, and be clear of the responsibility."

This series of reflections he wound up by recounting all the trouble he had had, and all his patience had endured—impertinence included—Master Ned not happening to be more fond of those who controlled him than other youths—the whole ending with remarks laudatory of his own judgment and discretion over a period of some twenty years.

The unhappy mother could only sit still and suffer. Who has not experienced that painful racking of the brain that ends but with exhaustion—solves nothing, and arrives at nothing; but leaves the subject of anxiety precisely as before? Whoever has experienced this distraction of mind, will understand us when we say, that, after a while, a kind of hopeful reaction followed the depression. Mrs. Walford began to think it was but an inquiry—things may not be so very bad—there was yet time to advise and to obviate. "Sir Buller says he will write. I only hope Ned will answer him without offence; and I will lose no time in exerting my influence, too."

Sir Buller's letter, it will readily be supposed, met with no very gracious reply, having first been read to Le Croix—that so discreet an adviser might give his opinion on the propriety of submitting to such a disgusting "interference." Ned informed Sir Buller that small thanks were due to him for disturbing a lady's mind with absurd and groundless apprehensions. He also assured Mrs. Walford, that nothing like any dealing with the estate had ever entered into his mind; neither could he at all understand how anything in which he was concerned could have caused those impertinent questions to be asked of the solicitor at Willingworth.

The good mother's fears were once more laid asleep, though this kind of sleep is never as composed as before. Each fresh alarm rendered Mrs. Walford more and more easily excited, and far more prepared for unfavourable news from Oxford.

A few words about the town and trade of

Oxford.—The law of demand and supply regulates every branch of trade; even to the due proportion of the knaves to the fools. As to "the credit system," "the harpies in the shape of tradesmen," and other wicked and designing persons, whom Mrs. Walford considered to infest the Universities alone; such characters are everywhere to be found, where rich young men are to be found; and the only reason we hear more of them at Oxford is, because at that City of Colleges there are more young men in a mood to take credit, and also with prospects to command it.

Of course, it is not to be supposed that Oxford tradesmen should care about any interest but their own, more than other tradesmen: but there is a sprinkling of good men everywhere; men who, amidst all the sharp practice of the trader, show forth the nobler qualities of the man. We have, therefore, a peculiar pleasure in approaching a part of Ned Walford's history, which will show that, if one righteous man can save a city from general condemnation, such a one was producible at the time of which we are speaking at Oxford.

Mr. Philip Buxton every one of our standing remembers as a dealer in various articles, both useful and ornamental, with the very best of goods on reasonable terms.

Buxton was sent forth from his parental home at about sixteen years of age, with no other stock-in-trade than a ten-pound note, and a good grammar-school education. To live by your learning is proverbially a precarious existence, but principally because men aim too high: they write for posterity, who cannot be supposed to pay in ready-money; or perhaps they soar aloft into the cloudy regions of imagination and theory, instead of keeping nearer to that market which is found upon earth.

Young Buxton took a practical view of things. Having been born and bred of an old Oxford tradesman, and having many a time heard his father talk of this gentleman and of that, whose name was crossed in the buttery, and, therefore, his Collegiate existence suspended, and perhaps himself confined to gates, till the said refractory youth had either turned a paper of the *Spectator* into Latin, or two or three hundred lines of Greek into English,—Buxton, like an original and inventive genius, espied the stream that would turn his mill. He very wisely observed, that if you stick up a notice that you cater for wisdom and virtue, your circle will be rather select; but once lay yourself out for folly and idleness, and you will never complain of want of customers.

Soon the very name of Buxton was a by-word in every College. Beginning with simple copying, either of the text or of translations, Buxton advanced to Latin Verse, as well as Prose, Essays on any subject, and a sketch of the Sermon at St. Mary's—according as idleness, ignorance, or Sabbath-breaking were the radical faults, which each kind of literary penance was supposed to cure.

We well remember Buxton's tariff:—Essays, four shillings; Sermons, two shillings and sixpence; *Spectator* (short pieces), one shilling and sixpence; copying, one shilling and sixpence a hundred lines; and anything done a little better, as for a Scholar was always charged extra; while the more liberal would add a bottle of wine, in pity for "the poor drudge" who lived by such dry work.

Oxford men have a respect for talent; and as Buxton showed alacrity, sometimes not as a mere hireling, but as a friend at need, he became a very popular character. This encouraged him at length to open a shop, which eventually superseded all the manufacture of Essays, Sermons, and Imposition-work, and landed Mr.

Philip Buxton among the most thriving and respectable tradesmen in the Corn Market.

At the time we knew him we well remember how firmly, yet how kindly, he would put on a deprecating smile, as of an older man, when some boyish scapegrace would boast his intention of committing any ruinous piece of extravagance or folly. If there was any danger of a man's falling into the clutches of any bill-discounter, or other beast of prey, there was no degree of trouble that Buxton would not take to save him: and in all these cases the wonder was how Buxton could ever have picked up his information, how he contrived to appear in the very nick of time to "confound their politics," or to "frustrate their knavish tricks," and to rescue some verdant, unsuspecting youth, from the gulf that yawned for his destruction, and bid him live a little wiser to the end of his days.

Such being the philanthropic bent of Mr. Buxton's disposition, one day he was concluding some Woodstock business over a glass of wine in the Commercial-room of the "Stag Inn," when his friend related, in the way of a little fun, the extreme mortification of a certain rich and well-to-do glover, who found all his efforts vain to make an impression on the pretty Alice Hengen. He added, that the old goose had not the sense to see, that while one Mr. Walford, from one of the Oxford Colleges, carried on so lively a diversion, no young girl would give a thought to a tradesman of forty-five.

Buxton's ears were open in a moment: he knew Walford well, and saw at a glance he was just that spoilt child of fortune who would rush blindly into misery for a life, rather than be denied the humour of the day.

After a few inquiries at Woodstock, followed up with a corresponding sifting of Le Croix and Walford's friends at Oxford, while they were lounging in his shop, and criticising his tempting wares, as their daily custom was—Buxton was soon convinced that the intimacy was all the more perilous to Walford, because of the soft and sentimental kind.

There is such a thing as a natural clairvoyance and a prophetic power in man, especially where a deep insight into men and manners is found in combination with a sanguine and untiring cast of mind.—This was decidedly the character of Buxton, leading him by a brief process of thought to a certain conclusion, and from that hour he overlooked no kind of incident which could have the remotest bearing upon the issue in which he had resolved to bear a part.

CHAPTER XIX.

A LADY FINDS SOME OTHER THINGS ARE NECESSARY BESIDES "ALL THE NECESSARIES OF LIFE."

THERE are many ways of looking at the same thing in this world: and perhaps the most delusive view of all is "the matter-of-fact view." This is commonly wider of the real fact than any view, especially as regards the ideas that middle-aged people form of the young—of what is best for them—and what they ought to be satisfied with, "if they only knew what's good for them."

Mrs. Hardaway's view of the position of Alice Hengen, and how happy she ought to be—"or it must needs be the fault of her own folly and unreasonableness"—is a case in point.

Mrs. Hardaway enjoyed quite a warm glow about the heart, when she summed up all she had done for "that poor, helpless young creature, with plenty to eat and drink, no rent or bills to pay, and a good bed to lie upon, and wages enough to put some in the savings' bank every quarter-day."—Little did Mrs. Hardaway realise the solemn truth, that here as hereafter "life is more than meat, and the body more than raiment." These things touch the outer life alone—whereas there is also an inner life, far more dear, the source of nearly all our best enjoyments, especially to womankind. With poor Alice Hengen, the food came with little appetite, the night came with no repose; and as to the sight of her quarter's wages, it was paid to one whose whole heart was sick and yearning for what no money could ever buy.

The lower orders, and that rough-and-ready, free, easy, and impertinent kind of people, who live and labour in the shops or the offices of a small country town, invariably look with jealousy on a girl of the refinement of Alice. "Proud"—"stuck-up"—"the like of her"—"not a penny to bless herself with, yet coming it so fine over us"—these are the remarks which a lady or a gentleman in reduced circumstances can never hope to escape when thrown into daily contact with persons in a lower grade of society.

We admit that, had Alice exemplified the warmest possible tone and the all-comprehensive charities of the Christian character, she might, in possibility, have carried with her the only spell and antidote against the spleen and venom which superior refinement inspires in the vulgar, small-town mind; but—we say it with sorrow; we say it as the result of a slow conviction against the fond belief of our earlier years—persons are not necessarily among the "poor in spirit" because they have been reduced to the number of the "poor in purse." Alice could toss her head as well as they—or, at all events, betray by her look that little she cared about pleasing them.

The result was, that Alice was generally unpopular; and those who have felt what it is to be continually meeting one person who passes sullen and scowling by, may understand, that when a poor girl could not go on an errand down the street without running the gauntlet of such chilling, curdling looks, she must have lived in a clime most ungenial to the heart.

Mrs. Winter heard nothing but complaints about her "fine lady," with impudent remarks, that she was "the sort for Oxford Collegers, no doubt," and she seemed to have a brooch and a chain already, more than honest earnings could be supposed to pay for.

Mrs. Winter thought, at last, what every one said must be true. Mrs. Winter arrived slowly and unwillingly at a serious apprehension that Alice must have one fault—the worst possible for any house of business—namely, very little care to please; and, after one or two sharp remarks on the one side, and sullen answers on the other, Alice found things not much more pleasant within doors than they were without. Alice realised that sad fate, which few indeed ever imagine till they feel it—*life without sympathy.* "None to bless us—none whom we can bless—none who, with kindred consciousness endued, if *she* were not, would seem to smile the less."

Steep me in poverty to the very lips—plunge me in a dungeon, where no struggling beam of day can pierce to cheer me—but let me know one heart in the world throbs in unison with mine, and I shall feel at least that there is an harmonious chord which thrills and links me to human kind. But woe to the poor creature who walks this wide world to find all bleak and blank around, with a heart that would speak, but none to answer—moving amidst the busy market crowd, all desolate and alone!

Of this wreck and ruin to the peace of Alice Hengen, Edward Walford was more or less the cause. It was he who had engrossed her heart and interest—it was he who had made her consider herself his alone; and from that moment careless and indifferent to all the world beside.

This might have been all very foolish, we admit: but Alice was quite as wise as many a well-lectured and chaperoned young lady under similar circumstances—those circumstances being a flat and stagnant state of things, from which she would catch at straws to escape—a warm heart in a flutter and a head in a whirl.

"Anger is a short madness," says the Latin proverb: beyond all doubt, Love is. It seems a providential kind of chloroform to lull our senses, and put our reason to sleep, pending those agitating and distracting arrangements which link a fond couple together for a life.

Alice Hengen was young; and, since it is by no means uncommon to see a lady, the most staid and prudential in worldly affairs, and numbering some fifty years, all of a sudden silly as any boarding-school miss, and defying all the efforts of her oldest friends to save her from staring misery and ruin, we can only exclaim, Think yourselves happy, lady friends, if you have some one to protect you in these mysterious hallucinations; and pity a poor girl like Alice, who is tossed at the mercy of her own surging emotions—unfriended and alone.

"Man is born to suffer:" more literally is this true of woman. Man is born to be diverted—to work, to act—and thus to take the full benefit of that resource and sedative for a troubled spirit,—*Labour;* the finest opiate ever vouchsafed to man. Some one has remarked that oxygen, that is, plenty of fresh air and exercise, is no small part of happiness. A gallop across country does send a healthful stream of nervous energy through the frame; does "rase out the written troubles of the brain:" but as to woman, it takes a great deal of crochet and constitutionalising "to cleanse the full bosom of that perilous stuff that weighs upon the heart."

So, true to their destiny, there was one lady at Richcourt and one at Woodstock; and the happiness of both centered in, and was at the mercy of, one thoughtless youth alone.

Both of these ladies—both the forlorn and loving Alice Hengen, and the fond and anxious Mrs. Walford, were doomed to feel, though in different ways, that they claimed just as much of Edward Walford's regard and attention as he could spare from the ever-varying amusements of the season, and no more. The Newnham party, and the other hospitalities of the summer term, acted on the popularity of Ned Walford in much the same way as a grand ball, which comes just in time to freshen up "attentions," will rescue from oblivion some superannuated lady in Belgravia. This kind of popularity, when you walk about with a genial glance from one, and a hearty word from another, was what brother Nat in one set, and John Hackles in another, enjoyed, quite without thinking about it: but men like Walford find it so rare and expensive, that when the party is over they are sure not to go out of the way till they have made the very most of the little consequence it gives them.

Alice counted the days to the long vacation. All that term she had had but one word from Walford: albeit one of those words, with that fire in the eye and that electricity in the fingers that stamp words as the coin of the heart — spoken all in a moment as he jumped off a tandem, that his friends might not see. This was little, indeed, to serve for the greetings and passages of love for two full months; and well did Alice know, that unless her "dear Edward" quickly came to see her, the term would be over, and then life to her would be one desolate blank from that day in June, at least, to the beginning of October, and all that time she trembled lest some other favoured fair should fall in his way, and she be left "to sigh alone."

Walford had now returned home for the long vacation. And where was brother Nat?

Nat had joined a reading party in Wales; for

Nat liked a quiet life: he was conscious that his ideas of things would continually clash and his feelings jar with those of Ned. He said he "was vexed to see Ned making so great a fool of himself;" and, therefore, now that Ned was come of age, and was lawful master of Richcourt, Nat thought it far better to "leave him alone in his glory," till the plagues of possession had had time to qualify Ned's sense of self-importance.

Nat was also aware that two men were coming on a visit — Le Croix, whom he heartily despised, and Dick Cheston, whom he regarded with suspicion, as too old a man to fraternise with a young fellow like Ned without an object. Expecting to be thrown unpleasantly in the way of two such visitors, Nat very properly remarked to a friend, "It would only create a breach between him and his brother if he remained in the house to cast sinister and depreciating looks at all that went on."

Mrs. Walford, as usual, could not look forward to Ned's return, however impatiently she counted the days to it, without a nervous pain to qualify her pleasure. After all that had passed, and her apprehensions as to money-lenders—wholly to avoid explanations was a course that her maternal anxieties forbade. But, on the other hand, to encounter such explanations was like raising a veil from what she dreaded more minutely to examine. However, Ned's short answers and allusions to his own age and presumed years of discretion, soon ended that part of his mother's duty: he also seemed so indignant at "the impertinent interference" to which he had been subjected, that Mrs. Walford feared an open rupture when he met Sir Buller Tawstock; she therefore touched upon the powers of a trustee, and the necessity of conciliatory measures.

Ned had no idea of this: like most other thoughtless and hot-headed youths, he was in a mood to kick away the ladder first, and awake to a sense of his difficulties afterwards. The consequence was, that Mrs. Walford was next day quite alarmed at hearing him say, that as Sir Buller came up "to act the Don over him," he had given him a little of his mind — he had taught him to talk business with his solicitor and not with himself; and least of all, to be coming to Richcourt Hall in his absence to scare his mother with groundless and ridiculous apprehensions.

But one thing Ned did not tell his mother, and, indeed, it was not for some time that he realised the importance of this little incident;

namely, that Sir Buller said, emphatically, as he turned away, that he "would take Mr. Walford at his word,—for the future he would limit himself to what a solicitor would advise, and not one step further would he go, happen what might—as Mr. Walford should feel to his cost, and, no doubt, bitterly rue the ingratitude and discourtesy of that hour."

As the world grows old, its arrangements grow complicated and anomalous, and in no respect more so than in these forms of law which, by entailed estates, with a mere jointure—a kind of pension—for the widow, allow the caprices of the dead to overrule the wisdom of the living—settling hundreds of acres on the eldest son, though all but demonstrably an idiot, and placing the parent at the mercy of the child.

Arrived at twenty-one years of age, Ned Walford had actually the power of giving his fond mother notice to quit. The *bipes implumis*—"the biped without feathers," as the logicians used to define the creature Man—could literally peck his own mother out of the nest!

And had Ned Walford the heart to do it?

No: he never thought of such a thing. But still, the unhappy lady soon began to feel that things had taken such a turn that the day might come when it would be by no means endurable for a lady of her feelings and habits to remain.

We have a distinct recollection of the following scene—which was, no doubt, no solitary instance, but one day of many in the life of Mrs. Walford.

The occasion was a village merry-making—a "barvest-home." The tenantry had been regaled, poles climbed for legs of mutton, greased pigs caught by the tail, and—which was much against the feelings of Mrs. Walford—a garment had been run for by such damsels of the parish as had the impudence to contend—the lightest, probably, in character, as well as foot.

Mrs. Walford watched all these rural sports from a tent, in which she was supported by the parson's wife, and occasionally by Dick Cheston, at this time on a visit to enlighten Ned on horses, dogs, and sporting things in general.

Dick was most attentive that day to Mrs. Walford: Dick was refinement and sensibility itself, in his lucid intervals. No man could be more proper or paternal when he pleased, or give better advice to a young man entering life. No man more naturally caught the hue and tone of any elderly lady by whom he had once confidentially taken his seat—the more prudish and particular she was, the better he could do it;

and therefore, though Dick's age seemed not quite in harmony with the boyish freaks in which he took a part, still Mrs. Walford, like all other ladies with so general a favourite as Dick Cheston, was flattered with his attentions, and fondly persuaded herself that a man who was so correct in his ideas could not be very fallible in his conduct.

Mrs. Walford did not consider that manners and morals form one of those subjects in which your theory may be very far ahead of your practice—still less did she consider that virtue and propriety are easy enough by fits and starts, though trying for a continuance. These qualities in Dick Cheston depended quite on the humour he was in, and were as evanescent as the good dinner and glass of wine so necessary to make them simmer up to virtue's mark—which creature-comforts had just then made goodness inexpressible sparkle in Cheston's brilliant hazel eye and soft, persuasive lips.

But though Mrs. Walford was not too old to enjoy complimentary attentions, and by no means too wise to be blinded to the faults of a fascinating man like Cheston, still, as regarded his eligibility as a companion for her son, her faith must have been tried somewhat hardly by the evening which followed.

Up to that time, Richcourt Hall, through the long minority, had been the very pattern of a well-ordered English home of the more affluent class. To watch over and to regulate the character and conduct of the whole household, had formed no small part of this good lady's ideas of daily duty to improve. As to drinking, smoking, gambling, and noisy revelry, they were horrors yet to come. The fine old Tudor hall had known none but gatherings of a widely different tone and spirit. The cursings of the profligate would make the very stones cry out, accustomed as they were to little else than the blessings of those her bounty clothed and fed. And true to the character of herself, and the home she had handed down unspotted to her son, methinks at this moment I see the good lady retiring to her own apartments, yet casting a certain wistful look behind, as much as to say, "Would that my boy would now, as years since, be contented to spend the evening with his mother!—these companions, I fear, will do him little good!"

It was about ten o'clock, on this occasion, when we left the young Squire of Richcourt. Le Croix and three of his party, determined to have a game of Van John and make a night of it, were talking, each louder than the other, in their own hollow, heartless way, while Dick Cheston's propriety was no longer upon guard.

One scene like this will be sufficient to show the tastes and the company with which the Heir of Richcourt was now entering on the enjoyment—if, indeed, it deserved the name—of his fine estate. As to Mrs. Walford, the mother, her thoughts and feelings—we must not pretend to see down into those dark depths to which she strove in vain to close her eyes. The Wise Man said, that no man could say whether his son would be a wise man or a fool. The more common disappointment is of another kind. We, unconsciously, invest our children with feelings and affections the most flattering and congenial to our own. And is it not among the severest of our trials to awaken to a sense of inclinations, and of interests, prevailing in a child, diametrically opposed to all the treasured wishes of a parent's life?

CHAPTER XX.

OCCASIONS WHEN OUR DEAR DEPARTED RELATIVES ARE APT TO COME TO LIFE AGAIN.

But all this time we have omitted to relate what had become of so striking a character as Alice Hengen's fond and anxious sister, Hannah.

Hannah, we said, had been early taught to suspect the truth of lovers. Truth! She had learnt, by cruel experience, to value, at its proper worth, that fashionable code of honour that treats woman as the conventional prey of man, and laughs when reminded of a lover's vow.

The cold scorn with which Hannah had, for some years, treated all the flattering attentions, on which others raised their buoyant hopes, was well remembered by the too-credulous younger sister: therefore was it that Alice, in her frequent letters, had spoken generally and enigmatically perhaps, but never seriously and distinctly, so as to ask the advice or to draw forth the opinion of Hannah.

Hannah was never without fearful apprehension that there either was, or would be, some adventure to put her sister's innocent credulity to the test. Her letters to Alice rarely failed to contain suggestions of caution, prudence, and all the virtues of a colder kind. But such topics could hardly prevail in Hannah's correspondence, without tending rather to check than to invite the confidence of Alice. Only imagine the poor, infatuated girl, when her head was running upon freaks of fortune, almost like those wrought by some good-natured fairy queen—imagine with what thoughts she would read a letter, melting her gorgeous castles into empty air, by a chilling reminder that the very position of a barmaid would, of itself, suffice to show the real character of any lover who pretended to high estate!

And this leads us to relate something of the situation of Hannah Hengen, as also of Mrs. Belmont, a rich old lady, whom she had the good fortune, through the kind offices of Mrs. Hardaway, to be serving in the capacity of "companion."

Hannah first came to Mrs. Belmont when that lady was hale and hearty, but in comparatively narrow circumstances. She was now up in the world in one sense, though down in another—having more to spend, but no strength to enjoy—the same wayward fortune that enabled her to set up her carriage, having deprived her of the use of her limbs.

That a young woman of the determined and impulsive character of Hannah should ever have bent to the whims and ways of this old lady of seventy-five, surprised Mrs. Hardaway and every one else who knew her.

"All the world have tempers as well as Hannah," said Mrs. Hardaway: "I am old enough to know, that if a girl will not keep her temper she will never keep a place."

But Mrs. Belmont made a lucky beginning: she began by striking the right chord to Hannah's heart. "A fellow feeling makes us wondrous kind," and Mrs. Belmont's experience with the gentlemen had not been much more flattering than Hannah's. It was whispered in her family—we should say, it was a tradition that had reached some saucy nieces—that Aunt Belmont had been jilted times without number, and made a very bad match at the last. It was therefore very natural that the old lady should jump to the conclusion that, in some form or other, "those shocking men" should have wrought that downfall, of which she had heard a little, in the history of Hannah and her sister.

Hannah was not naturally communicative, but words and looks of sympathy act like the spell of "Open, sesame!" on the heart. In course of time Mrs. Belmont's curiosity was destined to enjoy a treat, and Hannah told her story, or at least a modified version of it. What related to herself she sketched with hurried strokes, but when she came to her anxieties about her sister, her hopes, her fears, and gloomy apprehensions, were painted with a flowing brush, as her heart but too fondly sought relief in words. Mrs. Belmont's nature, it is true, was by this time somewhat soured; still, though she was always declaring that she had been lavishing her kindness all her life on selfish, thankless men, she had still some of the wine and oil of charity to pour into the wounds of woman: she therefore dropped "tears of natural pity" at the sister's tale, found some present for a parcel about to be sent from Hannah; and, what is yet more winning than any single act of charity, the old lady was ever inquiring of Alice's welfare, and looking approvingly on Hannah for all the care she was taking of her dear sister.

It was Hannah Hengen's character to do everything by impulse. Fierce and inexorable in her resentments, she equally prided herself on her untiring energy in requiting the kindness of a friend. She therefore threw herself, heart and soul, into all the duties of Mrs. Belmont's service. If the old lady were ill, Hannah was night and day at her side.—If any one at the boarding-house, at which she first lived, was kind, or the reverse, Hannah made them feel at once either the heartiness of her best attentions, or the withering aspect of her suddenly o'ercast brow.

But, "Where were Mrs. Belmont's friends?" she asked. "Had she outlived all her family, or nearly all?"—One or two had called with dutiful attentions; one lady had remained to see her through an illness; but where were the rest? Mrs. Belmont's reply was memorable.

"An old woman, child, has no friend but her money. My income is small, and drops with me, so most of my relatives have dropped off first."

"Then most of them are dead?"

"Yes; dead and buried, too, they might as well be, child: but you would find that they would come to life again pretty fast if—if—old Miss Wallis were to die before I do."

So, then, there was an old Miss Wallis on whom much depended! Why not? Has not almost every family an old Miss Wallis, or an old Mr. Wallis?—some one, at least, who is only interesting in his remains—some one who, in every family difficulty, is the subject of an "Only think! If it should but happen now—how smooth, how comfortable, it would make us all!"

Now, Mrs. Belmont had once five sisters. Every one of the five had speculated in their lives on the same Miss Wallis. "Old Miss Wallis" had been the *ignis fatuus* of their existence. It served to cheer and to amuse them, but nothing better; because they had all passed off before her, one after another, dying of good old age. Mrs. Belmont's existence on her small annuity would not have been half as endurable but for that sustaining cordial—that most exhilarating of extracts, which the alchemy of Hope can squeeze from the treasures of the future.

It was Miss Wallis's house that Mrs. Belmont must almost always pass in her drive—a lonely, old-fashioned house, at Brompton. The very scraper was rusty; the number on the door had faded, like the tenant, almost out of sight; and as to the paint upon the railings, time had eaten it all away—you would have thought the place was haunted, and long deserted by human kind.

"That's Miss Wallis's," said the old lady on the first occasion. "It is only that the blinds are down"—meaning to say, "I don't see the shutters up." "She is very old; her doctor is paid by the year; and her companion knows she will never find another such a place. This shows how much longer than they do doctors and nurses could keep people alive, if they had only a mind to it. A strange world is this! Her money is not a bit of good to her, and might be so—pleasant—to any one else."

Even Hannah began to catch the money fever. No one seems indifferent to money, however many degrees removed. Even a fortune falling in next door is interesting; how, then, can a "companion" help building her hopes on a quicker circulation of things easier in general? Hannah, therefore, found herself looking up, involuntarily, as they passed and eyed the premises—glancing, with reversionary looks of a longing kind, through the branches of the wild and unlopped trees, at those dark and smoky windows. Once in three months they called and made inquiries, and were diverted for days after in speculating on the symptoms—swelled legs, breathing bad, and other symptoms of decay.

Time went on. No one in the boarding-house could sit at table, day after day, and receive less observation or attention than Mrs. Belmont. Too economical for visitors, too old for flirtations, too indolent and sleepy to take part in a rubber, with little wine, no extra dishes, and nothing more stylish than an occasional cab or wheel-chair at the door—Mrs. Belmont was neither very interesting to the company, nor very profitable to the house. Mrs. Grindham regarded her as "a sacrifice—such boarders did not pay for their beds. No. 19 was never so unprofitably let before."

This state of things had gone on for twelve months, when, all of a sudden, the house was rendered dreadfully excited by the unusual announcement of a gentleman on business to see Mrs. Belmont. "A queer piece of business it is, too, I should not wonder," remarked Mrs. Bile—a lady who turned pale at the postman, and never moved out. In boarding-houses, a dashing young man on business means a lover, or a "cousin" at the least; but a man, such as now presented himself, in pepper-and-salt and spectacles, with papers, made half the house feel sympathetically nervous.

What could it all mean? Mrs. Belmont was closeted with this ominous personage for a considerable time; during which the companion hurried out for sal volatile, and seemed to be conciliating the enemy, by something as unusual as a glass of wine extra to the week's account. And when at last this mysterious gentleman disappeared, it was observed that the companion looked excited; and as to how Mrs. Belmont looked, Mrs. Bile had not an opportunity of scrutinising, because the old lady did not make her appearance for some hours.

But soon the news spread like wildfire. Mrs. Grindham had been applied to for her very best accommodation; but how was "three-pair-of-stairs-back" ever to pay for "the best bed-room front," with the mahogany wardrobe and marble slabs? Why, one Miss Wallis, an aged relative, given over by the faculty forty years ago, was dead at last; and a sum of two thousand pounds a-year had passed from an estate of lingering expectancy, into the actual possession of Mrs. Belmont.

There was nothing talked of in Mrs. Grindham's boarding establishment all that morning but Mrs. Belmont and her sudden fortune. Everybody felt as on their way to the diggings, or as if a gold mine had turned up in the very next field. Some were cross and envious; some were cool and calculating; every one felt as if, directly or indirectly, they ought to be the better for it: and not a few talked of "that pert Miss of a companion," and "the airs she now would give herself, beyond all bearing."

When the old lady, having recovered her composure, found her way back to the drawing-room, she felt, as she afterwards *naïvely* remarked, like the hare with many friends—she had stepped into quite a different climate—out of the frigid zone of cold indifference, into the very tropics of the warmest congratulations and glowing smiles. She was the focus of all eyes; their very chairs were instinctively radiating towards Mrs. Belmont as the centre of a complimentary circle—all giving ear to her sentiments, and echoing her remarks.

So much of the effect within the walls of Mrs. Grindham's boarding-house. As to the way in which the change of fortune operated without, the old lady's sarcastic remark was verified to the letter; her relations did, indeed, "come to life again." Some one likened the effect to that of a camel dropping in the desert. The sky, so late without a speck visible to the very horizon, becomes suddenly peopled with birds of prey.

"Yes," said the parlour-maid, "how they do come a eagling of the old lady! Why, if you'll believe me, I hadn't taken up nobody's cards, nor nobody's compliments, ever since I came to the place, and now a body had need have nothing else to do."

At dinner, all one end of the table was Mrs. Belmont's; and her decanters had learnt to travel a little wider than the circle of her self-invited relatives. And as to these relatives, to borrow a good thing from Goldsmith, it was wonderful what a lot of beggars

"Claimed kindred there, and had their claims allowed."

The most amusing thing was to see how dearly they loved each other. The old lady began to give little family dinner-parties—supposed to be most harmonious little gatherings: though the company blended so well, that every one seemed to wish the other far enough away. The only thing we remember seeing at all like this has been in trout-fishing, when the true Waltonian would pitch his own father into the water rather than have the pleasure of his company, knowing that he would whip his likely streams.

One would think that money was the mainspring that moves the world. Mightiest of despots, it sends its willing slaves to toil in Zembla's cold or Afric's heat—or sunless mines, or city offices and crowded courts, seething with human steam: it nerves the arm of labour, quickening the pace, the pulse, and all the energies of the man: but not least does it give a stir to the brain, whet the eye-teeth, and quicken the very dullest to feats of inventive ingenuity, worthy of a better cause. So truly are "the children of this world wiser"—more alive to possible contingencies, and provident of future interests—"than the children of light."

We never saw this more clearly than in the case of Mrs. Belmont and her money. Every one in the boarding-house, or out of it, must have the fingering of her money, or name the people who should earn it. One was forward to order her wine—another was red-hot about a carriage, with *his* coachmaker or *his* jobmaster—another had the cashing of her cheques: and, in short, the attentive friends in the house, and the never-failing relations from without, looked daggers at each other; and both sides looked daggers at Miss Hengen, who, by the negative and repulsive influence of that chilling, scornful, yet significant and searching look, which characterised her blighted and disnatured character, shot into the shabby souls of all of them the galling truth, which, in plain words, she had uttered to more than one,—namely, that there was a very curious coincidence, in point of time, between the commencement of their attentions and the news of the estate.

To be held in check by a mere companion, was a thing some persons wondered that any relatives, or even visitors, should endure; but Hannah Hengen stood in the relation of no ordinary companion to Mrs. Belmont — besides being a woman cast in no common mould. There was in Hannah that strong nature which ever sways the weak — an intensity of character and commanding energy that carries everything before it.

More than one relative, in the might of their right and the plenitude of their assurance, had called on purpose to tell Miss Hengen a little of their mind, but went away without their errand. She looked them through: she made them feel as if their very faces were "books in which she could read strange matters" — bold in the consciousness of her own ascendancy with a shrewd old lady, who deemed them more "akin" than "kind." Indeed, there was little fear of offending Mrs. Belmont by the part Hannah was disposed to take; for she was continually telling Hannah that, "as to half of them, they never let her know there were such people in the world till she had the fortune." We may almost affirm, that the further the companion kept certain members of the family away, the better the old lady was pleased. No one of them was so near or dear to her as Hannah Hengen. So the old lady reposed in her companion, and clung to her as a friend—for a true and faithful friend she was, indeed, exulting all the more in proving herself such, from the disgust and scorn with which she regarded the time-serving policy so glaring in those who were clustering around her.

It will be enough, in this part of our story, to relate, that Mrs. Belmont soon appeared with an establishment in proportion to her fortune.

We take leave of Hannah for the present, with the less compunction, because in the enjoyment of a comfortable home, and with duties which she took a pleasure in discharging. In the language of the world, Hannah had everything to make her happy. "She had feathered her nest pretty well"—"she had it all her own way; so, what more could she want?" For, this world ever will forget, that "man doth not live by bread alone;" and that there is also a yearning of the soul and a hunger of the heart. What more did Hannah want, indeed! Why, there was not a day but she would have given up all these seeming luxuries without, and cried, "Miserable comforters are ye all!" could she only have bridged over the gulf that parted her from Alice: and if, in the very weakness of that fond and unsuspecting girl, she could only have found a sphere for her restless energies, and a vent for that love which, though early thrown back, by man's unkindness, upon its gushing fountain, and, battling with fierce resentment, maintains an undying struggle in every true woman's heart.

It had not escaped the vigilance of Hannah's affection, that there was something significant in the fitful irregularity of Alice's letters — there was something more significant still in their altered tone, as also in the haste and impatience with which they had so evidently been written.

Alice's letters, at first, were all that Hannah could desire; they were, what letters should be, her written confidence — the resource and refuge of her spirit in every hour of its inquietude. But it is of the very nature of such letters, when read aright, to serve as a barometer, and to mark the rise and fall of the writer's spirits — timely significant of clouds or sunshine, and all the varying seasons of the heart. It was natural, therefore, that with the letters that now came more few and far between, Hannah should remark the falling off in the zest and punctuality of her correspondence, as also a want of candour and composure in the tone.

Think yourselves happy, ladies, reared in affluence and independence, that in all such trying seasons of painful doubts and fond anxiety you can rush away to the very spot where your heart has fled before you — that you can front and battle with the hideous spectre which at a distance denies you rest. As to the poor dependant, the envied companion, all this her "lot forbad"—"chill penury circumscribed the glowing virtues" of the devoted sister. Hannah could, therefore, only indulge in weaving those mental webs in which the anxious are so ingenious, and in solving imaginary problems, till her brain reeled and her head went round, and all the pieces were scattered to be set up afresh, without advancing one single move in the complex game of life.

CHAPTER XXI.

HOW TOM SNIPE LIVED BY HIS WITS.

DURING all the festivities and entertainments at Richcourt Hall, we shall naturally be asked, Where was Tom Snipe? Tom Snipe was absent—ostensibly with his own consent.

We have already remarked, that Tom did not feel his position or his influence the more secure for the presence of Dick Cheston. There is a peculiar cast of countenance by which a Detective, even in a strange locality, can pick out a sharper in a crowd. There is also a peculiar expression by which the same sharper can be made to understand that he is known—that his game is up, and that where the one is in attendance, the other must quickly disappear. The expression is one of lowered eye-brows and insinuating look, which signifies, as well as a dozen arguments—"It is no use talking: you and I understand each other."

When, by some such look as this, Dick Cheston told Snipe that he had "summed him up," "taken stock," and could exactly allow for the declension of his honour and the variation of his compass, Tom made up his mind that to measure himself against the popularity of this man—the most winsome with ladies, and the most jolly with gentlemen of all the country round—were playing a losing game; so, on the principle of "out of sight out of mind," Snipe resolved to spend part of the long vacation in London.

We have already hinted that Snipe was one of those men who are said to live by their wits in London; but it is not everybody who knows what kind of connexion there is between depending upon one's wits and three meals a-day, besides rent and tailors' bills, and no little spare cash for uses various: so we propose to follow Tom for awhile, and watch the course of his daily operations.

"The boy is father of the man," so says a very true proverb. Tom Snipe in London, was merely the later growth of Tom Snipe at Oxford, where we have a distinct remembrance that our first acquaintance with him was in this wise:—

"Do you see," said a friend, one December

afternoon, turning into Symmons's stables, "that knowing-looking little man, with true sporting cut—he and his horse part and parcel of each other?—Would not you declare by that man's appearance that he kept his hunters, and was quite in easy circumstances? Well, the chestnut mare he rides is Dorrell's of Oriel; the red coat he borrowed of Lindley of our College; the top-boots he dunned me into lending him; and even the whip and the spurs are not his own!"

Ten minutes after Tom met us, and passed the lender of the boots with a degree of coolness in his look and manner, that plainly told me that he felt all the happier for his tact and success in laying his friends under contribution for the sources of his amusements.

In London, at his club, the younger and the greener sort looked up to Snipe for the earliest information. Tom was of the same kind of service to them that a touter is to a racing-man; no man knew sooner, or appeared to know, if any "event" would turn upon its merits, or whether it was already "settled," and the bets made safe. In certain circles, a man who ranks as honest, but acts otherwise, and is known not to be over-scrupulous, has his value; and "sharp, keen, and knowing," are marketable qualities.

Snipe, therefore, in a certain circle, was well

worth humouring and conciliating. He insensibly gained an influence over young men of large estate; he contrived to lounge with them into the stables of a dealer in fine dashing "screws;" or, to enter their names on the books of wine-merchants, tailors, tobacconists, and dealers various. In short, many a golden stream would Snipe turn into the channels most profitable to himself.

Neither, unhappily, was Tom Snipe at a loss to know the conventional tap at certain green doors, that are always strongly barred against surprise from the officers of the law; and thus would he introduce some thoughtless fellow, at whose expense he had freely drunk and dined, to habits, ruinous to mind, manners, and estate.

For these introductions, directly or indirectly, either in money or in kind, Tom received his commission. One man would suggest, as a personal favour, he should be measured for a coat off the identical piece he had recommended to Lord Tom Noddy. Another would insist on his trying some of the same cigars; while, as to any horse he passed off, it was regarded as Tom's own, at the cost of the "blemished," and sold, as for him, at the price of the sound.

Less difficulty still had Tom about horses to make a figure in the Park, and to keep up appearances. No dealer could have a better agent; and little did the giddy crowd suspect that the stylish Tom Snipe, curvetting in Rotten Row, was only acting as the owner's groom, to show off the action and the effect of fashionable hacks.

But if Tom was riding one day, he might be seen driving another, in equipages various; but especially in a well-appointed chariot, with coachman and footman, and some members of Tom's family, as it appeared; and one tall, elegant-looking young lady, in particular, who seemed on pleasant terms with Tom. In this carriage he was often seen. Not a few thought the equipage was Snipe's own. It drove to and from the very door of the very house in a fashionable square that was engraved on the corner of his visiting card: so no one suspected that Tom's real establishment was one cheap bedroom near the Strand. Still less, that all his talk about going to Coutts's Bank—false nineteen times out of twenty—was only true when the owner of the carriage accepted his kind attentions, and let him drive to Coutts's in that carriage to cash her cheque.

But there was something about Tom with which ladies were, at all times, exceedingly interested—a point very much in his favour, as enabling him to lay married men, as well as bachelors, under contribution.

Tom was one of these easy-going men who would conform exactly to the ways, whims, and customs of the house in which he was entertained. Tom would make a very attentive appearance in a country family pew. Early associations and an instinct of devotion will hold their own, however choked with rank weeds or the entanglements of evil habits—men are more often self-deceivers than hypocrites. Even Palmer the murderer was, every Sunday, next pew to a friend of ours in Rugely Church: and why not? No doubt he had the same way of going on sinning and praying, and praying and sinning, of which we are all so painfully conscious. The difference is only a question of degree: and the "deceivableness of unrighteousness" —the nature of that poison that lulls while it kills—is among the mysteries of this mortal state.*

The art of living by your wits requires no little wit to live by. It requires considerable

* There is a case on record of a banker guilty of forgery, who lived with a Bible and a loaded pistol in his desk—daily reading the one and ready to blow his brains out with the other. At length an officer came to arrest him, and he shot himself on the spot!

personal and social qualifications. And Tom Snipe had a degree of tact and knowledge of character, coolness and penetration, that would have insured success in any honest calling. He soon saw that, while he found it a trouble to get money, the rich must be helped through the trouble of spending it. Some want even their thinking done by proxy; and to have their wants found out for them, is the greatest want of all.—We have often thought that Virgil meant to be satirical when he made Æolus say to Juno, "It is hard work enough for a lady, like you, to find out what to wish for."

If old General Ashton wanted his friends amused, Snipe would preside at the billiards and the smoking. Did the soft and silly Sir Alfred Manton want the credit of taste, of which he had none—of knowledge of horses, dogs, guns, or wine, of which he had as little—he had only to invite Snipe for a month, and all would be perfection. When Lord Marshfield wanted a manor, immediately there were two country-houses open to Snipe, by one and the same operation. There was a commission from Tom's old chum, Winkley of Christchurch, for letting his shooting in Hertfordshire, to stop a gap in his exchequer. There was an invitation from his Lordship to come down to the said manor, and point out the covers, and explain the locality.

As to Tom's social qualifications, there was a constitutional flow of spirits, and that rude health and buoyancy, which go a long way towards the character of a pleasant, good-natured fellow. Not easily tired, fretted, or worried with anything, no man could render great services in a house with so little sacrifice; and partly from a free, communicative, and generous humour—for a gleam of moral sunshine would break out occasionally—and partly because, full well Tom knew that "there is nothing for nothing in this world,"—Tom always did something as a pleasing remembrance of his visit, and to make everybody ask when he was coming again. Besides singing, and playing accompaniments on his flute, he would help the son with his holiday verses, mend his tackle, and teach him all kinds of sporting dodges. He would enliven an evening with conjuring tricks, act dwarfs, giants, ghosts, and get up charades in first-rate style. All this was worth paying for: and Tom thought it very fair "give and take," as neither party could do without the other.

We deemed it necessary to say so much of

Tom Snipe, and the secret of his success, because few persons would expect to find such a mixture of good and evil in those who play the baser parts in the broad farce of fashionable life. Unmixed evil, for a continuance, never could make its way —that cold, selfish cunning, and deep design, which are never for a moment relieved by one warm glow of genial feeling, would hardly enable the Tom Snipes of society to gain a position from which to carry on the sapping and the mining of so many fine estates.

But to return to our particular Tom Snipe. It was shrewdly suspected that he had succeeded in ingratiating himself with a lady possessed of untold riches. In London, where no one knows his next-door neighbour, the story amounted to little more than a vague rumour—the appearance, the age, and even the name of the lady, being as yet unknown. However, every one who knew Snipe was at all times ready to believe a report of his feathering his nest in a more comfortable way, and with a keener instinct, than common men; and Tom, when joked with on the subject, was not a likely man to deny anything which sounded complimentary to his own personal attractions.

In this part of our narrative, all we are concerned to remark is, that the report was well known to Ned Walford, and that Ned had the less difficulty in believing it, because he had more than once felt his own inferiority, as regards the impression he could make, and the smiles of sparkling interest he could elicit, whenever tutor and pupil were thrown together in the company of a few lively young ladies. It was not that Ned was so very dull and slow, but rather that Snipe was so provokingly fast. Indeed, Tom's spirits were ever up to proof. He had a dash of Irish in his blood, which accounted for the raciness of his humour and the glibness of his tongue—with just the slightest dash of impudence, too—so little, that he gained in piquancy without losing in taste: all which qualifications, the ladies must excuse us if we say, have a tendency to give these wild birds of society no slight advantage over the tame, though better bred, domestic fowl.

Snipe's success with the ladies caused anything but an agreeable sensation in the mind of Ned Walford. But there was no helping it. For though a rich and eligible young man will ever receive a full share of forced attention and well-simulated smiles, still there are moments when nature is too strong for flattery. And dull indeed must that man be who, in the midst of such hollow sounds, is not struck with the merry tones that ring with gladness when a young lady springs almost over the straight lines of stiff propriety, to greet one of those genial, happy fellows, who seem intuitively to touch the key-note of the heart.

CHAPTER XXII.

HOW CUPID IS MOST BUSY AT IDLE TIMES.

As all things, even the so-called Long Vacation, have an end, the hopeful son and the chosen tutor, by the middle of October, in spite of all the charms of pheasant-shooting, had returned to Oxford.

There is not much amusement at Oxford in the October term, except for the hunting men; and although at King's, in those days, it used to be thought an honour to the College that we turned out on a fine morning nearly as many "pinks," or red-coats, as Christchurch, yet Walford was not among the number—a slight accident from a thorn, while too eagerly following some pheasants over quickset, having rendered riding painful to him.

And as to this little thorn, we cannot think of it without observing how small may be the pivot on which shall turn the greatest of events.

It is very probable that, but for this little accident, Walford would have blown off his superfluous steam with his fellows in the hunting-field, and poor Alice would have found, that in the attentions of the gentlemen the ladies have few more formidable rivals than horses and dogs.

More than one man has fallen in love, and married, too, simply because he had nothing else to do. So generally is it true that Love catches us—even as Death overtook the Cambridge carrier taking holiday, in the well-known story—not while we are busily jogging along the high-road of life, but when we are laid up in ordinary by some accident, or snowed-up in a country house for long winter days.

The usual routine of College life went on again. From Rickworth's room the familiar sounds of heavy feet and sudden bounds announced that boxing-gloves and single-stick—if not the rat-and-porter invitations—had once more commenced. On Cowley Marsh, instead of the cricket-tents, and old King Cole standing as a sturdy janitor in front, you might see a man like our friend Norman, in high shoes and white stockings, sketching the cowshed or studying the picturesque. Take the usual round, and cross the river by Ifley Lock, and you would see none of the eight-oars practising, but one or two scratch-crews in a four-oars, perhaps, and, much more likely, a row of skiffs, left by men who had landed, to jump at the bars or play at skittles. If, after this, you returned home by the weirs, the quick report of some dozen guns would tell of pigeon-shooting, with sailing-vessels, on a blowing day, carrying a fearful load of canvas, as they ever used to do till two fine fellows (Graham and Surtees) one day sank to rise no more.

These were the amusements of the October term; yet in none of these did Walford care to take a part, from a certain private-school feeling of reluctance to measure his prowess with that of other men.

Very naturally, therefore, did he soon renew his drive to Woodstock.

No sooner did Mrs. Winter see him, than she shook her high-crowned cap, laid aside her spectacles—to reveal the deep significance of her clouded brow—and looked as much as to say to him, "What have you got to say for yourself, Mr. Edward Walford, before I let you know a little of my mind, and read you a pretty good homily on proper manners?"

"Why, what is the matter, Mrs. Winter?"

"You ask me, 'What's the matter,' indeed, Mr. Edward! Why, what should be the matter?

Perhaps you can answer me that question! What can you have had to say with that silly, addle-headed young creature, that she should have made herself the talk of all the town? Why, I can't as much as walk down the street without hearing of it! That girl will be the ruin of the 'Stag'—indeed she will: for all she has been a-doing ever since she saw you last, is a-breaking of glasses and a-forgetting of every one, and a 'offending of every one that comes into the house—I must get rid of her, indeed I must!"

After some casual and deprecatory reply from Walford, who began to look rather sheepish, Mrs. Winter continued:—

"Yes; I always will say that business is business, and charity is charity. Talk of charity, indeed! as Mrs. Hardaway did when first she went a-coming round me—if I had took out the best twenty-pound note that Lord and Lady Coverley ever paid me—and that was pretty many, all the years before I was turned out by those neck-breaking railway folks—and if I had put down that twenty-pound note and said, 'There, take that for charity, and then I've done with it'—why it would have been dirt cheap for all the custom I have lost, let alone the scandal, vexation, and the troubling of my spirit, ever since this poor creature came into the 'Stag!'

"'—Poor creature!' Yes, she is a poor creature! Not that I am angry with her—it is her nature, and she can't help it. I might speak sharp, or the like of that—but really, I do pity her!

"—But gentlefolks are poor creatures, and that's the truth! They are no more good in this bar-room than I should be in the Queen's palace—aye, that's just it!—I do feel awkward and all no-how, kind and condescending as they all are to me, when they've had me up to Coverley Hall; but still I can't feel more out of my place than born gentlefolks ever must feel here.

"—Yes, gentlefolks were made to spend money, and ride about elegant, and all that. But as to earning of any—may the Lord help 'em! for precious little can any of them help themselves, when once they come down in the world!"

This will serve as a sufficient sample of the strain in which Mrs. Winter's long-vacation grievances sought vent at last, when she found the much-wished for opportunity of speaking her mind to that offending "young Oxford Colleger."

Ned Walford was naturally soft-hearted. It was more his misfortune than his fault that, under the blighting curse of gold, all those thoughts and feelings, which should have been so turned as to flow warm and gushingly towards those around, had been made to circle in narrow eddies back upon himself; still, when these baneful causes did not operate — whenever no great effort of self-denial was required, and Ned's heart enjoyed fair play, his sentiments were good and generous. Only, with men of this character, you must ever strike the iron while it is hot. Call them at once to action while they are in the humour; otherwise their virtue, no longer patted on the back, grows chill and cautious—the head is too prudential for the heart, and their generosity cannot fight in cold blood.

"But you have not let me see my much-injured lady, Mrs. Winter. Really, that is hard. After all your lengthened indictment of high crimes and misdemeanours, the least you can do is to let me ask the lady's pardon, and to make some little amends."

This request was naturally accompanied with words, complimentary to Mrs. Winter's charity and forbearance.—He said, he was sure that her soft heart never yet repented a kind action — that as to loss of custom, where Mrs. Winter was, there all the wealth and the fashion of the country must come, too. The result was, that, added to the luxury of a good listener and free course for Mrs. Winter's own self-importance, the appeal was irresistible, and the good woman, though she still went on talking one way, proceeded forthwith to act the other; and poor Alice, looking very pale and pitiful, was called to take her seat on one end of the dimity-covered cushions in the bow-window of the "Stag."

It was not to the first call that the pale and trembling Alice—sick at heart as she was with hope delayed, and worn by one life-long struggle against the petty insolence of petty people—could sufficiently command her feelings to respond.

"Alice! Alice!—is the child deaf?" exclaimed Mrs. Winter. "Come, this is a pretty 'make-believe!'—as if Mr. Walford had come at last, and you not know he was in the house! Well—I—never——!"

But when Alice did come, the less she had the power to speak, the more Mrs. Winter found words for her: when, suddenly, "Coming!" she exclaimed, though no one called, and casting a good-natured look behind, she had disappeared in a moment, and left the young couple alone.

What Mrs. Winter's exact intention was, in this strange proceeding, it is hard to say. Those who trace every action to sordid interest, and make out human nature to be little better than a living Ready Reckoner, reducing things of all denominations into pounds, shillings, and pence — they, of course, would argue that all Mrs. Winter wanted was to get the poor girl off her hands; and took the most likely course to do so. But a more attentive study of womankind has taught us that they have one never-failing source of amusement to their dying day, namely, match-making; and that, just as a superannuated hunter in a paddock pricks up his ears at the music of the hounds, even so does an ancient lady snatch a pleasure from the past whenever she is conscious of aiding and abetting in what is pre-eminently called an "interesting affair."

If pity is akin to love — if the sense that one fond heart has for weeks and months been set upon himself, has any power to move a man not insensible to generous emotions, Ned Walford was just now in danger's way. The age of chivalry is not so far past — the position of Alice, tied and bound in the galling bonds of servitude, and threatened by Woodstock boors, was not so far unlike the romantic position of a captive maiden in ancient song—that our hero should feel no spirit of generous emulation or wild adventure.—How delightful the resolve to be the happy man to dry her tears and soothe her throbbing heart, and to hear her acknowledge her joyous deliverance as his proud act alone!

We say not of how many visits, stolen or allowed, such feelings were the growth. Had Alice been less virtuous, the result might have been different. There is a certain awe and reverence, far, indeed, removed from the idea of an easy conquest, which, if once it seizes on the heart of youth, holds him spell-bound, entranced, and captive.

From this moment two things are worthy of attentive consideration.—The first, that Edward Walford felt irresistibly attracted to Alice Hengen. The second, that the same Edward Walford had never yet learnt to weigh the present with the future, nor to obey any other law than his own impetuous will.

CHAPTER XXIII.

SOMETHING SEEMS LIKELY TO HAPPEN IN MORE WAYS THAN ONE.

If men were always in their sober senses, there are a great many foolish as well as wicked things in this mortal world which would remain undone. But there is a deal of "temporary insanity"—a deal of suicidal madness, as regards either body or estate, besides that—of which alone we are accustomed to hear — that falls under the cognisance of "crowners' quests."

We see this truth in the case of the gamester, when the dice have gone against him, who, exasperated to the highest pitch of frensy, stakes every acre upon a single throw!

We see it in the failing merchant, whose last acts, bordering on insolvency, run counter to all the prudence—to all the clear views and penetration — that have characterised his life.

We see it often in the reputed murderer, who

has harboured one vindictive thought till the evil spirit, grown dominant within him, hurries him into deeds of blood most foreign to his calmer nature.

When once frail man gives reins to an all-engrossing passion, it is vain indeed to say, "So far shalt thou go, and no further." "Though free," says Aristotle, "to hold back the rolling stone, man is not free to check its midway course in a precipitate descent." Ruminating on these infirmities, we often are reminded of the terrible appeal of a patient to the visitor of an asylum,—"Sir, have you thanked God for the use of your reason to-day?"

But of all temporary insanity of a milder form—for it is nothing less—there is no kind we see more frequently than that kind of infatuation of which Ned Walford was now the victim—when, under the form of sentiment or romantic feeling, passion, intensified by denial, produced a revulsion in his whole nature—the brain sympathising with the fevered and distempered body. Alice he felt "he could not live without"—"dearer than life itself." So it were idle to suppose that a man in such a mood should look beyond the humour of the hour, or weigh the common prizes and pursuits of life in the scale against it.

Ned Walford was not the first man of whom we may say that, while this fit was on him, he was literally "beside himself." That supposed "going out of himself," of which the Greeks used to speak, was, in his case, for the time, most evidently fulfilled. We should never have felt such interest in the strange chances and mischances of Ned Walford's life, if his follies or his failings had been wholly unredeemed by lucid intervals of sense and conscience, too: but in every part of the world's history, a Helen, a Cleopatra, or a Lady Hamilton, have played very conspicuous parts among even the greatest of the sons of little and short-sighted man.

Homer describes a council of fine old boys, heartily sick of the ten years' war—all caused by Helen's runaway match: a set of elderly gentlemen who, in all probability, had uttered many a malediction against her, and not sparing those canine epithets which Homer's heroes had ever so ungallantly on their tongue—when, all of a sudden, they happened to look around and catch a glimpse of this killing fair herself! The effect was like magic—utterly overpowering—all the severity of their judgment is softened as they gaze, till old Nestor cried out,—

"Small blame to the Greeks and the Trojans! I swear
To fight for ten years for that lovable fair;
And as to our trials by land and by sea,
I'd deem it a trifle if she'd run off with me."

It is only fair, therefore, to remember, for the seeming madness of Ned Walford, that there ever has been a fascination wholly beyond all reason as regards ladies' charms. Do not flatter yourselves, ladies: you are not all so killing, or so hallucinating—we only mean that some of you are. Neither is it always perfect beauty that owns that indescribable charm and spell which throws cold propriety into a state of thaw.

No. By no means. It were not enough to vote all beauty contraband: love is too erratic in its ways. Indeed perfect symmetry, and features faultless, command a very sober admiration: for we could hardly imagine a flirtation between the Belvidere Apollo and the Venus de Medici. But whoever made up the match between Venus and Vulcan, handed down to us the testimony of the earliest ages to that unaccountable caprice in choosing for themselves, which has descended in a right line to the young people of the present day.

But to our story. Action—action—action. Excuses are premature. As to Walford, it is too much to ask absolution for an offence he is only now going to commit.

We have heard of more than one run-away match, where the truant couple might just as well have walked away, when Cupid did not want his wings, and when no one either would or could have stood against their determination to be married, if once plainly and positively expressed.

Still, in the case of Edward Walford, yet *in statu pupillari*, or, leading-strings academical, at King's College, Oxford, and lord of Richcourt Hall, and therefore hampered by all the complex ties of "proper feelings," or duty to his family, as well as by the rules of the College;—in the case also of Alice Hengen, owing true and faithful service and obedience, and "one month's notice" at the least, to Mrs. Winter, of the "Stag Inn," Woodstock—it was natural their minds should feel that so many words, if not arguments, would be used to stop them, that the shortest and most sensible way was to marry first, and to let people talk about it afterwards.

No doubt they both said many times it was their own affair, and they did not care; but there was an indescribable feeling, that told them both that, in spite of all they might pretend, they did care: and that as to its being their own affair, no step so critical could possibly be indifferent to certain other persons also. It was easy to say "there was nothing to be afraid of," but still the heart will beat a little quicker on such occasions, and young persons *are* afraid. Our walk in this life is in the midst of ties and laws innumerable though invisible; like electric wires, to give a shock to all who trample on them. The deep voice of some viewless monitor will whisper powerfully unwelcome truths to those who go on still in their follies or iniquities.

Can any feeling mind imagine that Alice could help thinking what her kind old friend Mrs. Hardaway would say, and what Mrs. Winter would say, when they found her gone?—Could she help thinking what her anxious sister Hannah would say at never having been consulted, even although the grand match should prove an overwhelming surprise to charm away all possible reflections? But, added to these unpleasant scruples, there was one apprehension predominant over all; what if—if—anything should go wrong! if any ill-natured people should conspire to dash her from the very pinnacle of bliss! Full well she knew that all the town of Woodstock would be but too ready, open-mouthed, to join all Mrs. Winter's post-boys and hostlers in the hot pursuit, and to yell and hound her to the very death, rather than she should gain that proud position whence to launch her cold defiance at their petty malice.

The very plan proposed was fraught with nervous terror; the very arrangements that were making showed that even the rich, the independent Mr. Walford, was nervous and apprehensive, too. He was to come after dark—he was then to wait, with his dog-cart, outside the town—near the stile of the deer-park. At this hour she was to evade all suspicious eyes and casual questions, and to get away as best she could—and with her bundle, too—measures all full of many a slip to make such plots miscarry. Had it been the elder sister—had it been Hannah—her cool nerve and colder scepticism in the good faith of any confidant in female form, would have reduced the adverse chances to a cipher; but Alice's very weakness persuaded her that Martha, the chambermaid, must be trusted with both the bundle and the secret, too, and her fealty insured by the promise of the best of situations at Richcourt Hall. And Martha, again, from the hour she had this secret under her yellow neckerchief, felt, as she afterwards related, "like a tea-urn with a heater in it, a-burning its way out."

"La, my dear child!" said Martha, "you mind and not make a mess on it; for, as to them Oxford Collegers, there's no lies them won't lay tongue to to make fools of us poor girls."

Still, though secrets sentimental are of the most dangerous and explosive nature, Martha showed that both the secret and the bundle might have been intrusted to less worthy hands.

This being the situation of the lady, fluttering between hope and fear, let us turn to the other side.

Ned Walford was in a position which occurs rarely, if at all, in the life of most men—he was distracted by feelings yearning for expression, yet dare he not utter a word to any one. Alice's name had been canvassed at many a wine-party; and, to most of the company, one barmaid was no better than another—and, with nearly all, an affectation of lady-like manners was, in the neighbourhood of Oxford, deemed almost part of any fair tempter's place.—So, many a light remark had cut Walford to the quick, and showed him how little hope there was of any sympathy, either for himself or lady fair, whatever he might assert of her superior birth or conduct.

Nothing was better understood, so nothing was more readily taken for granted, than that any pretty girl, with that slight dash of the Finishing-

Academy manners which women are clever enough to pick-up wonderfully fast, should be engaged to draw custom to an inn.

Now, Walford was a man of no self-reliance —the last man to take the lead and "cut out the running"—so, being now, perforce, upon the silent system, the step he was venturing seemed, as the day drew near, to be one cold plunge, and to look rather different.

Whatever may be said of University studies, as forming a part of useful knowledge, Love and Logic are two things that are likely, very materially, to interfere with each other; and as to alternate hours with the "Heavy Euripides Coach," and the "Slow Herodotus Ten o'Clock" —this, with Hall and Chapel, and Wine, Supper, and Breakfast parties daily, and the "Rats and Porter" for a change—might well threaten a diversion, almost enough to set Ned Walford's wits upon their legs again.

As to his plans to carry Alice off—to be married as quickly as possible, and making their way to the North, to far-famed Gretna Green, unless some more ready means should occur to save them time and distance—this was the vague and indefinite form in which his ideas were contented to remain. Once off, he thought things would shake right, and he should manage somehow, as others had done before him. But whether the marriage ceremony was first and foremost in his mind, or whether it was not rather a matter-of-course concession to the innocence of one to whom he dare not speak of elopement in any any other terms, is another question. This naturally reminds us of the exceeding risk that Alice, like all other runaway young ladies, must ever incur. But there was the more excuse for her; because, as a lady similarly situated and dependent, like Alice, on daily labour for her daily bread, once pleaded in our hearing,—

"It is all very well to apply the strict rules of etiquette and propriety to young ladies blessed with kind parents to take care of them: but a poor, motherless girl, like me, through good report and ill report, must trust to her own conscious innocence to protect her."

But Walford, we said, felt the burthen of the silent system. His thoughts and feelings, struggling under high pressure, wanted vent. It was very natural, therefore, that what he dare not disclose to his equals—encountering the sneers of Le Croix, or the philosophic wit of Tom Norman quizzing him through his spectacles, and perhaps sketching on the spot a ridiculous caricature of the happy pair—that these ideas he should seek to ventilate in some other way, pouring half-truths and hints he deemed wholly enigmatical, into some sympathetic ears.

Every man of experience has observed that, on all great critical occasions, there is a singular fatality, that, by some very strange coincidence, prompts a man to make choice of exactly the very person it were better to avoid. So, to whom should Ned Walford betake himself, but to Mr. Philip Buxton!

Half-standing, half-sitting, on Buxton's counter, and swinging the string of his gown nervously in his hand, Ned had hardly begun casting about for a fair opening, when he was agreeably surprised by Buxton asking, rather significantly,—

"Have you been to Woodstock lately, Mr. Walford?"

"Woodstock! What makes you think of Woodstock, indeed? What a knowing fellow you are, Buxton!"

"I simply did hear that there was a very peculiar attraction at the 'Stag.'"

"Oh, certainly! Old Mrs. Winter is quite an original character—is she not?—quite an old ally. She comes from our side the country."

"And her young friend Alice Hengen, I suppose, comes from the same side, too?"

From this auspicious commencement a most lively confab ensued, in which Walford flattered himself that he said no more than would suffice to puzzle Mr. Buxton for the present, and be something to laugh over at a future time, when the dark prophecy had been interpreted by the event. But many a secret has been revealed by forgetfulness of one self-evident fact—that half-truths tell quite enough to the man who is already in possession of the other half. Buxton pursued his advantage, and led Walford on from point to point, until he said so much, that Buxton was convinced that no time was to be lost—now or never was the time to take measures to stop this egregious folly, which might otherwise be rued for a life.

Mr. Buxton, therefore, made inquiries at the stables, and thought he saw something ominous in the manner of the noted John Green. John Green was accordingly asked if he could not, for a consideration, give any information, supposing Walford's dog-cart should be ordered at any unusual hour, or anything else connected with Woodstock should fall under his notice?

John replied, that "it made no odds to him, or not much, seemingly, what he told"—"there ought to be plenty of stuff (money) about a job like this; it was only deceiving of one's self to try it otherwise."— As to Mr. Buxton, "every one knew he understood *business*, and never, without money paid, expected money's worth."—So, as Walford evidently had not specially retained John's secret services, he "would just mention— there might be something in it, or there might not—that he had been sent to book all the inside of the mail for Mr. Walford on the following night—to take up at Hatton toll-bar—just where the Woodstock cross-road runs into the London road—Mr. Walford to be there about ten o'clock at night."

"And how about the dog-cart?"

"Why, I am to come after Mr. Walford's portmanteau when the gentlemen are in at Hall. And the long and the short of the matter is, I am to keep the places inside the mail for fear of accidents, and to be ready at Hatton toll-bar to bring the dog-cart back to Oxford."

"Thank ye, John," said Buxton. "Now only do as I tell you—Keep your mouth shut and eyes open, till four o'clock to-morrow; at which hour, punctually, come down to my house, ready to do as I shall then require."

"But you 've a deal too much sense, Mr. Buxton, to let the young 'uns know where the old 'uns get their information,—haven't you, now?"

"Trust me for that, John. You may look as innocent as ever you please—I won't spoil your trade, depend upon it."

Buxton in this promise was sincere enough. No one knew better than Philip Buxton that the John Greens were far too useful to be treated with indifference when the plot was over.

Indeed, it is by the John Greens of society—by men with just that want of principle which invites confidence in the first place and betrays it to the highest bidder afterwards, that the balance of power is preserved on the side of honest men.

END OF VOL. I.

CPSIA information can be obtained
at www.ICGtesting.com
Printed in the USA
LVHW100435110522
718424LV00003B/135

9 783375 006457